BATTLE AT RIO PEDERNALES

ALSO BY MELODY GROVES

Lady of the Law

The Colton Brothers Saga

Trail to Tin Town

Showdown at Pinos Altos

Nolan Gang Unleashed Series

The Making of the Texas Kid

Eagan's Revenge

BATTLE AT RIO PEDERNALES

NOLAN GANG UNLEASHED
BOOK THREE

MELODY GROVES

WOLFPACK
PUBLISHING
— EST 2015 —

Battle at Rio Pedernales
Paperback Edition
Copyright © 2024 Melody Groves

Wolfpack Publishing
1707 E. Diana Street
Tampa, Florida 33609

wolfpackpublishing.com

Paperback ISBN 978-1-63977-672-6
eBook ISBN 978-1-63977-671-9
LCCN 2024940433

BATTLE AT RIO PEDERNALES

CHAPTER ONE

BLANCO HILL, TEXAS HILL COUNTRY—FALL 1871

"JOE, NEED YOU TO RUN THIS OVER TO THE bank."

I looked up from the idle telegrapher's code keypad and the desk's high seat, where I spent most of my time sitting these past few weeks, operating the town's telegraph station. Usually, I was busy sending out important bits of information. Or receiving them. But today, not many customers came in. I guessed nothing of major importance was happening.

Ed Whalen, my boss, held out a wad of cash. I must have blinked ten times. He'd never before had me take the week's earnings to be deposited. And today was Friday. As was his habit, he always left early to spend a bit of time flirting with the bank teller, Miss Amanda Freyling. I dipped my eyebrows but thought better of the face I must have made.

He pressed bills into my outstretched hand. "I trust you, Joe. There's over twenty dollars here, twenty-three and seventy-six cents to be exact, and all you need to do is deposit it all into the office account."

"Of course, Mr. Whalen." I focused on the regulator over his desk. Not quite four. Definitely enough time to get to the bank before they closed at half four.

When I didn't move immediately, he flapped his hands toward the door. "Now shoo. I'll lock up behind you." Whalen plucked his bowler from the peg near his desk and held the hat and door in his hands. "Go ahead. See you tomorrow."

"Yes, sir." Who was I to argue? I tucked the money into a pocket inside my vest. Ma, a piecemeal seamstress, had sewn me a special one with two secret pockets. They had come in handy more than once, and I thanked Ma every time I had needed them. Right now, with all this money, would be one of those times.

With an extra hour of freedom, we usually closed at five on Fridays and three on Saturdays, I figured I'd get a beer over at Sam's Emporium, the rowdiest and best saloon in town. A beer with my brother sounded like time well spent. But first, I'd make sure this money got into the bank.

As I walked down Main's creaky boardwalks, I tipped my hat to a couple of ladies walking toward me and gave a "howdy" to a man who seemed to be in a rush. Not many people were out and about. I figured the women were home starting supper, the men finishing up whatever they were doing so they could get home to that supper. My stomach rumbled. I was still a couple of hours away from said supper. Probably a beer would help.

I stopped in front of my da's meat shop, Nolan's Meat Market, and peered through the big front window. He'd owned the store since moving to Blanco Hill back aways.

I counted. Must be close to fifteen years. My youngest brother, Eagan, who now worked with Da at the store, was born a couple years before they arrived here. Now, he was just shy of eighteen.

Inside, Eagan and Da were busy helping a customer. I tapped on the window and Eagan looked over. A smile hooked ear to ear. I made a sign of drinking a beer, tipping an imaginary mug up to my mouth, then pointed up the street. He nodded. Maybe I'd see him there in an hour. Or maybe not until we both got home. Sometimes Eagan and Da worked past five, especially on a Friday.

I waved and went on my way and saw Da still talking to the customer. Two blocks down and on the same side of the street, stood the bank, a two-story imposing gray stone building. I'd heard this was the first permanent structure in town but, more than likely, Sam's was. When towns sprung up, the first thing they built was a saloon. Usually several. Blanco Hill, with a population of close to a thousand, hosted eight such Edens. But none as grand, or as much fun, as Sam's Emporium.

Pulling open the bank's ten-foot-high doors, gold lettering standing out on the windows, I stepped into a room with plush carpeting, mahogany paneled walls and, hanging on those wooden walls, paintings of old bearded men looking important. A high ceiling covered with silver-stamped tin completed the scene. Opulence at its finest.

I didn't go in there very often. No reason to. I didn't have much money and what I did have was at home stuffed in a dresser drawer.

Three cashiers stood behind the counter in what I believed they called teller's cages, each busy helping a customer. Miss Freyling's line was three deep, while the others had one. I stood behind the three, knowing Mr.

Whalen would want me to say "howdy" to this particular woman.

People ahead of me were in no hurry to get their business done and move on. Would they close the bank at half four and make us come back tomorrow? That didn't seem to be overly friendly, but then again, this was a bank, a place of business. But Da never threw out a customer who dawdled over pork chops past closing time.

One person now ahead of me and he'd just stepped up to Miss Freyling. Her smile flitted across her pretty face, while she reached up to pat her hair. It was all in place. If she'd concentrated more on helping this man and less on her hair, maybe I could've deposited this money and go have a beer with Eagan before going home to supper. If only the customer would hurry and quit leaning over the counter at her.

The doors flew open. I turned. Three men, masks covering their faces, pointed guns at all of us. "Hands up!"

My arms reached for that silver ceiling. Heart pounding, chest on fire, I couldn't breathe. All I could do was watch the men rough handle a man standing by the door. They whacked him upside the head and snickered as he crumpled to the floor. Miss Freyling's arms were up as well as everyone else's. Was she shaking? I know I was.

The men rushed inside, slamming, then locking the door. One pulled down the shade darkening the big room. A sense of foreboding covered me, and I was sure we would all die. We'd be shot and left on the luxurious rug; simply left to die a painful, lingering death. I wouldn't let that happen to Miss Freyling, no way. A plan. I needed a plan.

Two of the robbers dashed behind the counters,

pushing the tellers aside, including the pretty lady. I stepped forward until the third man shoved his revolver into my back.

"One more step, you're dead."

I froze. Doing a mental count of how many of us were on this side of the counter, I figured three, a fourth knocked out cold. If those other two customers were willing, maybe we could take down this bandit. However, there was a distinct possibility the tellers would get hurt or killed. I certainly didn't want that to happen. But could I simply stand by and let these masked men take money from the hard-working citizens of Blanco Hill? My da's money included. He banked there and had all his money sitting behind that door in the safe. If they took the money, Da and the others would be penniless.

A door leading into an office creaked open. Like prairie dogs in unison, the three bandits' heads swiveled to the door.

"Come out. Hands up!" the robber nearest to Miss Freyling hollered. "Now!"

An older man, one I recognized from coming into the telegraph office, stepped out, hands reaching upward. "Don't shoot. Please don't hurt anybody."

"Over here with the others." The outlaw near me waved his pistol at all of us. "Over there by the wall." The other two masked men snatched stacks of bills from the tellers' drawers.

I inched sideways until me and the other customers were shoulder to shoulder. Eyes on the only woman in the room, I made sure she wasn't molested. Muscles tensed, ready to spring into action, despite the gun in my back, I'd be the first to rescue her.

We stood on the far side of the room, waiting for the

men to finish emptying the drawers, then leave. The vault. Most of the money was stored there.

As if on cue, one of the bandits behind the counter yelled, "Got everything. Where's the vault?"

All eyes turned to the older man, the bank president. He pointed to a closed wooden door.

The closest bandit grabbed him by the collar, yanking him toward the door. The old man clutched his chest and sank to his knees, moaning. The outlaw growled, pushed him away, then grabbed my vest, pulling me toward the door.

"I don't work here. Don't know the combination." If I'd known it, truthfully, I would have opened the safe. But I didn't. Couldn't help at all.

Shortest of the outlaws rushed from behind the counter, waved a gun at the three of us. "Get their money. Let's go."

"Need lots of money," the other man hollered. Was that a bushy beard sticking out from his mask? "I aim to get rich. Now somebody open the damn safe." He grabbed the teller cowering against Miss Freyling. "You! Open it!"

The cash in my vest warmed. The pocket was hard to see and maybe they'd miss it. The outlaw still gripping me patted my vest. Finding a slight bulge where the twenty-three dollars rested, he chinned at me. "Money. Now!"

The gun barrel stuck in my face was the size of a cannon. I shook and no matter how hard I tried to open my vest, my hands wouldn't grab the material. Plus, it wasn't my money, and I couldn't let it simply be taken. Without much thought, I shoved the man back two steps hoping the other men would jump him.

Fast as a cat, the bandit swung his gun at my head.

Whack! Stars and black crowded my vision. The rug was soft.

* * *

"He's comin' around, Da."

"'Bout time. Thought he'd sleep all day." A sigh. "Second time this year he's been *banjaxed*."

"Let's sit him up."

Voices confused me. There were so many echoing in my head. Oh, my head. The left side throbbed and burned. I touched something crunchy. Someone pushed my hand away.

"Ye got cracked hard, son. Lookin' more like a melted welly. But ye'll be gran' in a day or two."

Was that Da? Didn't sound like him, but definitely wasn't Ma. I opened my eyes and sure enough, there was Da kneeling in front of me. On his right was Eagan. To his right, kneeled the town's deputy sheriff, Tommy... something.

I blinked into full consciousness, or what I assumed was full. "Where?" Did that word come out as croaky as I thought?

Da patted my shoulder. "Still at the bank. On the floor." He wagged his head. "Got robbed. Whole place got robbed."

Memories flooded into my brain. I blinked harder. Three men. Guns pointed. Hands up. Miss Freyling! I sat straighter. "The tellers...Miss Freyling..."

The deputy pointed over my shoulder toward the teller's cages. "All fine. They're shook up, like you, but the only injuries were to you and one other customer. Bank president had a mild heart attack. But looks like all y'all's gonna live."

And then it hit me. Assault. Robbery. Mr. Whalen's money. I patted my chest. No vest. Eagan pointed to a pile of material lying in tatters near me. He held up the pieces of the vest and I found the secret pocket wasn't so secret. It had been ripped apart which meant the money was gone.

"Let's get ye on yer feet, see if ye need the doc." Da came around behind me, slipped his arms under me and lifted. My knees held for a moment, then chose to buckle. I slumped. Normally, I'd have been embarrassed, but his strength was reassuring. I'd be embarrassed tomorrow.

The deputy grabbed one arm. "I'm gonna need you to answer some questions, Joe. Feel like it now?" He looked at me, Da, and then Eagan. "Need to get a posse together first thing in the morning."

"Not tonight?" Da's question was edged with outrage.

Tommy wagged his head. "Getting dark and Walter, uh, Sheriff Wagner's not in town. Supposed to be back later tonight, and since I'm...Eagan and me...are the only officers in town, need somebody to stay behind. Hopefully, that'll be Wagner." He nodded to Eagan. "I'd like you to come."

"Come with you? In the posse? Of course." Eagan cocked his head toward me. "Joe, too? He saw the men."

"Feel like going?" Tommy frowned at me, gripped my arm tighter.

Of course, I would go, but my world right now was spinning. I thought I'd answered him, but apparently not when Eagan said, "If he's up to it, he'll go, too. I can get his statement tonight when he's feeling better." He raised one shoulder at me. "Right?"

Da shook his head. "Sure, look it. For now, he's going home. We'll see about tomorrow."

As much as I wanted to snap at Da for telling me how I felt and whether I'd join the posse or not, I realized he was worried about me. I had no right to be angry.

Standing there, Da turned to Tommy. "I can ride with ye. Be happy ta."

The deputy looked around me at Da. "Appreciate the offer. But I'll take the younger men who can ride fast. No offense, Mr. Nolan."

Da looked a bit relieved. "None taken. But offers stands."

Going home seemed the best idea, but right now, lunch was busy making its way up. I pointed to the door and staggered that way, but before reaching outside, everything I'd ever eaten came boiling up, splatting onto the rug, my boots, and Da's boots.

Someone opened the big doors, and I stumbled outside, bringing up more breakfast and lunch parts. Once I quit shaking and gasping, I sat on the wooden boardwalk steps waiting for the world to stop spinning. Finally, all I had left was a blistering headache, one that felt familiar. Earlier this year I'd been hit on the head at the telegraph office and resulted in what the doc called a concussion. I'd suffered from bad headaches for a week afterward. I hoped we still had some of that painkiller mixture, laudanum, at home. Looked like I'd be needing some.

Da sat next to me while Eagan and Tommy talked to the robbery victims. Mind clearing, I needed answers. "Who were those robbers? Where are they? How'd you find out I was here?" There were more, but that was all I had right then.

Shaking his head, Da lowered his voice. "Got away.

Here and gone before anybody knew the bank was being robbed." He pointed behind us at the bank. "Tommy ran by the store telling Eagan about the robbery. Don't know how he found out. Eagan came back telling me ye were here."

"They took my money. Mr. Whalen's money." I looked over at Da. "He's gonna fire me."

Da rocked my knee. "Go way outta that. Twasn't yer fault at'all." His Irish accent on full display, he mumbled a couple of Irish phrases about "bodachs," and one short prayer I recognized from the supper table.

CHAPTER TWO

ALONE ON THE PORCH STEPS AFTER SUPPER, I sat holding my head and mentally kicking myself for not doing more to protect Mr. Whalen's money. And Da's money, although he seemed more concerned about my health than his life's savings. Probably tomorrow he'd worry, but tonight he'd spent too much time looking at me. Supper, ham and eggs, had been a trial.

I'd never forget the look on Ma's face when, with Da on one side, Eagan on the other, they walked me up the steps and into the front room. She'd rushed in fussing then fuming. Eagan helped me wash up and he was the one who told her about my shredded vest. Between losing all Da's store's money, my head and shredded vest, no wonder she ranted. Her Irish spoutings and then regular English sayings, muddled with her thick accent, made her impossible to understand. I hoped she'd calm down by bedtime.

Ma had fussed over me more than usual. As hoped, she found a tucked-away laudanum bottle and made sure I downed a big spoonful of the painkiller. Feeling the effects as I sat, my world didn't hurt much or spin like it had at supper. No, right then, I was furry. Soft, furry, like a kitten.

One thing was missing though. As much as I loved Ma and appreciated what she did for me and the rest of us men, I missed my wife. I needed a wife's touch on my tender head, not Ma's. I needed a woman to curl up against tonight who'd tell me I'd be all right. I needed my dear Frieda, now dead six weeks or so. She had been way too young to die. Barely twenty, both of us. But a miscarriage gone wrong took her life and that of what may have been a baby girl. Some said it had been too early to tell the gender, but an older midwife confirmed it was.

I'd never know for certain and wasn't sure I wanted to know. Tears trickled down my cheeks and nothing I could do would stop them. I ached inside and out. An emptiness in my chest, in my soul, brought more tears. Was that me sobbing? I'd done my share of crying right after she died and then once on the ride back from Denver when her parents forced me to leave. As Germans, they didn't approve of me. A lowly Irishman, they said. And Catholic to boot. They had hated the idea of Frieda and me getting married, but we loved each other despite our backgrounds and wed sooner than we'd planned. The surprise baby had helped that.

I loved Frieda and wished it was me in the ground instead. Good-intentioned people, Da included, said I'd find somebody else. Somebody I'd love as much as her. But they were wrong. The world was wrong. Life was wrong. I bawled into my hands.

I must've sat like that for a good ten minutes until, feeling like a fool, took down my hands and gazed into the dark Texas landscape. Would I simply sit here night after night feeling sorry for myself, or do something about it? Was it time to venture out into the world and be a man again? Or what did I really, truly want in life?

Those kinds of questions I hated. There were no clear answers. At least I had a job and family. They gave me love, support, a roof over my head, proper victuals, and a bed at night. Although the bed was lonely, I couldn't complain too much. I had it good. Better than most.

But I needed a woman. A wife.

Moon beams danced among branches of the towering Texas oaks and pecan trees down by the creek. If I'd felt better, I'd wander down there to throw rocks into the water. But my entire body ached like I'd run to hell and back. Or lifted a thousand-pound bull. Or climbed Pikes Peak, which I'd ridden past in Colorado.

The screen door creaked open behind me. Before I could turn halfway around, a glass of cold buttermilk appeared at my shoulder.

"Ma thinks this'll help." Eagan handed me the glass, eased down next to me on the steps, and sipped his own. He pointed to nothing in particular in the dark. "Head still hurt?"

I shrugged. "Not too bad. That laudanum works wonders."

"It does. Just be—"

"Careful. I know. It's addictive and I understand why." I held up my glass. "I feel so...so...soft."

Eagan chuckled. "Like a baby rabbit?" He shoulder bumped me. "Ma's hidden the bottle again, so enjoy the feeling while you can."

We sat in the cooling Texas air on the unforgiving porch planks, until my rear end turned quite numb. Eagan helped me stand, picked up both empty glasses, and hovered over me like a mother hen until I'd stepped inside. I said good night to Ma and Da now turning down the oil lamps' wicks, then blowing out the sputtering flames. Except for hesitant shafts of moonlight, the front room turned dark.

I managed to navigate the stairs up to the bedroom I shared with younger brother, Eagan. I used to share it with my older brother, Tate, also, but now he lived on a nearby ranch. The room had been crowded with three of us, but now it felt empty. Eagan came in, pulled off his boots and clothes, and snuggled into bed before I could unbutton my shirt. If I'd had a wife, I'd be fully undressed by now.

Pressure pushed behind my eyes.

* * *

THE SKY DAWNED light purple and blue as Eagan and I saddled our horses, tucked sandwiches Ma had made into the saddlebags, then led our mounts from the barn around to the front of the house. Ma and Da waited, both frowning, concern etching their faces. Da's arms folded across his chest made him look more like a warrior than a father wishing his boys a safe journey.

We tipped our hats to our folks and swung up into the saddles. "We'll find 'em, Da." I hoped those words came out as strongly as I wanted them to. Truthfully, I hadn't slept well the night before, despite the laudanum. And right now, Ma was growing fuzzy around the edges. But I couldn't, wouldn't, let them see me as anything but resilient. I could do this. So much of me, as it rolled around in my head last night, so much of me needed to get that money back. Da's future had been stolen and I wasn't going to let that set.

Mr. Whalen's money. His future. All the townspeople

who relied on that bank to safeguard their money...they needed it returned. Their future was at stake. No, I wouldn't let them down.

Eagan reached down from his saddle and hugged Ma. He was agile like that, like he'd been born on a horse. Da shook hands with me, then Eagan. Although I'd patted the top of Ma's head already, I leaned over and hugged her as best I could. It certainly wasn't as graceful as Eagan's, but my attempt was heartfelt, if not a bit wobbly.

We waved over our shoulders as we trotted up the street toward the sheriff's office. Hopefully, by now, Tommy had an idea where we were headed.

* * *

TO MY SURPRISE, four other horses were tied at the hitch rail next to the office. The door was open, and one fella I recognized, but couldn't name, leaned halfway out. Eagan and I tossed the reins around the rail and started toward the office when Tommy and Sheriff Wagner stepped out.

Wagner held up a hand. "Some fella came riding in from Fredericksburg complaining the sheriff over there wasn't keeping his eyes open for outlaws. So, since we're the next county over, bigger town than us, guess that leaves it to us. We'll head over there first."

He then introduced everyone. Three men I didn't know. One tall, lanky fella, Jim Blanchard, was the son-in-law of Mr. Krause who owned the gun shop. Another one went by Tiny, although there wasn't much tiny about him. He was mostly muscles and broad shoulders and a head taller than the rest of us. The third, the fella in the door, introduced himself as Montgomery Snyder, "originally from Alabama," he'd drawled. "Call me Monty." He stuck out a hand the size of Texas.

Deputy Tommy O'Sullivan nodded at me. "How ya feeling, Joe?" He pointed at my head.

"Fine, if we don't mention it." I held up a hand. "I'm ready to go. We both are."

"Good." Tommy looked back at the sheriff. "Joe might be able to identify the robbers." He turned to me. "Hope you can."

Memories flooded in. Fuzzy memories. It took time bringing images back, surprised how long it took. I shrugged. "Being they were all masked, nothing special about any of them. Just like I said. And I don't remember them saying anything other than 'Hands up!' No accent or such."

Tommy released a long sigh, like he'd assumed overnight I'd know exactly who those bandits were.

Sheriff Wagner waited until the six of us were gathered. His gaze roved over each of us then he nodded. "Good group of men. Thank you for volunteering for a posse. Got word late last night—well, closer to this morning, that a couple of men were throwin' around a lot of cash over in Fredericksburg. Now that doesn't guarantee they're the bandits, but most folks in these parts don't have that kind of money."

"How much money, Sheriff?" Tiny stood straight, hands in vest pocket.

"Sizable sum, apparently." Wagner took a deep breath. "Now, that doesn't guarantee they're the bandits."

"Makes 'em suspicious though." Jim adjusted his gun belt around his hips.

Tommy fit his hat down tight. "It does. Don't know

how long we'll be gone. Hopefully by dark today, but I hope you brought bedrolls and couple canteens."

We had. Da had made sure we were provisioned for a week. He also said he'd tell Mr. Whalen I wouldn't be in for a few days. Inside, I smiled at Da's reaction to not riding with the posse—relief. He hadn't protested too much about being left behind.

Along with the other men, I yanked the reins from the hitch post, put my foot in the stirrup, then glanced at my horse. She shifted her weight twice, favoring her back left hoof. "Wait up, boys." I lifted her hoof and sure enough, the shoe wiggled, not down tight like it should be. I couldn't ride her like that.

Eagan stood at my side and pointed. "My best lad, Jimmy, is the blacksmith down at Alphonso's Livery. He can get your horse re-shod in no time." He looked at the rising sun. "Should be there, 'bout now."

Perfect. What else could go wrong? The sheriff's office and my horse both tilted. I shut my eyes, rubbed my head, then straightened up. Hand against my horse helped the world return to normal.

"You good?" Tommy leaned from his seat in the saddle.

I waved a hand at him. "Stood up too fast, is all. I'm good." Shielding my eyes against the brilliant golden sunrays, I pointed west. "Gonna have to get a new shoe. Go ahead. I'll catch up."

Eagan, reins in hand, stood next to me. "We won't be far behind. My friend's the best farrier around."

Surprised my brother was willing to stay behind, if only for a half hour or so, yet I was glad he was there. I still wasn't feeling all that well and, if I fell off my horse, or some such, it would be good to have him at my side.

Plus, I enjoyed his company. He told great stories, some of which I figured might even be true.

Eagan and I walked our horses down Main Street, nodding to the few folks were now out and about. Start of just another day in paradise. Hopefully, we'd be home in time for supper, but I wasn't holding out much hope of that happening. Most likely, we'd be gone a day or two empty-handed. Those bandits were fast, organized, and knew what they wanted. Undoubtedly, they were out of the territory by now. Hell, maybe even in Mexico. I would be.

Eagan's friend, Jimmy, was tying his heavy leather apron around his wide chest when we arrived. An expansive grin and firm handshake greeted us.

"Eagan, me lad!" He clapped Eagan's shoulder. "Up a bit early, aren't ya?" He turned to me. "Joe! Good to see ya again." His grin turned into a frown. "Sorry to hear about Frieda. I liked her. She was nice."

My heart teetered on breaking, but instead I took a deep breath. "Yeah, she was."

Awkward silence wedged itself in between us. Jimmy finished tying the apron. "What's going on?"

Eagan jumped in before I could explain. "We're part of the posse lookin' for the bank robbers."

I swear he sounded like an eight-year-old. I almost laughed at his enthusiasm.

"Are ya now? Posse? Wow. Now I know you're important." Jimmy shoved coal into the forge.

"What he's trying to say is my horse threw a shoe. I need a new one if we're gonna catch the bad guys." I tossed an exasperated sigh at Eagan, who tossed me shrugged shoulders and an endless grin. Yep. An eight-year-old.

Jimmy inspected the hoof, pried the old shoe off, and

held it up. "See? Nail came out. And this one was about to." He nodded to me. "Shouldn't take but a few minutes soon's these coals heat up."

While Eagan and Jimmy chatted waiting, I wandered down the line of stalls, admiring one of the horses munching on hay. A large bay, had to be sixteen hands, turned her head to see who was standing nearby. I patted her rump, turned, and about ran into a man, taller than me, bushy beard. He eyed me like I was a piece of meat, or the enemy. Or both.

"Excuse me." I moved back. "She yours? Beautiful animal."

A glare is all he gave me. Something about him looked familiar. Something, but what? Had I seen him before? I doubted it. And he didn't seem to recognize me. Or did his eyeballing me up and down, say it all?

A nagging, gut-wrenching sensation climbed into my chest. Involuntarily, I shivered. Nothing about this man I liked. Instead of looking at the rest of the horses, and there seemed to be plenty, I picked up my pace back to Eagan and Jimmy.

Embroiled in a detailed conversation about fish, Eagan and Jimmy took a breath. Eagan frowned. "You all right, Joe? Better sit. You're more than gray. You're white."

I did need to sit. Jimmy led me to a stool where I plopped down. What was wrong with me? True, my head was now pounding, but why did I feel like I'd just met the Devil incarnate?

"Couple more minutes, Joe, then you'll be good to go." Jimmy held up a horseshoe. "Well, maybe not you, but your horse will."

I sat, leaning against a wooden fence rail, and closed my eyes. Memories from the holdup exploded in my head. My heart was about to explode out of my chest. Hands reaching for the ceiling. Being yanked toward the safe. My pulling on the bandit's mask. His bushy beard sticking out.

My eyes flew open. The man at the stall! Was that him? Was he one of the robbers? But who, in his right mind, would rob a bank and stay in town? Wouldn't it make sense to hightail it to hell and gone?

I stood so quickly that the fence post whirled. I held on until my world righted itself. Could I be sure this was one of the men? Probably, since he was so unpleasant when we met. Then, probably not. I couldn't be certain, and I'd hate for someone to hang when I wasn't totally sure.

"Horse's ready." Eagan's voice made me jump. "You all right? Still wanna go?"

Bushy Beard walked up to Jimmy and held out a coin. He glared at me again, then turned his dark eyes on Eagan, giving him a long, steady look. He frowned at the badge on Eagan's chest, then looked at my chest. No badge. I wasn't sure if that was a good thing or not.

"Thank you, sir." Jimmy pocketed the money. "Enjoyed your stay in Blanco Hill?"

The man shrugged, turned, headed for his horse, then gave a long glance over his shoulder at me.

"Friendly cuss." Jimmy raised an eyebrow and gave a glassy stare.

I pointed toward the man now riding away and lowered my voice. "Think that's one of the bandits. The one who hit me."

"What?" Eagan and Jimmy chimed in unison. "One of the robbers?"

"Couldn't be." Jimmy looked after the rider. "If I

remember right, came in couple days ago. Didn't say much, if anything. Good lookin' horse though."

"Fairly sure I'm right. Was he alone?"

Jimmy gazed toward the stalls as if they'd tell him. "Think so. Had two others come in, few hours apart, but they didn't seem to know each other. Real quiet. Just like this fella."

More than likely, I was wrong. But a feeling—something—nagged at my chest. I dug half a dollar out of my vest and handed the coin to Jimmy. "This'll cover it?"

"More than enough." Jimmy shook my hand. "You both be careful. If that *was* one of them, he knows you, Joe." He looked at Eagan. "Knows you too now."

I patted my horse, she and I had been through much together, swung up into the creaky saddle. "Think he's going to Fredericksburg?"

"Let's find out." Eagan pointed up the street. "How 'bout we go through town, see if he stopped for breakfast. Then head west?"

That sounded like a good plan to me. I thanked Jimmy once more and reined my horse toward town. Eagan and I took our time down Main and then peeked down alleys. No big bay horse. No Bushy Beard fella.

Without a word, we turned around at the end of town and headed west for Fredericksburg.

* * *

I KEPT a sharp eye out for the man. The longer I rode, the more convinced I was he was the bandit. My brother and I didn't say much. I'm sure he was as nervous as I was. Every half mile or so I swiveled around in the saddle and watched behind us. No dust clouds, no lone rider. Nobody. Of course, this early in the day, probably not a lot of people on the road. I expected more in an hour or two.

We couldn't gallop, which would have been preferable since we had to catch up, but my head wouldn't take the pounding. Couldn't trot, head hurt too much. A lope worked for a bit, but we didn't want to tire the horses. So we walked. And walked.

Getting to Fredericksburg, only twenty miles west of Blanco Hill, took under three hours. Usually. But this morning felt more like thirty.

We topped a rise about halfway between towns and spotted two men riding our way. Coming at a gallop, they raised a small dust cloud. I reined up, hoping to have a quick conversation, a customary stop, but even though Eagan and I waited on the side of the road, they gave a simple touch of the hat and continued roaring past.

"What d'ya think?" I unplugged the canteen and sipped over my question. My head throbbed, but otherwise, I was all right.

"In a hurry." Eagan stared after them. "Wonder why. And why they didn't stop. That's what we do, isn't it?"

"Most times. Only neighborly." A thought struck me. "Don't suppose it's the other two robbers hightailing it out of Fredericksburg cause the posses in town? Would that be a reason?"

Eagan turned his head toward me slowly. "Now, that's an idea." He bit his lower lip, a habit he'd had since he had teeth. "Think we oughta follow them?"

Now it was my turn to think. I gave it less than half a minute. "We should go meet up with the rest. Tell them what we saw. I got a pretty good look at the fella closest to us. Shorter than the other." I shrugged. "But that doesn't mean much."

"It might." Eagan plugged his canteen, wound the strap around the saddle horn. "Can you gallop for a bit? Get there faster."

I also returned my canteen and snugged down my hat. "Maybe a mile. Don't want to tire out the horses. They gotta get us back home." I nudged my mount into a trot, then lope, and finally a full-out gallop, Eagan next to me, his horse's stride matching mine's.

Farms dotted the landscape the closer we got to town. Cresting a hill, in front of us lay the German-founded town of Fredericksburg. I'd been there often enough to know it was easily twice the size of my home-town. Recently, I'd ridden through, once on my way to Denver and then back. But my family had attended Fourth of July celebrations there long before Blanco Hill grew big enough to have our own.

We met the others at the sheriff's office, all four standing on the boardwalk. Tommy was shaking hands with the county constable, Eldon Driggs, if the man's badge and sign by the window were accurate.

"Ah, here they are now!" Tommy introduced us to the sheriff. "Eagan Nolan's a deputy and his brother Joe, here, witnessed the holdup. He was at the bank when it was robbed. Got clobbered pretty good too." He pointed to my head, and I automatically stepped back, afraid he'd touch it.

I nodded at Driggs. He was about my height, looked to be around Da's age, graying hair at the temples, graying mustache, but otherwise clean shaven. "Sir."

Tommy pointed downtown. "Sheriff says two fellas were making large bets last night over at Gertude's Gast-shaus. Had quite the poker game going and then faro. Bought rounds for everyone...and there were over twenty men inside. More came in when they heard about free drinks."

Eagan's brow furrowed. "What'd these men look like?" He and I looked up and down the street like they'd be standing nearby, waiting for us.

Sheriff Driggs wagged his head. "That's the problem. Absolutely nothing special about either one. Mustaches, but no beards, brown hair under nondescript hats. One fella may have been shorter than the other, but not by much. No accents, no limps. Nothing."

Limps. Reminded me of Eagan. He limped from falling out of a wagon when he was a baby. At age four, oldest brother Tate was in charge of watching him while all three of us were riding in the back of the wagon. But Tate couldn't always keep squirmy Eagan contained. Out he went.

Apparently, his twisted, broken leg didn't heal properly. He'd always had a limp, but that didn't keep him from doing anything he wanted. I'd admired that about him.

I told them about the two men we'd passed, but Driggs didn't think that was them.

I regarded Tommy and the others, then pointed east. "This morning at the farrier's, we may have run into one of the bandits. Fella with a bushy beard. I think...I could be wrong. The man who hit me had a big beard like that."

"You sure, Joe?" Driggs stood straight, fingered his holstered gun.

"Not really. When I close my eyes, sometimes I get quick visions of a masked man with a beard right when I got buffaloed, but I can't tell if it's real or not." I raised one hand. "Sorry."

"All right, men. Fan out around town. Talk to as many

people as you can. I've already put the bank on alert, so no need to go there." Driggs eyed us all. "Meet back here in an hour."

Something about this sheriff set wrong on me. Couldn't put my finger on exactly what, but that nagging feeling wouldn't let me stay quiet. "How long were they at this Gastshaus, Sheriff? Know where they are now?"

Driggs studied the sky. "Started being rowdy around ten, I guess. Stayed a couple hours, then went to sleep it off, I suppose. Don't know where they are now." He narrowed his eyes at me. "That's *your* job, Joe."

Now I really didn't trust him. The others headed in various directions. I stepped toward town and then stopped, turned to Driggs. "Where were you yesterday afternoon, Sheriff? If you don't mind my asking."

Tommy slid to a stop beside me, leaned in and spoke softly. "What're you doing?"

Driggs shook a pointed finger in my face. "Don't like your attitude, boy. You questioning where I was? Think I was part of the robbery? You have some nerve insinuating—"

I held up a hand. "No sir, I wasn't meaning anything by that. Just wondering if you'd seen those two fellas beforehand, is all." So, I had to scramble to make that up. Yes, I thought he might somehow be involved. I knew lawmen didn't make much money. Generally, the town or county paid wages, but you couldn't live on them. Collecting taxes and getting a cut of those, supplemented their meager income. Wouldn't surprise me if he was corrupt. Our own Sheriff Wagner too.

Eagan stood on my left. Close. Was this Driggs going to arrest me? Or deck me? For asking a question?

Sheriff Driggs moved in close and growled. "If you must know, I was playing a private game of poker over at another saloon, the Texas Tumbler. There were five of us, closed to the public. Only the bartender, Gustav, knows exactly who was there, and he's not talking."

"Thank you, Sheriff. We'll spread out now." Tommy offered to shake with Driggs again, but the sheriff wouldn't take the outstretched hand. Tommy gripped my upper arm. "Need to see you."

Once out of Driggs's earshot, Tommy explained, loud and clear, that questioning the sheriff, who'd asked you to come help investigate, was not polite, nor a good idea. I was to apologize when I got back from canvassing the town.

I agreed to apologize but the first place I'd headed to was this Texas Tumbler. Eagan and I headed up West Main, briefly discussing why most towns had a Main Street. Why not call it something else, like First? Or Gold?

Locating the Tumbler wasn't hard. Getting in was difficult. Locked. The saloon was locked. And then I realized it was still early by saloon standards. I banged on the door and caught loud grumbling from the other side.

"Closed. Open in a half hour."

I turned to Eagan. "I've irritated enough people today. Let's come back in thirty minutes."

CHAPTER THREE

THIRTY MINUTES LATER, EAGAN PULLED OPEN the batwing doors and we both stepped inside the Texas Tumbler. Dark wood paneling lined the walls highlighted by streaks of daylight desperate to find their way through smudged windows. Odors of beer, whiskey, and well-saturated straw at the base of the wooden bar swirled around my head. I sneezed. My eyes watered. In my thinking, men should go around back to use the privy instead of stand at the bar and let go. Under that straw would be a shallow tin trough. Didn't contain the smell though.

Gustav was about as burly a man as I'd seen in quite a while. Shorter than me, and I was a thumb over six foot, this fella was built like an upside-down pyramid. Shoulders were at least ten axe handles wide, chest an ox would envy, waist of normal proportions, and legs, in comparison, were slim. I'd burned kindling thicker than his legs. But, no doubt, they served him well.

I stuck out a hand. "Gustav?"

He grunted and studied my hand like I had either coin or pox in the palm.

"Mr. Gustav?" Eagan looked around the room. "I'm Deputy Eagan Nolan from Blanco Hill." He pointed east. "And this is Joe, an eyewitness to the bank robbery there yesterday. Mind if I ask you some questions?"

Maybe Eagan, with youth written all over him, could get Gustav to tell us what we needed to know. The way that German eyed me, I was surprised he hadn't spit on me yet. He grunted again, tossed the stained rag he was holding onto the top of the bar, and chinned toward a round table with the chairs pushed under.

We sat, Gustav on my left, his body wedged into a wooden armchair. He studied my face, pointed to my left temple and frowned. "Got hit good, I see. *Der räubers* do dat?" He sported a light German accent; he'd probably been in this country since he was young.

So, the man spoke. I touched the side of my head, jerked it back. Damn tender, damn sore. From my chin to hairline it hurt. Was I bruised too? Probably. I nodded.

Eagan leaned back in his chair, crossed one leg over the other like he was spending the day visiting an old friend. "Understand you had quite the poker game going on yesterday afternoon." Before Gustav responded, my brother continued. "How long did it go on? When did it start?"

The barkeep regarded Eagan and then me. His chestnut brown eyes, slightly crossed and definitely bloodshot, roamed over us like he was deciding who to eat first. A chuckle rose from deep inside that broad chest. "I keep *das tür* closed," he pointed behind him at a shut, wooden door. "Private party. Didn't pay much attention. I go in, serve dem whiskey. Come back out."

Eagan repeated his question. "From when to when?"

Shrugging, Gustav's mouth rose on one side. "*Wer weiß*. Hard to tell."

Clearly, Eagan was on a roll. He uncrossed his legs and leaned forward. "You know those men? The ones playing poker? Seen them before? Understand Sheriff Driggs was part of it."

Glancing side to side as if the room was packed, when in fact, we were it, Gustav leaned forward also, lowered his voice. "Some I know, some no." He shook his head slowly.

"So, some have been in here before? How about Driggs?" I couldn't help but repeat the question.

Prying himself loose of the chair, Gustav stood. "You tink dey're the robbers?" He folded his arms across his chest. "Dey come in play cards. How dey rob bank, so far away?"

"Not sure. That's why we're asking around." Eagan stood. "Mind if we go back there?" He pointed to the closed door. "Just for a quick peek."

"I do mind. Not cleaned up yet."

"But—"

"You need *das Gewährleislung*."

I blinked. Twice.

"A warrant." Gustav narrowed his eyes, like I was supposed to know German.

Eagan regarded me, then raised one finger. "Just one more question."

"*Jah?*"

"Where were you yesterday afternoon?"

Gustav belly laughed. "You tink *I* be the bank robber?" He pointed at the door. "*Rau shier!* Get out."

We stood on the boardwalk a few businesses down from the Tumbler. "What d'you think?" What I really thought was that Eagan had asked a stupid question, but then again, did Gustav work all day, every day? Probably. I wasn't sure I believed Gustav but had no good reason not to.

"He's lying."

Surprised, I looked behind me at the saloon then back at Eagan. "Why?"

"Remember those 'gut feelings' you have?"

I nodded, still surprised.

"I got a big one from him. He's lying, and he's guilty. Probably one of the robbers."

I considered his words. "Couldn't be a robber; he was here, the whole time. If he was, it made a great alibi. But…"

Monty, one of our fellow posse members, walked up and thumbed over his shoulder. "Tommy wants us back at the sheriff's." He picked at something in his teeth. "Find anything?"

"Just more questions." Eagan shook his head. "You?"

"Same. I don't think those bandits came this way. Nobody's seen or heard hide nor hair. Nothing. Nada. Zilch. The big zero." He held both hands, palms out. "Hells, bells. I even went into one of them cat houses—for research purposes only, of course."

"Of course." I couldn't help but smile at Monty. I'd like to get to know him better, maybe have a beer with him at Sam's back home. "And?" I was dying to hear the rest of the story.

"Got propositioned coupla times. Met one fine-lookin' filly but didn't see who we're lookin' for. Fact is, most of them Mollies was asleep. Alone. All by them-selves. Had me a notion to remedy that situation, but…" He shrugged. "Duty calls."

Yep. I'd definitely enjoy getting to know him.

We squeezed in with the others inside Driggs's office.

The sheriff sat behind a paper-littered desk, pencil in hand, scowl on his face. "Well?"

Without exception, we all shrugged. Driggs, unhappy with the response, raised his voice. "Who checked at Gertrude's?"

Tiny, who had nothing tiny about him, raised a hand halfway up. "I did. Not much to tell. She mentioned men with money, spent some, then took the rest with 'em when they staggered out. Around ten, she said."

Sheriff Driggs and Tommy surveyed the rest of us posse. Tommy whipped off his hat and ran a hand across the top of his head. "Damn and double damn. Where the hell *are* these men?"

I wasn't about to say anything about Gustav and our doubts. Gut feelings didn't hold up in a court of law. But all this was taking way too long. With each passing moment, those bandits, those future-stealers, were farther away. Or were they?

Air was at a premium and I stood, leaning against a wall. Images grew gray and fuzzy. The room spun.

I nudged Eagan and pointed outside. He nodded. I pushed my way through the group and brought welcomed air into my lungs. Holding onto the side of the building, I pulled in more air. Horses trotting down Main lengthened, like being stretched. Their riders turned bright red. I stumbled to the steps and plunked down.

Pounding head in shaking hands, I shut my eyes, and breathed as deeply as I could. Breakfast, of what little there had been, decided now would be a good time to come back up. I gripped the wooden post, then pushed off, running toward the privy out back.

I didn't quite make it, but I was only a few feet away. I kneeled while this morning's apple and roll splatted onto the ground. Stomach roiling, I spit again and again.

Nothing left to come up, not even my toenails, I held onto the privy wall to stand and spotted a man with a bushy beard entering another privy about twenty yards away. Was it the same man? I wiped my eyes and waited. He had to come out some time.

I waited some more.

"There you are!" Eagan tapped my left arm. "What happened? You all right? Tommy says—"

"Shhhh." I pointed. "Bushy Beard's in there."

Eagan frowned at me. "What? He's here?"

I nodded and kept my voice low. "Spotted him maybe five minutes ago. Hasn't come out yet."

"Same fella? In there?" Eagan whispered.

Again, I nodded. Time was ticking and that money needed to be recovered and returned to the good people of Blanco Hill. But, while I stood against the privy, hopefully hidden from him, I considered all I knew.

First, the Blanco Hill bank got robbed around four, half four, yesterday. They took all the money from the vault and most from the teller's drawers. And mine from my vest. Second, twenty miles away, Sheriff Driggs and four others conveniently conducted a private poker game, yesterday afternoon. Third, last night, a couple of men were throwing around a lot of money. How did all that connect? Or did it?

A privy door squeaked. I peeked around the wall and sure enough, out stepped Bushy Beard, buttoning his trousers. Before I could say anything, Eagan headed for the man and the privy. He bumped into him.

"Sorry, sir." Eagan spoke loud enough for me to easily hear him. "I apologize. A bit in a hurry, I guess."

Bushy Beard stopped, growled, and stared at Eagan, his eyes roving up and down his length. To my surprise, just when I figured I'd have to come to Eagan's rescue,

Eagan pointed to the outhouse. "It's important." Eagan yanked open the door, stepped inside, and slammed it. Well, good on him for thinking of that. I probably wouldn't have.

The possible outlaw stared at the closed door, grunted, then turned and lumbered toward Main. When he was out of sight, I knocked on the privy door, waited for Eagan to open it, then I pointed to town. "Gonna follow him."

Eagan nodded. "Me, too."

We walked quietly, but quickly. It would probably be a good idea if the posse knew what we were doing. "How about you go tell Tommy what's going on?" I spotted the deputy sheriff in the next block talking to the posse. "I'll see if I can find ol' Bushy."

"Watch yourself." Eagan hurried toward Tommy. "I'll be right behind you."

Casting glances left and right and seeing nothing of importance, I focused on straight ahead. That fella sure could disappear easily. And quickly. He didn't have much of a lead and yet, where in the hell was he? I ducked into the General Mercantile, glanced down a row of bolts of calico, tools hanging on the walls, and a rack of men's trousers. On the checkout counter were large jars of black licorice, gumballs, and pickles. This place wasn't big enough to hide many people and I counted only four customers.

No Bushy Beard. My head sent jabbing pains from the temple into my jaw. My back teeth ached. If this turned out to be the fella who clobbered me, I'd be more than happy to repay him. My hand fisted. Give me the chance. Just one.

And then I thought of Da's money. And Mr. Whalen's. I wasn't any closer to finding it now than I was before dawn this morning. Were we on a fool's errand? Was this bearded fella even involved? And why was I growing more and more sure he was one of the robbers?

I stepped outside, focused on the saloon across the street. Ah. Gertrude's Gasthause. The saloon where supposedly two men were tossing around money last night. Although another posse member had asked inside, what would it hurt if I went over there? Should I wait for Eagan? No telling how long he'd be, and in all probability my quarry wasn't in there. First, I looked down toward the sheriff's and spotted one of our men sitting on the steps. Looked like we weren't leaving quite yet. I dashed across the street, dodging two passing wagons and three riders. Things had certainly picked up since we first arrived, this morning.

Inside was livelier than the Tumbler, at least there were people, besides a skinny bartender. Gertrude was nowhere to be seen. I counted six men—three standing at the bar, clinking glasses with each other, and three others at a table, a deck of cards spread on top. No one seemed to have a stack of cash. At least not yet.

I leaned on the bar and nodded to the men. They nodded back, eyeing me. The barkeep sauntered over. "*Bier?*"

No kind of alcohol sounded good, but maybe a beer would help my head. "*Bitte.*" I slid a dime across the bar, mentally thanking Frieda for teaching me a touch of German. Before I could straighten my borrowed vest, a mug full of yellow liquid slid in front of me. It sloshed over the side, but not much. I sipped. Warm and stale, a whiff of rusted nails wafted up. Ten cents was overpriced for this swill, but I wouldn't complain. I'd have a couple sips, ask questions, and move on.

The men at my elbow seemed friendly enough. I leaned my right side against the bar and spoke to the nearest man, a few years older than me, but not by much, maybe pushing late twenties, I'd say. "You come here often?" I reeled back. Oof. That sounded too much like a pickup line. I stuttered and stammered. "I mean... is this a good place for a beer? I'm new to town..."

He laughed. A good, honest laugh. "That's a line *I* use."

Immediately, I liked this man. "Sorry. Words get tangled up sometimes."

"They sure do." He put down his beer mug and stuck out a hand. "Felix Border and these are my friends, Larry and Rico."

"Howdy." I nodded to the other two. "You from around these parts? Heard there was quite the excitement in here last night." An attempt at sipping my beer made my eyes water.

"There was." Felix pointed a finger at my head. "But looks like you had some of your own. That's one helluva bruise."

With one eyebrow raised, I touched my head. More sore than yesterday. "Yep. One angry horse. Be all right in a day or two." At least I sure hoped so.

Rico leaned closer. "Never seen so much cash crossin' a table. I was at a table next to 'em and just itchin' to get my hands on some of it." He shrugged and looked at Larry. "Least got free whiskey. Guess that was something."

"So all of you were here?" I looked from Rico to Larry, who nodded. Felix made a wry mouth. I was close now to finding the robbers. "Who had all the money? Know 'em?"

Felix spoke first. "I was at home with the missus.

Expecting a baby, she is, and tethers me like a steer at dehorning time. Lets me out during the day only for a couple hours. Can't go anywhere at night." He stared into his half-empty mug.

Images of Frieda screaming in pain, crying about losing the baby, her writhing on the floor, blood everywhere, hit me in the chest. I couldn't breathe. I was there, holding her in my arms, gripping her hand, unable to do anything. Nothing. Helpless. I was so helpless. My fault. She shouldn't have died. All my fault. If we hadn't…

I looked up from my beer mug. The three men stared at me.

"There a problem?" Larry furrowed his forehead, which was considerable. "Got lost in recollections, it seemed."

"Sorry." I pulled back into the here and now. Da's money. Had to get it back. I repeated my question. "You know who had all that money?"

Rico and Larry passed a glance at each other. Rico nodded. "Seen 'em a time or two. Not regulars in here but seen 'em hanging around down by the livery. Guess maybe they work there."

"Got names?" Hope creeped into my chest and swirled. Maybe this day wasn't wasted after all.

The men studied the ceiling, then each other. "Heard one of 'em call the other 'Mex.' Least I think that's what he said." Rico sipped his beer. "Maybe it was 'Tex.'"

Not much help, but I'd take it. I couldn't help asking, "You know a fella with a big, bushy beard? Couple inches taller'n me? Live around here?"

Felix chuckled. "You sure you're not fishing for male companionship?"

My stomach churned. No way. I shook my head too

fast. The room spun and the few sips of beer I'd had, threatened to come up. I pointed toward the door. "Thanks for the talk." I took three long steps, reached for the door, but before I grasped the handle, the door swung inward. Bushy Beard lumbered in. We shoulder bumped trying to pass.

He grabbed my vest, spun me around. "You followin' me?"

"What?" Surprised I could speak, I pushed down rising beer.

"Third time today I seen you." He slammed me up against the wall, his Texas-sized hand around my throat.

Three times? Hell, he must've seen me by the privy.

"You make me mad." He squeezed tighter. "Don't make me mad."

Like a beetle stuck with a pin, I swung at his chest and grabbed at the hand strangling me. My hands clawed at his arms. I kicked out, found a knee. Breathing grew impossible. I wheezed while the room grayed.

Images of the three men crowded around. Voices rose, one over the other. I couldn't make out any specific word.

"Hold it!"

All talking stopped. Bushy Beard's grip increased, pushed me against the wall harder.

"Let 'im go!" Eagan's voice.

Bushy Beard growled.

"I'm Deputy Eagan Nolan. Release him. Step away." Gun in hand, he pointed it at the man's chest.

The man shoved my shoulders hard into the wall. My head cracked against the wood. Regarding Eagan, he growled again, then released me. I slumped but remained upright.

"You grand'?" Eagan spoke over his shoulder, and kept his gun aimed at my assailant.

Nodding, I struggled for air while massaging my sore throat. "Yeah."

Eagan wagged his gun at Bushy Beard, indicating an empty table. "You. Take a seat." He looked at the three men from the bar now standing like they'd done something wrong. "What's this all about?" Eagan's words turned hard, authoritative, confident. "You all part of this?"

Before they could answer, I croaked. "No. They were coming to help."

We spent a little while discussing who did what to whom. Felix, Larry, and Rico were more than happy to explain events. Bushy Beard simply sat and glared. I rubbed my throat and warbled my side of things.

About the time Eagan had decided he had things straight and no charges would be brought, a buxomly women, blonde hair tied up in braids on her head, yanked open a door from behind the bar and marched in, the skinny bartender close behind.

"*Was geht weiter?*" She halted next to Bushy Beard. "Vhat's going on?"

Eagan nodded at the man, then back at me. "This fella here, assaulted this man. Tried to kill him, he did."

"*Nien, nien.*" She stared at my assailant. "He a gut boy. A *mensch*. Cause no trouble."

Right, and I'm Queen Victoria. I wanted to laugh at the woman, but my throat was too sore. Words stuck.

Rico held a hand out to Eagan to gain his attention, then pointed at the woman. "That fella is Gert's brother. She's quite protective."

At least that part made sense. But besides that, what was his connection with the robbery?

Eagan turned to Rico. "Was he in here last night? When the fellas with the money were celebrating?"

Both Rico and Larry shook their heads. "Didn't see him. And he's hard to miss."

Eagan nodded and raised an eyebrow. "That he is." His gaze roved over all six of us, stopping on my assailant. "I won't arrest you today, Mr...." He frowned. "What *is* your name?"

He growled again. "Huber. August Huber."

"Well, Mr. Huber." Eagan holstered his gun. "I'll let you go this time, with a warning. Keep that temper of yours in check."

Huber sprung from his chair and pointed at Eagan. "Don't ever, ever tell me what to do, you *winzling*."

I wasn't sure what he'd just called my brother, but Gertrude smiled at it. Had to be derogatory, but it was simply a word. No physical harm done.

Eagan nodded to the three men. "Thanks for stepping in." He then turned to me. "Posse's waiting. Need to go."

I waved to Felix, Rico, and Larry. "Good meeting you," I gargled.

Eagan and I stepped into the warming Fredericksburg air. My stomach growled, this time from hunger. We walked up the street toward the Sheriff's office, where men I recognized were coming off the boardwalk, heading our way.

"Suppose we can get a sandwich or something before heading back?" I hoped maybe even a bowl of soup would stay down.

CHAPTER FOUR

THE SUN SAT ON THE HORIZON AS WE TROTTED into Blanco Hill. The entire ride back, I thought and rethought what I'd learned. None made much sense, but I was sure, convinced, that Bushy Beard—August Huber —was involved. One thing I knew for certain was we didn't get the town's money back and there would be terrible consequences. Businesses would have to close, including Da's. People would be forced to move...

The vegetable soup I'd slurped down for lunch didn't fill my hungry belly. If I was hungry, the others should've been famished. We tied up at the sheriff's office, where Wagner stepped out to greet us. A semblance of a smile immediately turned down when he spoke to Tommy.

Tommy shrugged. "Nothing. Just more questions."

Wagner ran an exasperated hand across his face, muttered several choice curse words, then looked at us posse men, standing, waiting, tired. The sheriff threw up his hands. "What the hell, now? I talked to everyone in town today. Nobody got a good look at those men. Nobody was sure which way they rode out of town. Hell, nobody knows nothing." He fisted both hands. "So, what...the...hell?"

While Tommy and a couple of others relayed the day's events, I took stock of my body. I was tired, my head hurt, my throat raging sore, and I needed to eat. Probably more soup would go down. While I stood there like a schoolboy getting blamed for something I didn't do, I wondered if the Shoo Fly Café would be open right now. Or would Ma have something on the stove? Certainly. She did every day, but I didn't think chunks of ham would go down my throat. As it was, it scratched and hurt when I swallowed broth.

Tommy dismissed us. "Might need you tomorrow though. Stick close by."

All of us mumbled agreement, then scattered for home.

Darkness was fast approaching. The buildings were turning dark gray and already someone had lit a lantern near a saloon. Soon, the street would be ablaze in gold lantern light. My stomach rumbled again. Having soup at the café would be easier and quicker than going home. We wouldn't have to wait for Ma to reheat supper.

Eagan and I walked our horses down Main, tied them in front of the Shoo Fly, and ordered soup for me, and a plate of beef and potatoes for Eagan. Aromas of baked chicken, bread, and stews emanating from the kitchen swirled together to create a version of heaven.

Strong, dark coffee went down well for both of us. The waitress, Mrs. Dearden, a woman I'd known for years—I'd gone to school with her daughter—stopped at the table to chat while we waited for our food.

"Find anything today, Joe? Eagan?" She played with a fork on the table. "You know, all my savings was stolen.

Left with only petty cash for customer change, and that'll go only so far. Don't know what I'm gonna do."

I hated like the dickens to give her more bad news. "Not yet, Mrs. D. Haven't found it yet. But we will. We'll find those men, get your money."

Eagan added, "Da lost his money too. It's a terrible thing."

"That it is. That it is." She sighed and headed off to the kitchen.

The vegetable-laced soup slid down my throat more easily than it had at noon. The softened chunks of carrots were easy to chew, and the few pieces of beef were cooked so tender they almost fell apart. A roll went down easily and at last my stomach was full. Thinking back over the last day, I really hadn't eaten much, and of that, most had come back up. No wonder I was hungry.

But now, I was tired. Sleepy-tired. I pushed my chair back.

Before I stood, Mrs. Dearden reappeared at the table. "You boys ready for pie?"

Eagan nearly danced in his seat. "Yes, ma'am. What kind?"

Her smile lit up a tired face. "Blueberry or fresh peaches. Last of the season." She touched my brother's shoulder. "You want one of each?"

"Oh, yes, ma'am. I do." Eagan about wiggled himself out of the chair. "And more coffee?"

As tired as I was, how could I say no? "Peach pie sounds good, ma'am. And more coffee, also." I relaxed back against the seat. Going home could wait a half hour. Plus, pie sounded like a healing ending to a disappointing day.

"It'll be right out, boys." Mrs. D. disappeared into the kitchen.

The café's door opened and in stepped fellow posse member Monty Snyder, and a man I vaguely recognized. I thought I'd seen him once or twice but didn't know his name. I waved them over, plenty of room at our table.

"You save any for us, Joe?" Monty sat on my right while the other man took a seat at the other end. "Howdy, Deputy."

"We're having pie." Eagan sounded like an eight-year-old. I couldn't help but smile. He sure didn't sound like a deputy.

Monty introduced his friend. "This here's my brother-in-law, Abe Montoya. Abe works on Anthony Carmichael's ranch and came in for supplies today."

Abe nodded. "Fellas."

Eagan glanced at me then at Abe. "Carmichael's ranch? That's where our brother Tate works. You know him?"

Abe chuckled, displaying two deep dimples on either side of a wide grin. A shave yesterday would have been in order, but his thick mustache was well groomed. His sepia-toned wide eyes looked from Eagan to me. "I'll be damned. Tate Nolan? *Sí, por supuesto.* How could I not know him? Worked with him up on the Big Blue. *El es un buen vaquero.* He's a good hand. Went back to the main rancho couple weeks ago now that fall roundup is over." He nodded. "We're all back. *Todos nosotros.*"

I studied Abe Montoya. Looked familiar and then I snapped. Earlier this summer at the Carmichael's ranch, they hosted a Sunday service luncheon. No doubt that's where I'd seen him.

We passed the next hour getting to know Abe, listening to stories about Tate, then talking over the robbery and our failure of finding the money or the bandits. Closing time for the café and Mrs. Dearden herded us outside, locking the door behind us. We stood on the boardwalk.

Monty turned to me. "Heard about your...well, loss, Joe. I'm sure sorry."

Wondering why he'd bring it up, I thanked him anyway.

He gripped my shoulder and leaned in close, but not too close. "Listen, when you're ready..."—he held up a hand—"and only then, well...my sister is unmarried. Not even seeing anyone that I know of." Monty rushed his words. "Nothing wrong with her. Coming up on twenty-one. She's comely, some say handsome even, and a great personality. She'd make a fine companion."

I couldn't help but laugh. If she was so perfect, why wasn't she at least betrothed? I let it slide. This had been quite the day and knowing he had a sister was the icing. Wagging my head, I thought about what he'd said. Was I ready yet? No. But soon? Maybe.

I thumped his chest. "I'll be sure to keep her in mind. When I'm ready. She live around here?"

It was Monty's turn to chuckle. "She does. Name's Clara Belle, but don't ever call her that. She's just Clara. Clara Snyder. Helps out at the school. Like a teacher's helper. Otherwise, she's at home taking care of our pa. Ma died a few years ago and Pa, well, he never learned how to be domestic...cook, clean, mend." He bumped my shoulder. "Don't think he ever wanted to learn."

I couldn't see my own da cooking, cleaning, and mending, either. "Maybe you could introduce us. Some day."

"Would like nothing more than that, my friend!" Monty held up a hand. "Gotta go. It was good riding with you today."

We waved goodbye and walked our horses home. The

peach pie, so delicious, so big, sat heavy in my belly and I needed to walk it off. The five blocks home didn't take long. Eagan had finally run out of words. I enjoyed a quiet few minutes.

* * *

I SURE AS hell didn't want to get out of bed the next morning. The sun tried its best to pry me out by sending happy beams right into my eyes. I groaned, whined, turned over, pulled the sheet up over my face. Nothing worked. I had to get up. Maybe I could be sick again. Say my head hurt too bad.

Eagan stuck his head in the bedroom doorway. "Rise and shine. Breakfast's about ready."

He disappeared before I could throw my pillow at him.

I glanced through the window as I pulled back the covers. Awfully bright for early morning. Then it hit me. I was late. Damn late. I threw on work clothes, ran a comb over my hair and a hand across my face, shaving would have to wait. I grabbed my borrowed vest as I rushed out the bedroom door, down the stairs.

I screeched to a halt in the dining room. Da and Eagan stared at me, their plates still full. They each had a cup raised to their lips, as if they had all the time in the world.

"Sorry I'm late. Guess I overslept." I pointed toward the door. "I'll get something to eat at work."

Ma appeared from the kitchen, plate of eggs and bacon in hand. "Where ye off to in such a hurry, this morn?" She placed breakfast on the table, then smiled at Da as he pulled out a chair for her. "An' why are ye dressed like that, Joe?"

"Work." I swiped a piece of bacon and chewed. "I'm late."

"Ara. Sit down, son." Da pointed to a chair. "'Sunday, it 'tis. *Faglais* isn't for another half hour." He and Eagan chuckled.

Feeling the fool, I sat and accepted a cup of strong tea. Sunday, huh? Right. The bank holdup was Friday, we rode to Fredericksburg Saturday. So, today was, indeed, Sunday. I relaxed and considered as I ate. After mass, we'd come home, have one of Ma's superb dinners, then Eagan and I could go down to the stream and see if we could catch fish. Hadn't done that in a while and I wondered if any fish were still there.

Or we could toss a ball like we did as kids. Or—

"Joe?" Da interrupted my daydreams. "Mr. Whalen came by this mornin'. Wonderin' if ye can come in to work for a bit, this afternoon."

"What? On Sunday?" Was I whining? Probably.

"Says the fella what took yer place yesterday couldn't keep up with all that come in. Needs your help."

Well, hell. I'd been looking forward to relaxing. "What d'you tell him?"

Da smiled. "Ye'd be there right after church."

* * *

BY THE TIME I'd finished my second cup of tea, wolfed down scrambled eggs and bacon, and polished off two rolls with blueberry jelly, I felt like a new man. Not new exactly, but certainly better than the last couple of days. At last, I no longer felt like I'd been thrown by the toughest bronc in Texas. My head was still sore to the touch but didn't thump like it had. Apparently, I was on the mend.

Which was good because it seemed someone learned I was in the office this afternoon, which meant it was possible to send telegrams on Sunday. Everyone wanted to send one. And about half the town received one. Although I kept telling people we were closed, come back tomorrow, they didn't listen.

I worked like a crazy person for a couple of hours and in my spare time, tried to decipher what had come in yesterday. While I was in the posse, Mr. Whalen had asked the fella who took my place when I'd moved to Denver to come back in and help. If these chicken scratches were any indication, he'd forgotten how to translate Morse Code. I had to guess at a few words.

Mr. Whalen had stopped in a time or two while I was working, and as soon as he returned to lock up, I'd say good night and head for home. Tomorrow morning would come soon enough, and I was sure there would be another slurry of messages to deal with.

Eventually, when Mr. Whalen stopped by for the last time, the frenzy slacked off, and I felt the tug of going home, changing out of my church clothes, and into going fishing clothes. According to the sun's slant, I still had time for parking my rear on the riverbank, luring fish to their demise and to my supper dish. Ma would probably appreciate a fish or two for dinner instead of more beef or pork. I'd catch the biggest trout in the area, and she'd pan fry it with greens from our garden. My mouth watered, actually watered, at the thought.

I'd missed the noon-day feast Ma had prepared, but breakfast had stuck to my ribs, and I wasn't especially hungry. Pan fried trout called. I managed to get home, changed, and down to the river while it was still light.

Eagan beat me to the river and the best spot, but I stood a bit upstream and wet my line. Again and again.

Eagan pulled in three large trout. About the time I was giving up, an even bigger one struck. I held it up and howled like I'd won a major award. We'd eat good that night.

And we did. Ma did our trout proud. Fresh greens along with boiled butter potatoes. It was a feast worth waiting for.

* * *

AND THERE WERE hundreds if not thousands of messages the next day. Seemed like everyone in the region, in the entire state of Texas for that matter, maybe the whole world, had something mighty important to say. Mondays were always busier than the rest of the week, but today was worse than usual. The bank robbery had everyone shook up, including Da. He hid it well, but I'd noticed dark circles under his eyes this morning. His mouth had been tighter as he sipped his tea. Even Eagan, with his almost-eighteen-year-old enthusiasm was tempered.

If Eagan, Tommy, and Sheriff Wagner couldn't recover the stolen money, even with a posse, then this town was in a world of hurt. If I understood banking here in Blanco Hill, this was a private bank, not covered by the State of Texas, and therefore had no insurance to cover losses. Yep, world of hurt. All of us.

Which meant we really, truly had to find those bandits and recover what we could. Hopefully, the bank had enough paperwork to figure out who lost how much. And then, if we didn't recover all the money, how much each depositor would get back. I didn't do ciphering well and that was a job I wouldn't want.

What I did want was the joy of catching those men.

But where to look next? Hell, by now, they should've been down in Mexico, drinking themselves a time with fine tequila with lovely *señoritas* on their laps. If I were prone to robbery, that's what I'd do. I'm sure a smile crawled up my face just thinking about that, when my stomach rumbled. Why was I hungry? I'd just had breakfast.

A glance at the hands of the regulator revealed half twelve. Really? This day had raced by and it was already more than half done. As soon as Mr. Whalen returned from wherever he'd gone, I'd take a bit of a break for the ham sandwich Ma had made. The door opened and in stepped Mr. Whalen. I relaxed. Time for lunch.

"I'm gonna walk down to Da's shop, have luncheon with my family. I'll be back in thirty minutes, Mr. Whalen." I pointed over my shoulder as I gathered my sack lunch. I was interested to see what Da had to say about surviving the hold up. He hadn't said much, if anything, at home. "Half hour. I promise."

"Enjoy yourself, Joe. I'll mind the store." Ed Whalen hung his hat on the peg by his desk.

A quick half hour passed with Eagan and Da, who said nothing about the future, but were busy with the one customer. Back at my desk at the telegraph station, I relaxed thinking it would be easy sailing the rest of the day.

Then *click, click, click*. I clicked back that I was here and ready for the message. Writing as fast as I could, the words started to make sense. Done, I sat in shock as it became clear: *Bank robbery. Stop. Johnsonville. Stop. Three outlaws. Stop. One teller dead. Stop. Robbers escaped.* I coded in return that the message had been received and transcribed.

I jumped out of my seat, yelling at Mr. Whalen. "Holy

Jesus! Another bank robbed. This one in Johnsonville." I waved the paper at my boss. "Gotta get this up to the sheriff right now."

He stood so quickly his chair scooted out from behind him. "After the sheriff's, stop by the bank and let them know too. Just in case."

Grabbing my hat, I tore out the door, up the street to the sheriff's office. I yanked open the door, startling both Sheriff Wagner and Deputy Tommy O'Sullivan.

I waved the message. "Another bank. Robbed." I struggled to catch my breath. Forgot I'd been running. "Johnsonville. Three robbers. One teller dead." I handed the paper to Wagner who read it, then tossed it to Tommy.

Wagner came to his feet. "Johnsonville's sixteen, eighteen miles from here. Small bank. Smaller'n ours."

"I'll get another posse together, right now." Tommy turned to me. "Can you ride?"

"Of course. I'll tell Mr. Whalen and be back here in ten minutes." I pointed over my shoulder. "Make that fifteen. Gotta go by the bank, then get my horse."

"Fine." Sheriff Wagner rubbed his lower back. "Tommy, you lead the posse. I'll stay here and keep a lid on things."

"Yes, sir." Tommy grabbed his hat and gun belt from the peg near the door. He eyed me. "Ask Eagan to come too. Would ya?"

I nodded and rushed into the warm afternoon air. At least Johnsonville was closer and the scenery better than the road to Fredericksburg.

When I shared the news, Da frowned, rubbed a hand across his face, and let out a couple of choice oaths I was surprised he knew. Eagan untied his apron, hung it in the storeroom and returned with his gun belt around his waist. I'd forgotten he took that rig with him everywhere now.

"Da, we'll be back when we can. Maybe tonight. I don't know." I opened the door for Eagan. "We'll let Ma know right now."

Eagan patted Da's shoulder. "Don't worry about us. We're always careful." And with that, we both rushed into the street and hoofed it the five blocks to home. With Eagan's limp, we couldn't go as fast as I wanted.

Ma wasn't happy, of course, but said she was proud of us boys. She insisted on whipping up road food along with a tin container of buttermilk, which we slipped into our saddlebags. We tied rolled-up blankets behind the saddles, just in case we were gone overnight.

Within five minutes, horses were saddled, equipped for a trip, canteens were filled, and most importantly, we were sandwiched. We each gave Ma a quick peck on the cheek, mounted up, and trotted to the sheriff's office.

Tommy, Monty, Tiny, and Jim were waiting for us outside the office.

"Men, you know the drill. Johnsonville has one lone deputy to watch over less than five hundred folks. He needs us." Tommy eyed each of the men. "Looks like the outlaws're getting more desperate, more violent. Killed a clerk. Be careful. Keep yer eyes open."

We mounted our horses, reined around aiming for what we hoped was apprehending the bad guys.

We were out of town within minutes, ranches and farms growing farther and farther apart the more northwest we rode. This time, my brother and I were in the middle of the posse, not half an hour behind like we were Saturday. It felt good.

The trip took about an hour, according to the sun shadows. We trotted into town, so much smaller than

Blanco Hill. People were milling in the street, one distraught woman sitting in a chair by the General Mercantile fanning herself, two other bonneted women patting her hand, fawning over her. If this hadn't been so deadly serious, I would have laughed. A bit melodramatic, I figured. But, then again, maybe it was her husband who'd been killed. I sobered up.

The five of us made quite the scene arriving in front of the bank. The crowd moved aside, allowing us room to tie up our horses at the hitch rail. They stared at us like we were either the robbers come back to kill everyone, or the Savior Himself come to make life whole again. Chatter, distant wailing of a female, and people scurrying about greeted us.

Tommy pushed his way inside the bank, located the deputy and shook hands with the man. The rest of us followed, talking to victims, locating eyewitnesses, and dismissing people who "saw it all" from home.

This time, I'd remembered to bring a small pad and pencil. I took notes—names and details—I'd most likely otherwise forget. The scene was scarcely a notch below full-blown panic. From what I could gather, the entire town had their life savings in this bank. A direct hit of a tornado couldn't do more damage. In an odd way, a tornado would be better. At least they'd still have cash. Blown around cash, but it still would be there, somewhere.

I spoke with a man who said he'd been in the bank when three masked men, one shorter than the others, burst inside, held up the two tellers. I shuddered. Had to be the same robbers. But nobody had mentioned a bandit with a bushy beard. The outlaws hadn't said much except the usual, "Hands up!" and "Where's the vault?" When the teller was too slow in opening the safe, one of the men shot him. The other teller managed to fumble open the safe.

I know I wouldn't have had the courage to remember combination numbers and twirl that lock in the right directions. I remembered being so shook I couldn't even hold open my vest. At least he hadn't shot me like he did the teller. Seemed I was lucky.

The biggest question of "Which way did they go?" was met with a myriad of answers. Two people pointed south, one north, two shrugged, and one chinned southwest.

After what felt like a full day, the posse met on the boardwalk, Johnsonville Deputy Lionel Lieberman, standing next to Tommy. The bank's president, a Mr. Dahlberg, joined us.

"Here's what we know," Tommy regarded all of us. "Looks like the bandits were the same ones from Friday."

Mr. Dahlberg licked his lips, swallowed hard. "They took everything. We're estimating over two thousand in paper cash. But no coins."

I whistled. That was a lot of money. How could a town recover from a loss like that? Especially such a small town?

Tommy wagged his head, something most of us were already doing. "As I said earlier, looks like they're getting more violent."

"Since we're not all that far away," Eagan pointed southwest. "Should we go back to Fredericksburg, see if anything new's come up?"

Monty shifted his weight. "Maybe those bandits high-tailed it back there, back to Gertrude's for more beer and throwing around money."

We mumbled our agreement while Tommy thought. He muttered to Deputy Lieberman, nodded, then turned to us. "Probably a good idea to go to Fredericksburg. I have a feeling there's more to the sheriff than he claims." He raised one shoulder. "Hate to say that about a fellow lawman, but..."

I wanted to share my feelings, but before I could, we all headed for our horses.

Deputy Lieberman and the bank president stood forlornly on the boardwalk and watched us ride away.

On the edge of town, I reined up, stomach busy deciding if it was sending back lunch. My head was about to explode, and the ground was spinning. Guess I wasn't as healed as I thought.

Tommy reined back around. "What's going on?"

Eagan had stopped with me and explained. "Headache's upsetting his stomach. We'll rest here a couple minutes, then catch up. All right?"

He nodded and waved as he spurred his horse.

Back a block was a café where I thought I could at least sit on the boardwalk steps. Maybe have an iced ginger tea, if they had ice. That should help. Eagan and I backtracked, stepped inside, enjoying the coolness the walls exuded.

No ice, but the tea was fresh. I sat at a table, held my head, and wished I had laudanum. Maybe a town doc would. I asked the waitress. No doc. They went into Blanco Hill for that.

Ten minutes and I felt much better. We paid the lady and opened the screen door in time to spot Bushy Beard —August Huber—ride by, headed west.

CHAPTER FIVE

Do we follow Bushy Beard at a safe distance? HAD HE
seen us? Or should we have caught up and passed him
on our way to Fredericksburg? Given a friendly nod and
wave? I stood on the boardwalk holding my breath. This
was too much of a coincidence to ignore. No doubt he
was involved in the robberies, somehow, some way.

Eagan stood at my shoulder, neither of us speaking.
Breaking the moment, I turned to him and shrugged. He
shrugged back, wagging his head. My gaze swept the dirt
road in front of me as if it held the answer I so desperately needed. Across the street, a woman stepped into a
store, the Sew 'n' Sew Millinery Shop, the sign
proclaimed. Clever name.

"There a way to get to Fredericksburg other than this
road? Maybe a back way?" I kept my voice low as if
Bushy Beard would hear me. "I'm thinking we need to
join the posse fast but should go around him."

Eagan shrugged a second time. "Don't come up here
all that often. Da and me deliver to their meat shop

sometimes. Maybe two, three times a year." He pointed behind him. "Somebody in there should know."

We asked the three customers and the one waitress and walked away with four different opinions. Eagan and I once again stood on the boardwalk looking south and west.

He pointed south. "I say follow the ravine and then gully like that one fella said. That'll get us closer and probably in front of Bushy Beard."

"Or…" I didn't have a better idea. "All right. Just know, I'm not happy about any of this. Seems like we always get separated from the posse. And now look at us."

We untied our horses, swung up into our creaky saddles, and headed south toward a wide ravine that we were told turns west in a mile or two. I prayed that bandit wouldn't know we were so close. That bandit. As I rode, I considered. He was one of the outlaws, the holdup men. Had to be. This was what, the fourth time we'd seen him? In four days? Maybe he hadn't done the actual robbing, but no doubt he was in on it. He'd know where the money had been hidden, if he didn't have it on his person in his saddlebags. Now the big question—how would we find out?

As we rode, at times the top of the ravine over our heads, I thought about where to hide that amount of cash. Mostly paper currency, a few coins. But where? Too much for the saddlebags on one horse. So, probably the men divided the loot and did what with it? Where would they put it?

Part of that answer was obvious. Have a great time at Gertrude's Gasthause. Throw the cash around like there was plenty more where that came from. *It came from the Blanco Hills Bank.* That had been some of Da's money.

And Johnsonville. I couldn't get back that part, but I'd sure as hell keep them from spending more.

Now...where to find these men. And the loot they hadn't yet spent.

The ravine narrowed, grew more shallow, and within several yards emptied out onto the desert, smoothing the sand. A gully to our right offered a bit of protection. A hill to our left would hopefully provide us a clear view of the area.

I topped the hill and, in the distance, spotted a band of brown, indicating one lone wagon plodding east toward Johnsonville. Must be what we wanted. But were we ahead of or behind Bushy Beard? I thought we'd made good time in the ravine, but if he'd galloped a bit, there was a chance he was still ahead.

Eagan unplugged his canteen and pointed it toward the road. "We gonna follow that, now?" He took two long pulls, recorked it, then re-hung the strap around the saddle horn.

Nodding, I wasn't sure at all, but had no good alternative. We reined west and a bit south, then stepped onto the road. Despite the distinct possibility of getting a nasty headache, we gigged our horses into a mile-eating gallop, hoping to make up for lost time.

Apparently, we did, as we found the posse's horses tied at the hitching rail in front of the sheriff's office. Sliding my hand across the closest mount revealed sweat and heat. He hadn't been standing there long. Despite the shade my hat provided, I shielded my eyes to stare down the street, both ends. No Bushy Beard. Were we ahead or behind him?

Eagan and I bolted up the steps and yanked open the door. Inside stood our posse, Sheriff Driggs, and another fella with a badge on his chest. Probably the deputy. I couldn't squeeze in close enough to tell for sure. It was obvious, though, he was the shortest man in the room. Not a dwarf, simply shorter. Probably quite a fighter. In my limited experience, the smaller men tended to be meaner, like they had something to prove.

Conversation stopped and everyone looked at us. Tommy's shoulders relaxed. "Finally here."

I wanted to explain right then and there who we saw and why we were late, but I took one look at the scowl on Driggs's face and the questioning look on the deputy's and decided to wait. When we were alone, I'd tell Tommy what I suspected.

Driggs let out a soft growl. "We were just talking about the robbery in Johnsonville." He nodded toward the man with the badge. "Deputy Randolph rode over soon as he heard about it." He turned to the man. "Tell 'em what you found, Randy."

Randy Randolph? Please. Couldn't his parents find anything more creative to name him?

The oh-so-self-important deputy thrust out his chest and raised his chin. "I rushed over there fast as lightning. People running all around, crying, complaining, scared half to death." His gaze focused on Eagan, who I guess he took as an adversary, and lowered his voice. "Three masked men. One shorter than the others. Didn't say much. Took everything they had. Ended up killing one of the tellers. Young man by the name of…he searched the ceiling.

"McDougal," Eagan supplied. "Eric McDougal. Just came over from Ireland. Been in the country six months. Maybe eight."

This was chest bumping at its finest. I wanted to grin at my brother, but so as not to distract anybody, I let him have all the glory. Randolph seethed at being shown up.

"Right. Eric McDougal. Off the boat few months back." The deputy shook his head and mumbled. "That's what he gets for being Irish."

Both of my hands fisted, and I moved forward. Plowing into that jerk would feel great. Eagan held my arm, keeping me from pounding him. Plus, he was on the other side of the tightly packed room. No way could I have reached him. Not easily, anyway. He wore a badge. I'd have to save my rage for later.

Driggs picked up a short pencil, scrounged around for a piece of paper. Finding one, he positioned the stub. "So, let's get down what we know."

We told him in detail, and he wrote, frowned, wrote, and frowned some more. We all stood quiet, waiting for further instructions or an epiphany. At this point I'd have settled for simply a name. Just one. Anything. But nothing came.

Driggs tapped the end against his lower lip. "Not much to go on. Like last time."

Tommy reset his hat. "First Blanco Hill, now Johnsonville." He scanned the room. "I'd bet Fredericksburg is next. Makes sense."

"They wouldn't dare." Driggs glared up at Tommy, then the rest of us. "We know they're coming' and we're ready."

"Hope so." Tommy shifted his weight. "They're getting bolder. Now that they've killed once, probably won't hesitate to do it again."

Those chilling words brought the Blanco Hill robbery into focus. The confusion, terror, disbelief and getting buffaloed came crashing down around me. I shook. My head throbbed, especially on the left side. I tasted pain. Eagan squeezed my arm, bringing me back to the here and now. I pulled in air and nodded at him. I was all right, again.

Tommy continued. "Boys, it's getting too late to ride back to Blanco Hill." He glanced out the window and then I realized the sun's ray were at a slant. The day had slipped away. And it had been a long day.

"Let's bunk down here tonight. If you want a hotel room, the town will buy one for you." Tommy regarded us. "Right after breakfast tomorrow, let's ride back over to Johnsonville, see if anybody remembers something else. Then we'll head home."

I had questions for Driggs. I should have saved them for later but couldn't keep my mouth shut. "Why d'you send your deputy to Johnsonville, instead of you going? When did Deputy Randolph leave? Were you at the Texas Tumbler playing poker this afternoon?"

Driggs stood so quickly, I thought for sure he'd reach across the desk and punch me. I stepped back.

"Told you once." He pointed an angry finger at my face. "Don't ever question me. I do what I do because I'm the authority around here. Do what's best for my town." Driggs cocked his head toward the door. "Best you get out. Now."

The five of us posse men mumbled our agreement, then shouldered our way outside into fresh air. Eagan and I stood at the bottom of the steps, waiting for Tommy, who stepped out last.

The three of us met in the center of the main street. I scanned the road and streets for any sign of Bushy Beard. Not many people out and about, especially the one man in question.

Tommy stood in front of me, glanced over his shoulder at the closed office door. "You best not rile him again, Joe. Besides, what're you getting at with all those questions?"

I pursed my lips, a habit I'd been trying to quit. "Don't know, Tommy. He's in on it. Somehow. Can't say how or why I know. Just got this feeling."

"Best you keep quiet around him, until you do know. And for certain."

He was right, of course. Before Eagan could relay why we were late, I jumped in. "About five, ten minutes behind you this afternoon, ol' Bushy Beard rode out toward here."

Tommy frowned. "The fella who you think clobbered you? The one who tried to strangle you? The one you think—"

"One and the same." I ran a hand across my mouth and tasted dirt. I lowered my voice, just in case. "Four times now in four days. Too much of a coincidence. He's one of them, I'm sure."

"Think he's in town now?" Tommy looked left.

Eagan nodded. "Don't know where else he'd go. We were behind him but off the road a bit. Don't think he saw us."

Pulling in air, then letting it out in a slow stream, Tommy regarded both Eagan and me. "Be damn careful tonight. Best stay in your hotel room 'til mornin'."

"Probably a smart idea." I hitched up my pants which seemed to be sagging. "Right after supper, we'll do just that."

I said good night to Tiny, Monty, and Jim who promised they'd stay out of trouble, right after a beer or two.

With that, Tommy headed up Main and Eagan and I walked the other way, down toward the hotel. Hopefully, they had a room available. If not, we'd throw our bedrolls down...well, I wasn't sure exactly where. Maybe down in the stable. But the gurgle of a stream with me lying beside it, put me to sleep faster than anything. Still, a bed would be my first choice.

Fortunately, they did have a room available with two beds, and especially with Blanco Hill paying for it, I looked forward to spending time in there. Although I was worried about our safety—Bushy Beard's hand around my neck reminded me to stay on my toes—I was tired. This had been a long day, and I was ready for supper and a good, long sleep.

Second floor, room eight, flowered wallpaper on all four walls. A white planked ceiling looked freshly painted. A nightstand sat between the two beds, lace doily covering the top, oil lamp on top. Across from the beds was a stand with a water pitcher on top. A mirror reflected the small room. Eagan plunked onto one bed and I tried the other. Firm enough. I would sleep just fine tonight.

But first, supper. My stomach rumbled. I hadn't eaten much these past few days and what went down, didn't stay down long. Maybe this evening's meal would change that pattern.

"Let's fill our bellies, then come back. Get some sleep for a change." I poked Eagan. "What d'ya say?"

He sat up. "Guess I could eat." He patted his stomach. "A whole cow. Or maybe an elephant!" Springing to his feet, he gripped the doorknob. "Heard there's a good place down the street."

Even with his limp, Eagan made it to the restaurant in record time. He must've been truly hungry. We took our time with the meal, enjoying a second cup of coffee with blueberry pie. I leaned across the table to Eagan. "This's almost as good as Ma's." I looked around at the patrons as if Ma was standing at my shoulder. I raised an eyebrow. "Almost."

"Agreed." Eagan placed coins on the table, then stood, stretching. "Could use a beer before calling it a night. You want one?"

I considered and followed him outside. "So far, we haven't had any trouble. Seems to me if we go to a saloon, we'd be inviting some." Main Street and the saloons were quiet. "Think we should go back to the room. Keep a low profile. Sure as hell don't need any more trouble."

"Just one?" Eagan walked down the two steps to the street. "Doesn't sound like anything's going on. C'mon, just one and we'll turn in."

Against my better judgment, I consented. "Just one at the Tumbler. Then we go."

"Fine." Eagan headed for the quiet saloon where the sheriff and friends had played poker all one afternoon, last Friday.

Maybe somebody would remember something from last week. Maybe not. Probably not. This investigation wasn't going anywhere and I was about to give up. Then, as we walked, I thought about Da and his meat market business. He'd have to close up. Maybe sell the house, move away. Work for somebody else. He'd hate all that.

No. I'd keep searching and asking until I found the money.

Eagan pushed open the batwings and we stepped into a golden lit room, kerosene lanterns providing circles of light. Enough to see who was in the saloon. I counted eight men, one hostess in a frilly blue dress, shot glass tray in hand, and the unfriendly bartender we'd met Friday. Of the eight patrons, three were at one table, one by himself, and four at another table, a deck of cards in one man's hand.

Seemed like everyone stopped to stare as we entered. Two beats, three, then they disregarded us. Even the bartender.

We leaned against the bar, ordered a beer each, then waited for the barkeep to slide the mugs in front of us. A clear glass full of foamy, yellow liquid appeared. Eagan and I tapped glasses and sipped. Warm and flat, a bit sour.

Would all of this swill even go down? I'd probably have to leave half behind. Eagan took a second long drink. Just watching him made my eyes water. Blinking hard, I surveyed the room. The surly bartender moved down toward us, close enough for me to ask. "Heard about another big poker game back there today." I nodded toward the closed back room and leaned closer to him. "We, my brother and me here, would like to get in on that. Understand the stakes are high."

Maybe, just maybe, if I came across as a high roller, a big spender, we'd get invited in. If not, I hadn't lost anything. The bartender eyed me and then Eagan. "Takes more'n money to get in. Certain men have to tell me who's invited." He leaned across that wooden bar, and then so close to me that I spotted pockmarks on his forehead. He growled. "And you ain't it."

"How d'we find these certain men?" Eagan took his cue and dug a hand into his vest pocket like he was searching for cash. "We're interested in...well, enriching ourselves."

If this hadn't been so serious, I would have laughed. But I didn't. Seriousness occupied my chest. I could barely breathe.

The barkeep leaned back, pointing his hand, a drying

cloth over it, at Eagan. "You couldn't afford to enrich yourself." He chuckled, turned, and moved down the bar to the other end.

I sipped the bitter, yellow water and considered. We learned a bit, but not enough. Eagan and I were still leaning against the bar when the lone man stood, scooted back his chair, and walked toward us. Something about him. His stature? He was shorter than most men but didn't seem menacing. Hat snugged on his head, dark hair at his shoulders, a mustache covering his upper lip. Immediately, I reached for my gun, my hand resting on the walnut grip. A bit too wound up, I figured. I needed to relax. Not everyone was out to get us.

I nodded as he passed, a bit too close I figured. His shoulder brushed Eagan, who was bringing his glass to his mouth. The beer sloshed onto both men's shirts.

"Hey, watch it!" The man brushed the front of his shirt.

"You bumped into me. Your fault, mister." Eagan plopped his beer glass onto the bar.

"*Your* fault." The man swung at my brother, connecting with Eagan's shoulder.

Eagan swung in return, his fist plowing into the man's chest. Before I could stop them, they pushed each other, Eagan crashing against the wooden bar.

"Stop it!" I stepped between them, now on the receiving end of the man's fist. I swung, connecting with his shoulder.

The man grabbed my beer mug, doused me in beer, then punched my jaw. I flew back against the bar, then sank to my knees. Stars replaced lights. Men hollered and shouted encouragement. Eagan grabbed the man's vest, but as he did so, the man reached for Eagan's half-full beer glass, flinging the contents into my brother's face.

I sprung upright, and threw all of my weight at him. We crashed to the floor. Eagan pulled at me, but I used every ounce of strength to punch this guy. The three of us rolled back and forth, bumping into chair and table legs, then a spittoon, back to table legs. Blood ran down my throat and I coughed.

Suddenly, a bucket of beer rained down over the three of us. I blinked up at the bartender, an empty bucket in hand, then back down only to catch a fist on my chin. The world turned gray, zig-zaggy, and then black.

* * *

SOMEONE GROANED. Forcing an eye open, I turned my head. Big mistake. More metallic streaks raced in front of me. My head didn't throb or pound. It simply felt like a balloon was inflated inside, stretching out my skull, and about to burst.

Another groan. Wasn't me. Who then? I ran a hand over my face and picked at dried blood coating my other eye. It crunched open. Gray lines running up and down came into focus. Bars? Steel bars? I gently rubbed both eyes, blinked and refocused. Certainly looked like bars. Jail bars.

Using both hands, I managed to push upright. Under me was hard. A cot. Like in a jail. Not in my hotel room. My world came together and in the next cell lay my brother.

"Eagan? Eagan?" I shouted. "Eagan?" Was he alive?

Another shout and he moved. Thank God. We would get through this. Questions bombarded my brain. What happened? Why? Who was that man? How'd we end up here? How long would we stay locked up? But most important was my brother. Was he all right?

Sun warmed in what looked to be the back room of the sheriff's office and I discovered we were in Fredericksburg's jail. It was morning and my clothes reeked of beer. Was that whiskey as well? I sniffed harder and coughed. Images of that scoundrel pouring swill over my head came back. Why? Why pick on us?

The wooden door to the office banged open. Sheriff Driggs stood at the door as in stepped Tommy, the three posse members behind him. "There you are!" Tommy wagged his head. "Told you, both of you, to stay out of trouble."

I ran a tongue around the inside of my mouth, tasted blood. "Tried to. One beer. Fella bumped into Eagan. He picked a fight."

Tommy gripped the cell bars where Eagan lay still and glanced over his shoulder at Driggs. "How's my deputy? You get the doc?"

Driggs pushed his way closer to Tommy. "Doc's finishing breakfast. He'll come when he's done."

"Open this door. I want to check him." Tommy glared at Driggs. "He's hurt."

I made it to my feet and gripped the bars. "Wasn't his fault, Tommy. Not mine." Were my words as clear as I hoped? "This fella—"

"Take it easy, Joe." Tommy turned to me. "Rest. We'll get you both out of here."

Monty, quiet until now, moved in as close as he could. "Ever seen that man before, Joe? Think he was one of the…"

I shrugged. Nothing made sense right now. Nothing, except what I knew would be a righteous headache in a matter of minutes. My jaw complained as well.

Driggs found keys and opened Eagan's door. My brother moaned and rolled onto his back. I sent more thanks heavenward. I vowed I'd find whoever hurt him. That *scut* from last night. Maybe not kill him, exactly, but hurt him. Bad.

Tommy knelt by Eagan. "Eagan? You hear me?"

Eagan nodded and one eye opened. Glory, hallelujah! He mumbled something too soft to hear but thank God, he was alive.

Patting his shoulder, Tommy said, "You're one tough *hombre*; you'll be fine." He stood. "Let's get you out of here."

"Not today." Sheriff Driggs glared at my brother and then at me. "These two were arrested for drunk, disorderly, public brawling and assaulting a law officer."

"What?" Tommy and I spoke in unison.

"I wasn't drunk, or disorderly, last night. I had two sips of a beer."

Driggs cocked his head to one side. "Smelled yourself, lately? You reek." He turned to Tommy. "Can't hold his liquor, I see. Poured most of it on himself, some on an innocent bystander. Him and Eagan. Two of a kind. Both troublemakers."

Tommy's hands fisted and unfisted. His mouth a taut line. "I know these men. They're not troublemakers. They're not drunks. Release them to my custody. Please."

Shaking his head, a scant smile crawled up one side of his face. "No can do. They assaulted my deputy after picking a fight with one of our town's leading citizens. Obviously, they were drunk, guzzling way too much. Hell, ask the bartender."

"Oh, I will. You can count on that."

"All these charges—"

"All these charges, hell!" Tommy's face turned red. "I want my men out, now!"

Driggs relocked Eagan's cell door. "Not 'til the circuit judge comes by." He pocketed the key.

"When'll that be, Sheriff?" Monty nodded at me.

Driggs studied the ceiling, then out the window. "Let's see. He was here 'bout two weeks ago. Should be back three, four months."

"Months?" Tommy stepped toward Driggs. "Remand them to me."

"Sorry. You're out of your jurisdiction, O'Sullivan. You're over county lines. Your badge means shit out here." Driggs sneered. "I asked for your help last week and you weren't any." He pointed to the door. "So, now it's time for you to go."

"Not without my men."

"I've half a mind to throw you in here, too, *Deputy* O'Sullivan." Driggs pushed through the group to his office. "You and *all* your men. Best leave while you can." He held open the outside door.

Monty nodded to me, then Jim and Tiny followed him into the office and then outside.

Tommy reached through the bars and gripped my forearm. "We'll get you out. Soon." He nodded at Eagan and then me. "I'll tell your folks you're, uh, detained. I know they'd come rushing over here, otherwise. Wouldn't be helpful for either them or you boys."

"Thanks, Tommy." I nodded back. "Might find us a good lawyer too."

CHAPTER SIX

EAGAN AND I SPENT TIME MAKING UP VARIOUS excuses Tommy would give Da and Ma as to why we didn't return with the posse. We laughed at what he would tell Mr. Whalen. "Joe spotted a lovely *señorita* heading down to Mexico. He followed her."

Or to Ma and Da. "Sorry, but your boys like German goulash better than your Irish stew. Decided to stay in Fredericksburg."

And about Eagan. "Mr. Nolan, your son is tired of hauling ice and chopping up dead cow parts. He decided to stay in Fredericksburg and work making pies in a bakery."

All sorts of scenarios danced in our heads, and then what Da and Ma would say in return. Creating wild stories was better than nothing. I didn't enjoy sitting or lying on hard cots and worrying about what was going to happen to us.

The next few days I spent listening, as best I could, to the comings and goings of Sheriff Driggs. People came in to visit, sat in a chair, coffee cup in hand, to shoot the breeze. They told tales and were generally *cacks*.

My frustration continued to grow. Driggs wasn't doing anything to get the money back from Johnsonville and he sure as hell wasn't helping with Blanco Hill. I paced, thought, figured. My anger built.

Eagan, every bit as frustrated as me, tended to pace back and forth like a caged tiger, while I generally sat and thought—when not pacing. My head had at long last no longer throbbed, in no thanks to the doc who stopped by. I asked for laudanum, but he refused, saying it was addictive. For three days, I held my head, rocked side to side, threw up on occasion, and, admittedly, cried. Tears rolled down my cheeks and onto my beer-infused shirt.

Eagan's face looked like it had kissed the moving end of a freight wagon. Many days gone past, the bruises had blossomed to ugly green and purple, but the swelling had gone down around one eye and mouth. He could now see and eat.

Not that eating was a treat. I wasn't sure what they served at the café where Driggs got our food, but surely no customer would actually *pay* for the meal. We were provided two meals daily, breakfast and supper. The first was usually a thin porridge, or *haferflocken*, as it was called here. For supper, overcooked beef drenched in watery gravy. At times, a spoonful of peas and carrots would accompany the beef, sometimes not. It didn't really matter. Everything tasted the same. And there were no heady aromas or mouth-watering smells. Just something that looked like gray paste.

If my count was correct, we'd spent seven full days behind bars. And in that time, I neither heard nor saw anything suspicious. At times, Driggs or his Deputy Randolph would forget to close the wooden door between the cells and outer office. That's when I could see who came and went. The longer we stayed behind bars, the more often the door stayed open.

Church bells brought Eagan to his feet and he peered out the window. I didn't have one, so I had to rely on his descriptions. He gripped the bars over the window and spoke to the outside. "Must be Sunday. Bells are nice." He glanced over his shoulder at me. "Church steeple is all white. Stands out above the whole town. Sure is pretty."

"What else you see?" I slumped back against the wall, the cot under me harder than usual.

Eagan stood on tiptoes and peered at something outside on the right that caught his attention. "Huh."

I perked up. "Huh? What d'you mean 'huh'?"

He remained quiet way too long. I asked again. "See something interesting?"

Shrugging, my brother released the bars and walked the five steps closer to me. "Thought maybe I saw some-body looked like Tate."

"Tate?" I jumped to my feet. "You mean, our brother Tate? That Tate?"

He nodded and shrugged again. "Fella walked like him is all. Same size, is all. Looked like he was coming this way." Eagan studied the brick floor. "Guess I just wanted it to be him."

We both sank to our cots, lost in thought. I held my head in my hands. The outside door opened, and since my cell was positioned to where I could see it, I watched who came in and out. To my surprise, in stepped our oldest brother Tate.

I nodded at Eagan. "Look who's here."

He leaped to his feet and grabbed the bars. I had already done the same. As much as I wanted to call out to him, I kept quiet. It would be interesting to see what the deputy would say, being that he was the only one in the office this morning. Sheriff Driggs was off doing whatever it was he did. He seemed to be gone most of the time.

Tate's words were loud enough for me to hear. They were polite. "Hello, Deputy."

"What can I do for you, sir?"

"I'm Tate Nolan." He extended a hand and surprisingly, the deputy shook it. Tate continued. "Understand you've got my two brothers locked up here. Wondering if I could visit with them."

Randolph looked him up one side and down the other like he was about to buy a prized bull. The deputy pushed to his feet and held out a hand. "I'll keep that rig of yours 'til you leave."

"Fair enough." Tate unbuckled his gun belt then handed it to the deputy.

Randolph cocked his head to the left. "In there."

"Much obliged."

Tate stood between the two cells and looked from Eagan to me and then back again. "Got your own private rooms, I see. Pretty fancy." A grin stretched his cheeks. We shook hands between the bars.

Questions came fast and furious, but the one we both asked was, "How'd you find out we were here?"

"Understand you met Abe Montoya." He waited for us to nod. "He told me. And before you ask, Mr. Carmichael gave me a few days off to come deal with you two."

"What about Da and Ma? They know?" Eagan spit out the questions before I could.

"Been expecting you home any day. I stayed over with 'em last night. Looks like Tommy told them you were on a special mission for him. Might be a week or two." Tate chuckled and held one of the bars. "Special mission, my ass."

I let out a few choice curse words, ones which Ma would have stuffed a bar of soap into my mouth for and thrown me out of the house. A long stream of air came next.

Tate stepped back and peered around the room. "Yep. Looks familiar. Spent couple days in here myself." He studied the ceiling. "Yep. Earlier this summer."

Eagan leaned against the bars closest to Tate. "Can you get us outta here?"

"Depends. What'd you do?"

It was my turn to clutch the bars. "Drunk. Disorderly. Harassing fine citizens. Assaulting a peace officer." I shrugged. "Nothing major."

"But you didn't, right?"

"Right. He threw beer on *us*. He hit us. Short fella. Started the whole damn thing. No idea why." Eagan rubbed his bruised jaw. "Sure packed a punch though."

Tate peered at his face. "Looks like you're healing up. Sore?"

Eagan nodded. "Like Hell exploded."

I knew exactly how he felt. My head had exploded a time or two.

Eagan took a breath, ready to rant and rail, but Tate jumped in.

"And let me guess." Tate held up a hand. "Circuit judge doesn't come for months, right?"

"Pretty much." The world crashed down around my entire body. I slumped back against the wall. I'd never get out of here, never get Da's money returned. Never even live to get married again. Or have children again. My life was ruined, over.

"How's Da holding up, Tate? How's the town doing without any money?" Eagan, emotions under control, appeared to have his full senses going, better than me.

Both of Tate's eyebrows rose. "That crafty Da of ours had hidden some money in a sock drawer. Says it's enough to stay afloat a month or so. After that..." Tate shrugged. "Who knows?"

"But the rest of the town—"

"Your boss, Joe. Whalen's raking in the money." Tate shifted his weight. "Seems everybody is either sending telegrams or receiving them." He gave a soft chuckle. "Fact is, he's had to hire a youngster to deliver those 'grams. Too busy for your replacement to go himself."

"Where'd they get the money?" If they'd just been robbed, where'd the money come from?

Tate shrugged. "Good question. Probably had some tucked in their own sock drawers."

So, the world wasn't so dark, after all. But with each passing day...

"Who's this back here?" Sheriff Driggs stepped into the room. His eyes narrowed as he surveyed Tate. "Well, well. Mr. Seamus O'Brien. Thought you might show up."

Seamus O'Brien? Who? And then I remembered Eagan telling me about Tate's stint here in Fredericksburg under the name Seamus.

Tate rubbed his shoulder. "Wound's about healed. Your bullet dug in deep."

Ow, was all I could think. Then again, maybe Tate shouldn't do any more chest bumping with the man who held the keys. Two of us in here was bad enough. All three wouldn't be good at all.

Tate and Driggs stood, eyeing each other. Neither said a word, simply stared. I guessed Tate chose to take the low road.

"Just came in to see my brothers, Sheriff." He pointed east. "I'm workin' over at the Carmichael ranch south of Blanco Hill. Stayin' out of mischief, too." Tate produced an innocent smile. One I'd seen him use when Da was angry at him.

Driggs's shoulders relaxed. "Good to hear." His gaze roved over Eagan and me. "Be quick about your visit."

To my surprise, leaving the door open, he strode back to his desk and sat.

* * *

TATE HAD PROMISED to stay in town a couple of days, ask around, see what he could find out. More importantly, he'd promised...*promised* to stay out of trouble. To stay on the straight and narrow. If he ended up in jail with us, we were all doomed. The entire towns of Johnsonville and Blanco Hill were doomed. He had to behave himself, which in this town might be hard.

Before he left, he'd mentioned visiting a woman named Hilda who ran a German bakery. Her da was influential around town and maybe, possibly, he could help. At the least, Tate promised to bring back some of Hilda's finest. I could hardly wait.

But I had to wait until Monday afternoon, when he walked in with a nice-looking woman beside him. Aromas of cinnamon and baked apples wafted into my cell. Eagan, the always-hungry teenager, bolted to the bars and hung his arm through them.

In the outer office, Hilda and Tate made a showing of presenting some sort of baked goods to the deputy. It could have been a pie or tart, I wasn't sure. As usual, Sheriff Driggs was nowhere around. I hadn't seen him since the evening before.

Deputy Randolph stood from behind his desk and escorted Tate and this woman back to where we wiggled like hungry puppies.

Tate nodded at the blonde woman, couple years older than me, slim, smiling, a tray of delicious-smelling, tantalizing treats held in her hands. "This is my friend, Miss Reinstein, Hilda, the lady I told you about. She owns a bakery here in town."

Both Eagan and I extended our hands to shake, and she smiled, holding up the tray. "Nice to meet you, Miss Reinstein." I meant it. Seeing someone besides the dumb deputy or surly sheriff was a real pleasure.

"Hilda's got...well, I'll let her tell you." Tate stepped back to present her like royalty.

"These are some blueberry *obstkuchen* and one peach." Hilda glanced at Tate. "I sold all the other peach. *Ich bedaure.*"

It didn't matter to me. I'd eat about anything that didn't look or taste like paste. "Thank you so very much, ma'am." Would groveling at her feet help?

"Ma'am." Eagan leaned as close to her as he could. "We appreciate anything and everything. Sure smells good." He closed his eyes and sniffed, hard.

She laughed. An outright laugh. "*Dumeine Güte,* I wish I'd known you were here sooner. I'd have brought something last week."

I wished that too, but I'd enjoy it, now. Right now. My stomach rumbled and grumbled. Breakfast had been a while back and supper, probably more beef gruel, was still hours away.

Hilda held the tray in front of Eagan first. "*Bitte, nehmen Sie sich.*"

He selected two tarts and a handheld pie, she called it. I got the remaining three and bit into a blueberry tart.

If I'd died right then, I'd have died happy. Heaven was in my mouth and nothing, *nothing* could have been better.

Eagan's entire face blossomed into a sappy smile with bits of purple around his lower lip. I wasn't sure which of us made louder sighs of satisfaction, but my verbal thanks were drowned out by my too-stuffed mouth. Overwhelmed with gratitude, a little moisture came to my eyes. Was I about to cry? Over a blueberry tart?

I swallowed, this time tasting, actually tasting the treat. And I still had two more! "Miss Reinstein," I swiped a hand across my mouth, "Miss Reinstein. I think you've just saved my soul. You have no idea what this means to me. To us."

"Hilda, please. Call me Hilda." She reached between the bars and patted my arm. "*Sie unglücklich Mann.* When Seamus told me about you, of course, I had to come to help. To do what I could." She looked up at Tate. "*Meine enger Freund.* He's still special to me."

Obviously, there was a story there, but now wasn't the time to hear it.

Tray in one hand, she turned a bit toward the door. "I need to get back to the store. *Meine vater* is closing up for me, but—"

"Thank you, ma'am. Miss Hilda." Eagan stuck out a hand. "Thanks is not enough, but guess it'll have to do until we can thank you properly."

Hilda smiled up at Tate. "Your brothers *are* charming. I see where you get it."

"They get it from me. I was first." Tate took Hilda's offered hand and kissed the back of it. Her dimpled smile chased all misery from the room.

He fished a deck of playing cards out of a small sack he'd been carrying. I'd been too focused on food to wonder what was in there. He handed me the deck.

"Something to pass the time. Sharpen those poker skills. Something you desperately need to do, little brother."

Before I could refute, he handed a book to Eagan. Our youngest brother enjoyed reading ever since he learned how. He always had a novel under his bed. Ma had made him quit reading at the supper table years ago. Otherwise, that was all he'd do.

Eagan put down the tart remnants, wiped his hands on his filthy pants, and studied the cover. "*California Joe, the Mysterious Plainsman*." He looked up at Tate. "Hey. This's a Beadle's Boy's Library Dime Novel! It's new. Where'd you get it at?"

Tate raised an eyebrow. "I've got my sources." He glanced at Hilda. "Thought you'd like it."

"Sure will. Thanks."

The floor creaked. Deputy Randolph leaned against the door jamb. I guessed that was his way of suggesting visiting time was over. His stare centered on Hilda, but he managed to rip his gaze away momentarily to look at us. Then back to Hilda and her quite generous bosom.

Ignoring the deputy, Hilda fairly cooed, "*Meine Lieben*. I'm sorry you're in here, but glad I could make you happy for a minute or two."

"Thank you again, Miss Hilda." I regarded the two tarts now sitting on my cot. "I'll savor these for a couple of days."

"Mine, too." Eagan nodded.

Tate started for the door, then stopped and turned. "I'll see you before I go."

"Go? Where're you going?" Eagan frowned. "When're you coming back?"

Tate waved and stepped into the outer office. Within moments, he and Hilda walked outside, disappearing into the street.

Eagan carefully placed the tarts on one end of his cot, then sat at the other end and drew up his knees. Forehead on his knees, he covered his head with his long arms. If I'd had words to comfort him, I'd have shared them. But I had nothing.

I slumped to my cot, the hardness reminding me of where I was. There for a moment, the world had been right. But now? All that was left was merely a big dose of uncertainty, a bit of fear, and a lot of nothing but worry. And wonder.

CHAPTER SEVEN

OVER THE NEXT FEW DAYS, TATE STOPPED BY twice. Once with more tarts of strawberry and peach, another book for Eagan, and a magazine for me. This second time was to say goodbye.

"Need to get back to the ranch. They're expecting me."

Both Eagan and I frowned, our gazes sweeping the brick floor. I hated to see him go. With him in town, I'd felt secure, in an odd way. But now?

"Promise I'll stop by Da and Ma's. See how they're doing. I'll tell them I saw you." Tate shrugged. "Saw you doing what, I'm not sure." His grin went ear to ear. "But I'll think of something. I'll be sure you come home heroes!"

Even from in my cell, I heard two men arguing in the street—something about a horse. They were getting louder and if the confrontation didn't end in a shooting, at the very least a good fistfight would break out. The outer door squeaked open, and Deputy Randolph stepped outside.

Tate used that opportunity to tell us he'd been asking around town, trying to figure out who stole the money. He'd met with a lot of head shaking, sideways glances, and couple of whopping, made-up stories. "But," he said, "I'll ride through Johnsonville on my way back and see if anything new came up."

He shook hands with both of us, his grip stronger than I'd remembered. Him walking through that door, disappearing into the free world, made my insides sink. Although Hilda had promised to visit, it was Tate I needed.

Since I had nothing better to do, I kept mental track of who came and went in the outer office. Thursday seemed to be busier than usual, but Bushy Beard hadn't stopped by, nor had a short fella. That third bank robber had been nondescript. Nothing unusual about him, at all. Hell, for all I knew, it could be Deputy Randolph. That thought kept me occupied for over an hour. All the possibilities...

As usual, the deputy brought in our tray of gruel, Thursday evening. Eagan and I tried to choke down what we could. At least the coffee was warm and good. A second cup would have been greatly welcomed, but that wouldn't come again until morning.

Half an hour later, Randolph collected our bowls and cups, then closed the thick wooden door between us and the office. Had I heard a lock click? Maybe. Were we locked in here? Not only behind steel bars, but a wooden door as well? What was going on?

We spent a restless night, tossing and turning, mumbling theories to each other. We'd long passed the point of conversation. After being locked up so close together for so long, there wasn't anything left to say. We grunted at each other, stretched, cocked our heads left and right once in a while, but mostly sat and read and played cards.

Friday morning dawned clear with blue skies. Already wind was swirling past the open window, announcing a looming fall dust storm. Didn't matter to us. We were inside, mostly protected.

Deputy Randolph unlocked the door, shouldered it open and delivered our morning delight. Eagan insisted he needed the privy first, so while the deputy escorted my brother out back, I dove into what passed for breakfast. The coffee went down first, then the rest.

Before I finished, Eagan was back, and it was my turn. Despite swirling dust, outdoor air rejuvenated me and, on the return trip, hope filled my chest. Maybe today we'd be released.

As the deputy locked my cell door, I put on my best innocent charm. "We've been locked up here for quite a while now. Any chance we can take a walk...around the block? You come with us?" What I wanted, needed, was not to stretch my legs but to get a good look at the sheriff's office and then outside. Something was going on and I wanted to know what.

Randolph locked my cell door, stepped back and regarded me, then Eagan. "It *has* been like ten days. And y'all *are* damn ripe." He shrugged. "I'll check with the sheriff. See what he says."

We were making progress. It wasn't an immediate no. I spoke over what may have been bacon at some point. "Haven't seen Driggs around. Not for a couple of days."

Eagan picked up on the idea immediately. "He go off somewhere, looking for those bandits?" From his seat on the cot, he pointed up at the window. "Hear he's real good at tracking. Bet he comes riding in today with all three robbers in tow."

Randolph wagged his head. "Keep thinking all you want. Sheriff's holed up in another poker game. Over at the Tumbler."

"Poker?" I picked up my deck of cards. "Wish I'd been invited. I can play. Real well." I eyed Eagan. "Win most hands, don't I, Eagan?"

"Uh-huh."

"Can't be invited if you're in jail." The deputy chuckled. "Besides, it's high stakes only and, from the looks of you two here, I'd say you couldn't even buy in." He continued chuckling as he closed the inner door.

"Can you believe that, Joe?" Eagan jumped to his feet, gripped the bars. "Think the sheriff's in on it?" He frowned. "I mean. Why'd a sheriff do that? Rob his own bank? That's crazy."

Maybe. Maybe not. But what to do? How do we get word to Tommy? Or Tate? I'd hesitate about Blanco Hill's Sheriff Wagner. He might be in on this too. More information would be helpful.

Half an hour passed, the door opened again and in walked Deputy Randolph. "I'll take those plates. Young lady normally comes and gets them, but Joe, if you promise to behave, you and I can walk over there and surprise her with them. Give your legs a stretch."

"Promise I'll be on best behavior, Deputy." I couldn't believe my good fortune. Finally, a chance to get more information, see the world, stretch my legs.

Randolph chinned at Eagan's empty plate and coffee cup. "Get his and yours, then I'll handcuff you."

I managed to stack our plates in one hand, put a cup on top, then slip my finger through the handle of the other. In the outer office, Randolph handcuffed my wrists so tightly, my hands tingled. But I wouldn't complain. This was getting out and I'd savor every minute.

Part of me felt bad for leaving Eagan alone, but he'd manage. I knew he was disappointed, but maybe his turn would come later. After locking the handcuffs, Randolph locked the inner door.

"Usually, one of us is in the office, but I think your brother wouldn't dare try to escape, right now." He led me down the two steps to the boardwalk. "If he did, I'd probably have to shoot you and I don't really want to. Waste of a bullet."

He locked the outside door, which meant Eagan would have three locks to get through if he tried to escape. Probably wouldn't happen.

I squinted against blinding sun, but it felt good. The earlier trip to the privy had been one of urgency. This seemed more like a vacation. We walked two blocks up the street, while men passing by glared and women stopped to stare. Two recoiled. Did I have the pox? Still, my little trip to the café renewed my energy. I would get out of jail, soon. Eagan and I. Together. Soon. We'd find the money. Soon.

A young woman opened the café's screen door as we walked up to it. "Howdy, Deputy. I was just coming to get them dishes."

"Miss Ida." Randolph tipped his hat. "Thought I'd save you a trip."

"You're too kind."

The shape of her clover-green eyes reminded me of a cat. One I'd had as a kid. He'd lived in the barn and caught all sorts of vermin. A good ratter. Miss Ida's eyelashes, the darkest and densest I'd ever seen, fluttered at the deputy. Good Lord. They were an item.

"I'll let my *prisoner* bring them in for you." The deputy nudged me up the step and into the café. Smells of cooking pot roast and potatoes brought moisture to my mouth and a gurgle to my stomach. If it smelled so good in here, why was our food so bad?

At this time of day, somewhere between the end of breakfast and the beginning of the noon meal, there weren't many customers in the café. I glanced around and spotted two men at two separate tables. Miss Ida slid the cup from my finger and then plucked the two plates and one cup from my other hand. She nodded at me but kept her distance, like I was a cougar about to attack. She was safe from me, being as I was not only handcuffed, but a badge with a gun stood at my shoulder. Besides, I wasn't about to try anything "funny." I wanted out of jail, but as a free man. And I wanted Eagan free too.

The two flirted with each other, while I stood inhaling aromas of meals I would never get to eat. If I didn't leave soon, I'd start gnawing the closest table. They chitchatted for a full three minutes, then Miss Ida asked the deputy, "How do your prisoners like their food?" She spoke as if I was invisible.

"They eat everything you bring over. So they must like it." Randolph smiled at her. "You know, everything you fix is wonderful."

I couldn't help myself. "A second cup of coffee would be nice." And then I remembered my manners. "Ma'am." I nodded.

Miss Ida jumped back like I'd jabbed her. Maybe she'd forgotten I was right there. She looked at my handcuffed hands, then up to my face. "I guess...I guess a second cup would be all right."

"For both me and my brother, ma'am." I smiled. "He likes your coffee as much as I do."

Shoulders relaxing a bit, she pointed toward the kitchen. "I'll send two with you now, when you leave."

Randolph moved in close and dropped his voice, but I

heard every word. "I'd like another one, too, if you don't mind. Will I see you tonight?"

Both of her arched eyebrows reached for her hairline. Without saying a word, she gave an ever-so-slight nod, turned, and headed for the kitchen. She returned moments later with two cups of steaming coffee, which she handed to me, then a third cup, which she handed to Randolph.

He tipped his hat. "Ma'am." The deputy nudged me toward the door, opened it and I stepped down onto the boardwalk.

He didn't say a word the couple of blocks back to the sheriff's office. I was busy taking in the sights and sounds, relishing every second of "freedom." Could I figure out where the money was simply by walking the street with coffee in hand? Probably not.

I handed Eagan his cup, put mine on the brick floor. The jail cell lock clicked, and I was back. A captive. Caged like wild animals in a zoo. Suddenly, rage engulfed me. I gripped the bars, shook them, yelled as many curse words as I knew. I even made up some, when the others seemed bland.

I ranted and raved until exhausted. I picked up the still-full cup, thankful I hadn't thrown it across the room as I'd wanted, sank to the cot. Eyes closed, I sipped, slumped back against the stone wall. Cup in one hand, I used the other to run through my shoulder-length hair. Fingers catching on tangles, I yanked. Bits of hair hung from my fingers. I shook them off, sipped again, then regarded Eagan.

He stood leaning against the bars, sipping coffee, watching me. "You done?"

I glared up at him, sucked in a long drink of air, studied the brick floor. "Yeah." I considered my tirade. So appropriate, so needed, but so rude. "Sorry."

Eagan finished his coffee, ran the cup across a few bars. Tin on metal did nothing to calm my nerves.

"Stop it!" I should have tempered my demand, but apparently, my nerves remained on edge. I hated feeling like this, but anger surfaced more quickly than I'd imagined. More curse words flew around the room as I hurled the rest of my cold coffee against a far wall. A thin trickle ran down. Cup in hand, I reared back, ready to throw it too, when the door opened.

Miss Hilda, the woman of Tate and bakery fame, stepped in, Deputy Randolph right behind. He wore a smirk that told of him getting an entire pie as an entry fee. Part of me was jealous, the other simply happy to see her. And whatever she carried on a tray smelled heavenly. I relaxed. Someday, I'd get out of here and be able to thank her properly. Maybe she'd enjoy supper with me over at the café.

"I've brought you more blueberry *Obstkundel*. And…" She pointed to two brown crusted treats, "cherry strudel. I used the last of my cherries for this."

First, a second cup of coffee, and now two pieces of pure sin. If I died right then, I'd have died happy. "Thank you, Miss Hilda. Thank you for this."

Eagan reached through the bars and selected one of each. I got the other two.

Miss Hilda held the tray by her side and looked from me to Eagan and back. She held a handkerchief to her nose, her pretty eyes watering. Looking at Randolph, she blinked, hard. "Do your prisoners ever get a bath, Deputy? A chance to clean up? Maybe soap and water? A shave?"

Strudel in hand, I sniffed at my shirt. Dried, old beer,

encrusted sweat and a bit of dirt made up my clothes. I guess I was "ripe" as Ma said sometimes. And seven days without a razor definitely had taken its toll on my face. Scraping it when the time came could be painful. Maybe I'd simply grow a beard.

Randolph leaned in closer. "I'll see what I can do, ma'am."

I regarded Miss Hilda again. For the first time, I noticed tiny lines jutting out from the sides of her eyes. Pretty. Her eyes were pretty, which made her even more attractive.

She glanced behind her at the deputy, then focused on us. "Just received a note from your brother." She dug into her apron pocket and pulled out a folded piece of paper. "Says to tell you, 'Folks are fine,' and 'nothing else new.'"

I gripped the bars, studied the floor. No news about Johnsonville or especially Blanco Hill. Obviously, Tommy hadn't arrested the bank robbers yet, which meant the merchants and citizens were still out of money. Their life savings gone. I could imagine the anguish some of them were going through.

Miss Hilda, Eagan, and the deputy chatted, while I thought. How to put it all together. Sheriff Wagner? Sheriff Driggs? Bushy Beard? A short bank robber? High stakes poker games? The Texas Tumbler Saloon? What else did I know? One man dead.

I missed something. Tired of guessing, I tuned into the conversation.

Eagan flapped a hand through the bars. "Ma bakes chokecherry pies when it's season." He swiped the other hand across his mouth. "'Bout drips with filling. And it's sweet and tart at the same time. That's one of my favorite pies."

Mine too, but I didn't feel like talking about fruit, right now. More like when do I get released? Can I go on another walk?

The three of them chuckled at some joke when the outer door flew open, a man yelling, "Bank's been robbed! Bank's been robbed! Where's the sheriff? Where's the Deputy? Where the hell are you? Anybody?"

Deputy Randolph whirled around, bolting into the outer office. "Here! Bank's been robbed?" He grabbed the shotgun from the rack behind his desk, slammed on his hat, bolted for the door, then skidded to a stop. He hollered at Miss Hilda. "Sorry. You gotta go."

She flicked a slight smile on us, then scurried outside. Randolph locked the inside door and no doubt, locked the outside one as well.

Eagan stood on tiptoes at his window. "Yep. Every-body's running every which-a-way."

Bang! Bang!

Gunshots echoed down the street. Women screamed. Men hollered. Horses whinnied, some stampeding up the street.

I stood on my cot, hoping to catch a glimpse of the action. But even as high as I was, could see only a square of blue sky. Sounds of pure panic sailed in through the open window, filling the small room. More men yelling, women in hysterics, even a dog in the distance yowled.

But what caught my attention was the distinct sound of hooves pounding against the packed dirt street. Probably the bandits getting away.

"Looky there! Three men galloping up the street!" Eagan turned back to me. "Gotta be those robbers."

"Can you tell if one's got a bushy beard? Maybe one of 'em's short?"

He shook his head. "Nah. Went by too fast." Eagan

spent half a minute gazing outside, then sat on the cot. "Bet it was them, though. Bet the town'll never see its money again."

I had no good answer. Nothing to say. I sat and thought.

The lock to our door clicked open. Sheriff Driggs stood there, key in hand. "Somebody's just robbed the bank." He glared at us. "Know anything about it?"

As much as I knew to keep quiet, the anger and frustration I'd bottled up, vented, spewing all over the cells. I threw myself at the cell door bars. "Why the hell would we know anything? You've kept us cooped up here until we...well, hell, Sheriff. Until we can't even think straight. Why would we know anything about your stupid bank being robbed?"

There was more. Lots more. Before I could continue, Driggs had his hands around my throat, choking off any chance of air. I clutched his wrists, but damn, he was strong.

"Shut the hell up! Just shut up!" Driggs squeezed tighter. "I'm sick of your attitude! All you Irish're alike. Always talkin'. Talk, talk, talkin'. You and your brothers. Just shut the hell up!" He released me and I flew back, wheezing, rubbing my neck.

Eagan smartly chose not to say anything, staying as far away as possible.

CHAPTER EIGHT

EAGAN STRETCHED ON TIPTOES GAZING OUT the window to watch the good citizens of Fredericksburg panic about the robbery. I stood at the cell bars and gripped them so tightly my fingers turned white. What the hell? What was going on? We'd already predicted their bank would be robbed. I remembered Tommy telling Sheriff Driggs this would happen. It was a logical assumption and, sure enough, bandits struck.

But who were the culprits? Who was brash and bold enough to go into banks, in broad daylight, and hold them up?

The questions hurt my head. I sat on the cot, picked up a magazine, and let my eyes scan the pages. Not a thing I read made sense, but what else to do? Otherwise, the frustration coursing through my mind would cause me to explode. I'd end up in little pieces all over the cell. The image made me smile. I looked. There's my head under the cot, my left foot stuck between two bars, a hand still grasped—

"What's so funny over there?" Eagan's voice interrupted my scenario.

I shrugged. "Envisioning my body scattered all around this cell."

"Well, that's a cheery thought."

In an odd way, it was. Made me laugh, though. It was better than trying to figure out the bank puzzle. And then...

"All this time spent in here's made me daffy, Eagan. Try this one—what if Sheriff Driggs was the leader of the bandits?" I whispered, in case he was around. "What if he hid the money for the bandits? Took a cut of the loot?"

Eagan jumped down from the cot. "And what if... what if he hid the cash here in his office? Nobody would think of looking in the sheriff's safe."

"How big of one does he have?" Hope filled my chest. Maybe we'd figured this out. "How much did he get? In total, do you suppose?"

Eagan shrugged. "Hard to tell. But enough for them to go waving it around town." He gripped the bars, tightly. "Some of that money was Da's."

Nodding, I made a mental map of the outer office. No safe. However, off to one side was a door, usually partially opened. More than likely that room held supplies, and maybe the safe. "You seen a safe when you go outside to the privy?"

It was his turn to think. Finally, he shook his head. "No, but he's gotta have one. Someplace to keep important papers and such."

"Maybe it's in that room off to the right of the deputy's desk. Usually, it's open when I walk past. Haven't taken much notice, though."

We agreed next time either of us got out, somehow,

we'd find the safe. We sunk to our respective cots and thought.

The chance came about an hour later, when Driggs unlocked the wooden door, pushed it open and brought in our evening supper. This time an aroma of cooked steak and corn wafted around my nose. Had Miss Ida made us real food this time? Oh yes, please.

"Over there, against the wall." Driggs chinned. "You know the drill."

"Yes, sir, I do." If I didn't get into the outer office, I'd not sleep at all tonight. "But before we eat, I need the privy. If you don't mind."

"I *do* mind." Driggs unlocked Eagan's door, slid the tray inside, then locked it like he expected Eagan to dart out or attack him. "Deputy usually does all this, but he's out leading the posse."

"Posse? He need some help?" I couldn't help but goad him a bit, even though my neck was still sore and probably had bruises from his fingers.

"Shut up, stinkin' Mick." Driggs stood at the cell door, glaring. "Have a mind not to let you out, at all. Ever again. How'd you like that?"

What I wanted to say was that was fine. He'd have to clean up the mess, but I didn't. If I was going to get through the office and outside ever again, I'd need to be polite. "Wouldn't like it at all, sir." And then added, "But I still need to go. Bad."

"Back over there." He chinned to the far side of the cell, unlocked the door, set the plate down and pulled his gun. "Don't try anything. After I shoot you, I'll shoot him."

"Why?"

"Just because I can."

I glanced at Eagan, whose eyes were wider than

normal, and made my way into the office. To the right was the door in question, partially open. I pretended to trip on the desk leg and stumbled into the doorway.

I gripped the door jamb, then fell to my knees partway into the room. Sure enough, in the corner sat a safe. Good sized one, at that. Probably big enough to hold all the cash from three towns.

"Get up, Paddy. Imbecile!" Driggs gripped my shoulder, yanking me to my feet. "Blundering bogtrotter."

He could call me whatever he wanted because I was sure, definitely sure, that safe held the towns' money—what wasn't spent yet. Now, how to get it open and retrieve the cash would be another matter.

Driggs shoved me outside, down two steps to the street, marched me past the side of the building, then out back to the privy. I closed the door, sat thinking. Nothing sprung to mind, but no way could I let the money simply sit in that safe. I had to figure out how to open it.

Banging on the door interrupted my thoughts. "Button 'em up. Let's go." Driggs pounded harder. "Now!"

I swung open the door, hoping I'd smack him with it, but he stepped back just out of range. He aimed his revolver at me, like I'd just tried to escape. Hell, I wasn't going anywhere, not with Eagan still locked up. No way would I leave him behind bars when I was free.

I held up my hands shoulder high, feeling frustrated, a bit silly, and quietly angry while being marched back to jail. The cell door clicked locked. Driggs sneered at me, then nodded to the tray of food he'd brought.

"Eat up. Maybe that's all you'll get for days. Maybe I'll forget you're back here." He cackled, actually cackled, as he walked away.

Over a much more palatable supper—nicely cooked slabs of beef and fresh corn off the cob—Eagan and I discussed the safe and what it probably held. We kept voices low since the door between us and the outer office was halfway open. Neither could come up with a plan. We needed outside help. But who?

Driggs returned with Miss Ida in tow. Her smile lit up an otherwise dreary room.

"Howdy, Miss Ida." I patted my stomach. "Supper was delicious." I turned to Eagan. "This's my brother, Eagan."

"Howdy, ma'am." He nodded a greeting. "Like he said, it was delicious. Thank you."

Cheeks pinking, she gave a slight smile. "You're welcome. Glad you liked it." She waited for Driggs to unlock my door, gathered my plate and cup, then did the same with Eagan. Plates and cups cradled in her arms, she waited in the doorway. "I'll see you in the morning."

"Looking forward to it, ma'am." Eagan and I spoke in unison.

* * *

THE SOUND of slow hoofbeats stopping, low voices of tired men wafted into our cells long after the moon had disappeared. I sat up. Who or what had disturbed my sleep? Eagan stirred also. The outside door squeaked open, heavy boot steps plodded across the floor. Someone peeked through the inside door. Even though the only light was from a turned down oil lantern on Driggs' desk, I made out Randolph's silhouette easily. I assumed making sure we were still there.

So...the posse had returned empty handed. Otherwise, I'd have company in my cell by now. I wasn't totally surprised, but disappointed, nevertheless. The town was quiet, which meant I could easily hear any discussion between Driggs and Randolph.

Their voices low, I detected exhaustion and frustration on Randolph's part. "Sorry. Couldn't find hide nor hair. How can three men disappear so quickly?"

"Incompetent posse, that's how." Driggs paused, then continued. "Got an idea I'll run past you, tomorrow." Another pause. "Go get some sleep."

"Be happy to, Sheriff."

Boots scuffed along the plank flooring, and the outside door opened and shut. Footfalls softened and soon vanished. I lay back on the cot wondering what Driggs had in mind.

* * *

BREAKFAST WAS late and I wondered if we'd get any at all. My stomach growled and complained. A trip to the privy would be welcomed as well. Maybe we truly *had* been forgotten.

At long last the inner door opened completely and in stepped Driggs and the deputy, tray in hand. Eagan and I automatically stepped far back from our cell doors, not needing a command from the lawmen. Randolph slid the plates and coffee cups into our respective cells.

"I get first crack at the privy this morning, Deputy." I wasn't sure I'd make it all the way without embarrassing myself.

He cocked his head at the front door, and I bolted toward it. Randolph, on my heels, rushed to keep up as I racewalked to relief. I didn't dare run for fear of being shot, but at this point, I almost didn't care.

I made it to the privy barely in time.

Once Eagan returned from his own short trip outside, we dug in on breakfast, which was considerably more substantial than the past week. On my plate lay real scrambled eggs, what looked and smelled like real bacon, and not one, but two biscuits. Two! And coffee.

Rudolph produced a tin coffee pot. "When you're done with the first, here's seconds."

Seconds? Really? I guessed my visit with Miss Ida helped. Or maybe it was Deputy Randolph's influence. Most importantly, I figured it was my charming personality.

We sat on our cots eating like we'd never seen food before, while the two lawmen stood and watched. They didn't seem to be in a hurry even though the bank had just been robbed. Wasn't there more pressing business than making sure we ate our food?

Driggs leaned against a wall. "Joe, Deputy Randolph tells me that you can identify one or maybe two of the bank robbers." He eyed me like I was one of them. "That true?"

A biscuit stuck in my throat. What did he want? I pushed down confusion and nodded. "But I didn't get a good look."

Eagan, ever so helpful, put down his fork. "Saw the three of 'em yesterday, right off. Looked like the ones Joe saw in Blanco Hill. One shorter than the others."

Driggs turned to Eagan. The intensity of his stare reminded me of a cougar about to take down a deer. "You saw 'em, too?"

He leaned back slightly, pointed his fork over his shoulder. "Just from a distance. From this window."

Driggs stood straight, glanced at Randolph, and then narrowed his eyes at me. "Understand you can identify the man who buffaloed you in Blanco Hill. That right?"

Well, hell. I hated being cornered like that. "I'm...I'm not sure, Sheriff. I mean, he'd just hit me, wearing a mask and all—"

"Big man with a beard? Taller'n you?"

Words wouldn't form. I nodded.

Driggs turned to Randolph. "Let's give it a try."

The deputy shrugged. "You're the boss."

A knot of ice chilled my chest. Whatever they'd cooked up, I wasn't going to like. I put down my cup and waited.

Driggs stepped in between our cells, looked at each of us, drew a long breath. "How'd you like to get out of here?"

"I'd like that fine, Sheriff." Eagan stood holding the bars.

"And you?" He eyed me up and down.

"Depends. What do we have to do?"

"Figured since you both were riding with a posse, and Eagan there being a certified deputy, and you, Joe, being an eyewitness, you two wouldn't mind trading the rest of your jail time for riding in another posse."

"Posse?" Both of us spoke in unison.

Driggs nodded. "We'd leave today. Few minutes."

So, that was why we got such a hearty breakfast. And I'd hoped it had been my charm.

I stood ever so slowly, coming out of hibernation. "Give my brother and me time to talk. We'll let you know in a minute."

Driggs shook his head. "It's either yes or no. No discussion." He drilled through me with his stare. "What'll it be?"

"You'll let us go, no questions asked, no 'coming to get us' later?" I looked from him to Randolph. "We'd be cleared of all charges?"

They both nodded.

Eagan held an arm through the bars toward me. "Say yes. We can find those men and be home for supper. What d'you say, Joe?" He mouthed, *say yes*.

Against my better judgment and because I couldn't see ever getting out of this jail, otherwise, I agreed. "All right, Sheriff. We'll ride in your posse. But the deputy here is an eyewitness to your letting us go, after we find them."

Driggs's smile went wide. "Of course. I'm a man of my word." He waved at our coffee cups. "Now finish up. We got riding to do."

"We?" Surely the deputy would lead the charge.

"I'm going. Randy rode last night. He stays behind to watch the town." He marched through the inner door to his desk, straightened papers, then went for a rifle stored on the wall.

The deputy unlocked both doors and stepped back.

I couldn't help but ask. "You sure this's a good idea?"

CHAPTER NINE

SHERIFF DRIGGS, EAGAN, AND I STOOD BY THE office hitch rail. "We waiting for the others, Sheriff?" I glanced up and down the street. No one leading a horse walked toward us.

"Couldn't find anybody else on such short notice. The ones from yesterday won't go, they said." Driggs regarded me and then Eagan. "You'll do just fine. Especially since you can identify them."

My uneasiness grew until I was sure my chest would explode. Something wasn't right. But what? Here was a lawman in search of robbers of his own bank. One witness and one deputy from another county riding along. And nobody else would come? If my money had been stolen, and it was, I'd be happy to ride after them.

I stood at the hitch rail, patting my horse's neck. She'd done nothing but stand in the stable for a week and a half. Being well rested, she seemed ready to go. Somebody had saddled her and even placed road food in my saddlebag and filled my canteen. From the confused expression on Eagan's face, looked like they'd done the same for him.

Before we mounted, that nagging feel of dread spurred my muddled head. I needed to get word to Tommy and Tate as to what was happening. But who could I tell, here? A letter might take a couple of weeks to get to Tommy. But a telegram would be much faster. Miss Hilda over at the bakery! She'd be perfect.

I turned to Sheriff Driggs adjusting his cinch. "Need to run by the bakery first. Gotta say goodbye."

The lawman rolled his eyes. "Make it fast. Those bandits are getting away."

It was faster to dash across the street and down a block than to get on my horse and ride. I ran and within three minutes was inside the store, catching my breath.

Miss Hilda's deep blue eyes opened wide. "Herr Nolan! You're out of *das Gefängis*?"

"Jail? Yes, ma'am." I pulled off my hat and nodded. "I need to ask a favor of you, and I don't have much time." A glance over my shoulder revealed no sheriff following.

"*Natürlich*. What can I do?"

Her Texas-German dialect and soft accent were delightful. Maybe when I got back, we could go to supper. Remembering my urgency, I lowered my voice as if Driggs was right behind me. "Eagan and I are going with Sheriff Driggs to search for the bank robbers. Right now. Could you, please, get word to Tate…uh, Seamus… that we're riding with him? Then send a telegram to the deputy, Tommy O'Sullivan in Blanco Hill." I shrugged and looked behind me again. "I don't trust Driggs."

Hilda's blonde eyebrows lowered. "*Ja, ja*. I'll write him a note, right now. *Vater* will get it to the telegraph office." She patted my hand. "You'll be fine, I'm sure. *Wer sonst?* Anybody else?"

"No, but thanks."

"*Ja, ja.*" She reached into the display case and brought out three tarts. "Blueberry. For your trip."

I wanted to smile, wanted to ask her to supper, but panic wouldn't let me. "Thank you."

She wrapped the tarts in brown paper and handed them over. For the first time I noticed a dimple in her left cheek. Before, I'd concentrated on her wavy blonde hair, neatly tied in a bun. But now...

"*Aufpassen.* Be safe, Joe." She smiled, and I melted. "I will see you when you return."

"I would like that." Had I said it out loud or just thought it? Either way, I waved as I opened the door in time to meet Driggs and Eagan riding up the street, my horse in tow.

Driggs pointed west. "Eagan says they went this way." He stuffed the tart I gave him into the saddlebag. He reined his horse to where he faced us. "I've returned your guns. They're loaded." He leaned in close. "Make no mistake. If I don't come back in one piece, the deputy will fill you both full of holes. Won't be enough left of you to bury. Got it?"

At least he was succinct.

I swallowed. We nodded.

"Let's go." Driggs reined west, gigged his horse, and trotted away.

We did the same. I turned, looking over my shoulder and waved to Hilda standing in the front window. Following the lawman, Fredericksburg became a memory within minutes.

* * *

I COULDN'T REMEMBER what was west of Fredericksburg, even though I'd ridden through there a few months ago. My thoughts busy on starting a new life in Denver, truly, I hadn't paid any attention. And then returning so full of pain, I didn't take in anything except the road.

Now I took time to look, really look, at the surroundings. The area was called the Hill Country for a reason. Rolling green hills towered on either side of the road. For a mile or two I figured they would close around our little party and fall on top of us. Surprisingly, we'd met few riders coming into town and none of them remotely resembled our quarry. We waved, but no one pulled rein to talk. And we hadn't passed anyone leaving town.

On occasion I studied hoofprints. Was there anything special about one of the imprints? A loose or thrown shoe? A horse with an unusual stride? Nothing.

We galloped for a bit, then slowed, needing to keep our horses in good condition. Our route took us generally along the Pedernales River, the longest waterway in Texas, I'd been told. Long or short, didn't matter. All I wanted was to find those bandits, retrieve the money, and go home. Back to Blanco Hill. And to my job. I'd sort out my future later.

A quick stop near the stream, we let the horses drink while we ate a sandwich.

"How're we supposed to find these men, Sheriff?" Frustration seeped out from every pore. I was tired, dirty, and ready to call it quits.

"Keep on riding west. Where else would they go?" Driggs pointed. "Don't have much of a lead on us. Maybe a few hours, but I'll bet they didn't ride at night."

"Why not?" Eagan spoke over a mouthful of sandwich.

"You know as well as I do." He threw up his hands. "Don't want your horse breaking a leg in a chuckhole. If you can't see where you're going, you'll hole up someplace, keep yourself and your mount safe. Wait 'til morning, then ride."

Eagan grunted then swigged from his canteen.

Rolling hills blanketed with Texas live oak, prickly pear, Ashe juniper, and other assorted greenery, plus the river, gave me no hope of locating the bandits. There must be a million hiding places.

On the road again, we trotted, taking our time, watching for errant hoofprints. About three hours into our excursion, I spotted marks that could have been the bandits'. Three distinct sets of prints heading west. Maybe this wasn't such a waste of time anyway.

I pulled rein and pointed down. "Think these're them." I pointed. "Looks like they're still heading west, just like you said, Sheriff."

Driggs dismounted, knelt, and ran a hand through the dirt, tracing one print. "Could be. Could very well be." He stared off into the distance, due west. A smile crawled up the right side of his needing-a-shave face. "Got ya!"

We continued our search, occasionally stopping to check the prints. Still on course. The sun was but a full hand above the horizon. Shadows lengthened, birds stopped chattering, even the breeze ceased. Within moments, the world was dark.

"We'll stop up ahead. I see a place near the river to make camp." Driggs chinned. "Get a good night's sleep. Then we'll find those hombres first thing tomorrow."

I wasn't so sure. But I did know we didn't dare ride the horses when we couldn't see hands in front of our faces.

The stopping area seemed to lend itself to camping. Dead brush was easy to snap and would make great kindling. Once we had a fire going, we unsaddled our horses, fed, watered then hobbled them. Chores done, we sat around the fire, finished another sandwich, then warmed our hands as the temperature had dropped. I stared into the flames.

Hilda's face sprung into my mind. Her sunlit blue eyes, light eyebrows, creamy skin, little bow mouth. And she was single? How'd that happen? Was I now ready to start courting again? Maybe. Probably.

A glance at Eagan told me he was tired and nervous. His eye twitched, which it only did when he was scared. I'd first noticed it when he was four and cornered by a bobcat. Somehow, I managed to chase the predator away, but that eye twitched and he shook. Right now, he wasn't his normal bubbly teenaged self. Quiet, he picked up a stick, examined it, tossed the wood into the fire.

Driggs held up an unburned twig and pointed it at me. "What exactly did those men look like? Tell me again."

Warning bells raced up and down my body. I'm not sure why, but that question scared me more than his threat to shoot me if he didn't make it back to town in one piece. I stared at Eagan, his eyebrows knitted.

I held a hand over my head. "One of 'em was tall. I think had a bushy beard." I didn't want to continue, but he'd heard the story before, so I couldn't hide facts. "Not sure if it was him who buffaloed me. Mostly I remember seeing the floor rushing up and then black."

"The others?"

I shrugged. "One's shorter. Maybe five-five."

"Five-three, I'm thinking." Eagan was trying to be helpful.

"Uh-huh." Driggs poked the fire, flames crackling and reaching higher. "And?"

How to answer? "Nondescript, Sheriff. Just a basic man. Not too tall, not fat, not skinny. All three were masked, though."

"Huh." The sheriff grunted again, then fell silent.

I studied the gazillion stars overhead. What was he planning?

CHAPTER TEN

Riding the trail, we followed the Pedernales River, stopping for a drink, a get down, and where I had a nip of the last sandwich in my saddlebag. I'd saved Hilda's blueberry tart for a celebratory time, when we would have those robbers in custody. If we didn't hurry, I'd have to eat it for tonight's supper.

Even though we didn't seem to be gaining on the bandits, I did enjoy the scenery. Green, tree-studded hills, a rimstone pool, dark blue water rushing toward a merger with the Colorado River. I vaguely remembered riding past the confluence as Frieda's family stopped here on the way to Denver, resting for a full day.

I relaxed but didn't relax. Thinking was not relaxing, and I had enough questions to keep me on edge for years. By now, our quarry surely had to be south down in Mexico, or west in New Mexico Territory, or someplace else far away. Hell, I would be. If I'd robbed three banks, I'd ride like Satan himself was on my tail. I envisioned a horned red devil riding a black stallion, flames and smoke spouting from his nostrils. Purple clouds surrounded him, while I sped on.

I smelled it before something wet hit my hat. Was that the devil's spit? Maybe sweat from the horse? Another plop, this time on my chest. More taps on my clothes. Wet. I looked up. Dark skies. Wind shaking the trees. And now rain. No! If heavy enough, the impact was sure to wash out any signs of those bandits, what little signs there still were.

Thunder rolled on our right, then echoing off the hills producing twice the sound. If I hadn't been so frustrated, I would have enjoyed the sensation. As it was, I hated getting wet.

Blinding blue lightning bolts zigzagged down a tree, splitting it in half. The horses bucked and reared. Half deafened, I held on tight, and I knew Eagan could stay on. He was the best horseman I knew, like he was born in the saddle. As much as I hated getting caught in the rain, I hated even worse getting struck by lightning.

Driggs, clutching the saddle horn, turned to us and yelled over the roaring wind, nerve-shattering thunder, and now incessant lightning. "Cave's not far from here." He pointed and spurred his mount. "We'll be safe inside."

Eagan tore out ahead of us, and I was right behind. We arrived at a cave's mouth just as the sky ripped open. As luck would have it, the cave was tall enough for our horses to come inside. And I could stand with a couple inches to spare. It was cozy, but at least we would dry out, in time.

We spent most of the next hour soothing our horses, running hands over their muzzles, down their necks. The best thing to do, we decided, was to unsaddle them, run the blanket over their backs as best we could and simply hold their reins.

And wait.

The stench of wet animals and soaked men permeated the entire rock room. I couldn't tell if my eyes watered because of that or due to the slices of rain that made their way inside. My hat had protected my head and hair. Thank goodness for the stampede string, though. Otherwise, the hat would have been lost to the wind.

An hour passed and the storm did, too. Thunder rolled in soft swells now and an occasional lightning bolt danced across the sky in the distance. Wind subsided into a gentle breeze. Rain stopped completely. Birds again hopped from branch to branch. Streaks of sun hit the silvery trees. I stepped out of the cave and surveyed the world. The air was clean, pure. Fresh.

Eagan sat cross-legged in the cave, rethreading the latigo on his saddle. Driggs stood with me. We didn't speak, simply enjoyed the moment. He pulled in a long breath. "How about you take the canteens down to the river, fill 'em up, then we'll saddle the horses and go?"

Seemed a fair request and plan. I nodded, retrieved the canteens, and headed off toward the river. Muddy underfoot, I slid across wet leaves and had to suck my boot out of the mire twice. Rocks were wet and my boots had trouble navigating over them. But, somehow, I managed to fill the three canteens then cautiously head back to the cave.

As expected, the horses were outside, tethered to a low branch. I held up the canteens as I neared. "We ready?"

A glance left and right revealed no Eagan. He was either still in the cave or had moved into the forest for privacy. I stepped inside, eyes adjusting to the dim light. No brother. Driggs, standing near a close wall, back to me, turned and pointed his gun at my chest.

"Drop the water. Toss your gun belt." He waved his revolver to my left. "Hands up."

"What're you doing?" I stuttered.

"Shut up. Turn around. Hands behind you." He cocked his gun. "Said toss your gun belt. Over there."

Every fiber of my being knew not to obey. I should pull my gun and shoot. But how could I? I wasn't a killer. And, if I actually shot or killed him, I'd be strung up for sure. Shooting a lawman wasn't the best idea.

I two-fingered my gun from its holster, tossed it toward Driggs's boots, unbuckled my gun belt, and threw that, too. Naked. I felt totally naked. And vulnerable.

Should I yell for Eagan? Or keep quiet and not get shot? What the hell was going on? I chose to turn and put my hands behind me. I shook all over and my heart thundered. I struggled for air.

Driggs snapped handcuffs around my wrists. The iron lock's *click* took the rest of my air. The cave spun.

"Over there." He shoved me against a far rock wall. The impact crumpled me to the ground. He untied my neckerchief to use as a gag. Dirty material filled my mouth. Rope wrapped around my ankles. I struggled against the binding, yelling. Intelligent sound didn't get past my mouth.

"What's going on?" Eagan stepped into the dark.

Driggs rushed forward, buffaloing him. A sickening *whack* echoed off the walls. I cringed, remembering that feeling all too well. Eagan grabbed for the left side of his head as he sank to his knees. Blood coated his face.

Nothing I could do, while Driggs rolled him over,

wrenched his hands behind his back and tied them. He yanked on the rope knot, making sure it was tight. He used more thick rope to bind his ankles and last, wrapped my unconscious brother's neckerchief around his mouth.

The sheriff stood back, eyed his handiwork, then dragged Eagan across the cave, depositing him close to me. Driggs saddled his horse, leaving the other two saddles in the cave. He took our saddlebags and slung them over his horse. He hung all three canteens around the saddle horn.

He made a show of removing our horses' bridles, then slapped them both on the rear, and waved his hands. "Yee haw! Get goin'." They threw their heads upward, happy to be free, and galloped into the forest. He stood at the cave's entrance, chuckled, eyed us again, then swung up onto his horse, spurred her, and disappeared. I listened hard for his direction, but heard only the pounding of my heart, Eagan's raspy breathing, and the sigh of wind through the trees.

I wriggled, grunted, thought about rolling to the entrance, but what would that do? If it rained again, I'd get wet. Or hit by lightning. On the other hand, someone riding by might spot us. Could I roll up to the road?

But most important—Eagan. There wasn't a damn thing I could do to help him. Eventually, when he came to, he could rub his ropes against a rock and release his hands. Could I do that with my bound ankles? The handcuffs would be much harder to break. The key had ridden off with Driggs and busting the iron was close to impossible. Besides, with less than four inches between cuffs, my palms turned away from each other, no way could I fumble with his rope and get him untied. I yanked the cuffs, but they held fast. My wrists were too big to slip through.

All I could do was wait for Eagan to open his eyes. He might need help to wake. I scooted over, close enough to nudge him.

"Eagan?" I mumbled under my gag. The word was mushed, garbled. I used my shoulder to push his, and then my feet to gently kick. "Eagan? Wake up." They didn't sound like real words, but it was the best I could do.

He mumbled and tried to turn onto his side. He muttered something. One eye fluttered open, the other glued shut with blood. When he realized he was bound, he frowned, and eyed me with questions. He wriggled and bucked. And screamed.

Although inside the cave was dim, I could make out a pointed rock or two, possibly a couple that had rung a campfire at some point. I needed to talk. Make sense. Out loud. This gag had to come off. Like an inchworm, I wiggled over to the nearest rock, lay my face against the stone and sawed back and forth. Surely, my handkerchief would wear away much quicker than the thick rope binding my ankles.

Raw. My right cheek turned raw within seconds. But even if I lost all my skin, I'd get this damn rag out of my mouth. Eagan muttered. I rubbed. My cheek stung, burned, like it was on fire. About the time I couldn't take the self-inflected pain anymore, the material snapped apart. I spit.

"My god!" I spit more fabric pieces. "That was nasty." I looked at Eagan's wide eyes. He chinned at my face. Something wet and sticky ran down to my chin, then dripped onto my shirt. I eyed drops of blood. Must've done a number on my cheek, now burning like a red-hot branding iron still stuck to my skin.

I sat hurting and thinking, wishing Eagan could talk, too. Ideas needed discussing. At least I could talk to him, and he could nod. I'd try that.

"We were right. Driggs was in on the robberies."

He growled.

"Two questions." I studied the cave. Solid rock. One way in and out. "First, does Driggs have the money? And second, how do we get out of here?"

Eagan grunted, shouted, wriggled, kicked out, thrashed.

"So, I'm thinking getting out of here is priority. We'll worry about the money later."

More grunts.

We quieted while we thought. Mentally, I listed ideas. Finally, I decided to try these out loud. "We could try to roll up the embankment to the road and hope somebody friendly comes along."

Eagan's eyebrows raised. At least one did, the other still glued with dried blood.

"We could stay here and holler if we hear hoofbeats."

Nothing.

"We could try to get your ropes worn away like I did the neckerchief."

That received a nod. Eagan slid to the rock I'd used, placed his ankles on top, and sawed. I searched for a second rock, found one and scooted to it. We spent all the daylight we had left gyrating against rock.

* * *

NEXT MORNING, the moment I could make out shapes in front of my face, I knew to continue sawing. I scooted close to the sharpest one in the cave, the one I'd used yesterday, and rolled from my side onto my back. My shackled wrists and hands felt more like a boulder in the small of my back. But I couldn't do anything about that. I'd simply have to ignore the lump. Carefully, I placed my rope-bound ankles on top of the rock. I pushed, pulled, and rubbed the rope until I was sure my trousers would catch on fire.

My legs, still sore from yesterday, gyrated back and forth, while Eagan snored louder, apparently trying to drown out my grunts. I sawed harder, with an occasional word Ma wouldn't approve of echoing off the walls.

"Mmmhhh?"

He was awake. I smiled at Eagan's attempt to ask a question, and I understood what he'd mumbled. "Success?" Of course, that was a silly question since I wasn't up walking around. I would be soon, though. I sawed harder.

Eagan found the rock he'd been working on yesterday, placed his bound ankles on top, and began.

And then...*Pop!* The ropes that once hobbled me like a bucking bronc, released. "All right!" I wanted to pump my fists in the air, but they were still shackled behind me. Instead, I rolled, wriggled, shook out my legs, then managed to get to my knees and finally, stood upright.

"Ggrrmmmht!" Eagan nodded at my success, then concentrated on his own ankles.

"Feels good!" I walked across the cave to the entrance and peered out. Blue skies, birds chirping and flitting from treetop to treetop, the rush of water over rocks, ten yards off.

Otherwise, the world was silent, except for Eagan's grunts.

I turned around just as the ropes broke. "Hallelujah!" I rushed to him. "We're both upright again!"

He nodded, mumbled, shook his legs, then got to his knees and feet much faster than I had done. We stood, side by side, in the cave's mouth, peering out at the world. Questions bombarded my mind. I chose only one to ask.

"Now what?" I was happy to be upright and able to speak, but my shoulders had long ago grown numb along with my hands. Would I ever get feeling back?

I studied Eagan on my right. For a man his age, which wasn't yet eighteen, he looked tired and old. Neither of us had slept well for a couple of weeks and it showed on his face. Probably mine too. On his chin, bits of fuzz glowed in the morning light. Since he was the fairest of us three brothers, I wondered if he'd ever be able to grow a beard worth having. Maybe not even a mustache. But still, he looked aged. And not in a good way.

"Wish I could get that rag outta of your mouth, but..."

He grunted and shook his head. Between us, we had four legs and one mouth we could use. I chinned toward the river, which was more of a stream right now. It would stay like that until spring runoff. Looking at the water made my mouth turn desert dry. "Gotta get a drink. Wanna come?"

We made our way past shrubs and large rocks down to the water. I kneeled at the edge and realized I couldn't scoop up anything. I'd have to lie down to drink. My numb hands clenched. I'd punch Driggs first chance I got. Maybe tie *him* up. See how *he* liked it.

My face and hair received a sorely needed bath, while I slurped fresh river water. Sated, I rolled over, enjoying the moisture in my mouth. Eagan knelt beside me, his eyes wistfully scanning the river. He shoved his face under the water, I guessed hoping to get some relief. He came up looking like a wild cat thrown into a bath.

We sat, watching the water burble its way to the Rio Grande. "Wanna follow this? See where it goes to?"

Eagan shrugged.

"Or how about we climb up to the road, flag down whoever comes by?" I liked that idea best, but not if Eagan didn't.

He nodded, clambering to his feet. Whatever he grunted at me didn't mean much, but we headed off toward the road that was at least fifty yards up the hill. Shale and shrubs made the going tougher than I'd wanted, especially since I couldn't use my arms to help, and I face-planted several times. Within a quarter hour we both stood on the packed dirt tracks they called a road.

We stood, peering west toward New Mexico Territory, then turned around toward the rising sun, and peered toward Fredericksburg. Both ways were nothing but empty. No buggies, wagons, lone riders...not even a coyote.

I considered sitting, but I'd done way too much of that recently. Instead, I leaned against a tree near the road and thought out loud. "I'd say we've lost their trail. No telling where they are now."

Eagan grunted and shook his head. He walked over to me.

"Guess we have to go back." I hated to say it, but that was all I had. "Avoid the sheriff if we can. Get us some horses and go home."

More mumbling and grunting, this time louder. Eagan shoulder bumped me. Shook his head.

"I know. We gotta find the money. But where?" I

moved so that I could see his eyes. "Tell me where and I'll go get it." I sighed. "Where?"

He muttered, then loud, muffled words almost made sense.

"I agree. I'd bet the money's in the safe." I gazed into a stand of trees, not seeing trees. "What if it isn't? Then what?"

A shrug. Eagan hung his head. Defeat. We both hated to admit defeat, but there it was. Nowhere else to look. Bile rose to my throat. Looked like Blanco Hill, Johnsonville, and Fredericksburg were all out of luck. Now, for sure, Da would go bust. And damn, there was nothing we could do. Nothing.

At least for right now.

We stood, kicked at rocks, walked a bit, anything to keep going. As much as I wanted to believe we'd come out of this alive, doubts crept in. What if nobody rode by? Could we walk back to town? Did we have the strength? What if we were attacked by a bear? Or bandits? What if we starved to death? Eagan couldn't drink. He'd die of thirst long before I died of starvation.

I paced up and down the road, peering into the dusty distance. A morning breeze picked up, indicating there would be high winds by noon. Great. All we needed for a perfect day.

Eagan mumbled something, but I shushed him. In the distance. A rumble. Deep, throaty rumble, yet definitely not thunder. He stepped onto the road, looking west, I did the same, looking east. And then I spotted it.

A wagon. Two horses pulling a heavy farm wagon, two men on the seat. I jumped up and down. Help was on its way.

"Eagan!" I hollered. "We're saved. Thank God!"

He walked up next to me, as we both stood in the middle of the road and waited. The team didn't appear to be in a big hurry, but I sure was. Would they ever get here? Maybe we could walk to them? Instead, we stood and waited.

The driver, a big man, wide square jaw covered with uncombed beard, pulled up the team and set the brake. Sprigs of sepia-brown hair jutted out from under a well-worn floppy hat. "How do?" His accent? Somewhere in the South. I'd heard something like it when friends of our folks from Louisiana had stopped by the house last year.

"Hmmppff." Eagan muttered.

The other man, younger than the driver, but with the same square jaw and hair color, nodded. "What d'ya say?"

"Please, help us. We were captured by a crazy man yesterday, tied up. As you can see, my brother's still gagged. And I can't help him." I raised one shoulder while dried blood crackled on the side of my face, where I'd scraped it yesterday.

"What'd he do that fer?" The driver sat, head cocked. "Seems mighty unfriendly, to me."

I moved in closer. Should I tell him the truth? Probably not. "Three of us were out here deer hunting when all of a sudden, he went crazy. Hit us both over the head, and when we came to…well, here we are."

The driver twirled his meaty finger indicating for us to turn around. I cringed, waiting for a blow to the head or some such, but instead, he grunted. "Looks like you got yourself strangled by a law man. Those're lawman cuffs." He pointed at Eagan. "But not you."

"Surprised us too. Didn't know he'd carry those just to shoot some deer." Was I stuttering?

Eagan muttered, mumbled and shook his head. I took that as a cue.

"You mind giving us a lift? Anywhere you're going is fine." I cocked my head at Eagan. "Could you get that gag off him? He's powerful thirsty." I raised my arms as best I could. "And these? At least his are only ropes."

The two men exchanged glances. The younger one picked up a well-used shotgun and pointed it at us. "Get in. Don't do no funny business. If'n all y'all do, neither o'you'll won't see tomorry."

CHAPTER ELEVEN

GETTING INTO THE WAGON TURNED OUT TO BE nearly impossible. The younger man, shotgun in the crook of his arm, stood at the tail of the wagon, while we threw our chests and then the rest of our bodies into the bed. He shoved our butts a time or two, but generally just stood holding the weapon—pointed at us. No doubt he would shoot if we didn't get in. Running away was not an option.

Eagan and I wound around boxes, slid over three burlap sacks full of flour or beans. Up near the front, directly behind the seat, we wedged ourselves in tight between more boxes topped with what looked to be a parcel from the mercantile. It was in brown wrapping paper and soft when I fell against it. Could this be for a ma or sweetheart?

I hoped we would continue west, putting us as far away from Fredericksburg as possible. No doubt, Driggs had returned by now and was more than likely busy counting his money, thinking we were dead or, at the very least, wouldn't come looking for him.

Right now, all I hoped for was getting to a town, cutting these binds off both of us, finding horses, saddles, and returning to Blanco Hill. We'd go to Tommy, let him know all that had happened, and make new plans. Somehow, we had to get the money. Somehow.

All that rattled in my head, until the wagon lurched forward, plodded half a mile west, then, to my dismay, turned around in a wide spot in the road. My arms sweated through my shirtsleeves and I found breathing hard. We couldn't be going to Fredericksburg. No!

"Why we goin' back, Pa?" The younger man frowned, turning his eyes on him for a second, then rested the shotgun in his other crooked elbow and returned his stare at us.

"Don't believe for one second they got the right story." Pa glanced at his son. "Probably got a large reward for them two, and I aim to collect it."

The son snickered. "So, we'll get rich!" He eyed us like we were a prize cut of beef from Da's store. His crooked, jack-o'-lantern grin revealed three holes, where teeth belonged. "Looks like you all're gonna get us a proper house. And Pa and me won't hafta work no more."

"That's rightful thinkin', Junior." Pa flicked the reins over the horses' backs. "Giddy up now." He nodded. "Once we get that re-ward, we can get Mammy two new aprons, 'stead of jest the one we got back there."

Great. Perfect. I closed my eyes hoping the entire world would disappear. I stayed like that, until we hit a chuckhole and my shoulder rammed against a box. I glanced at Eagan. His eyes were also shut, a grimace on his face. I shut mine again and prayed.

The ride back was much shorter than I'd remembered going the other way. It seemed like, within a quick hour or two, farms and ranches sitting on both sides of the road came into view. Then, more and more houses.

And then…Fredericksburg itself.

We pulled up in front of the sheriff's office. The man set the brake, nodded to Junior, jumped off the high seat and marched inside. Within moments, Sheriff Driggs, Pa on his heels, flew out of the office and stood at the wagon.

"See, Sheriff?" Pa pointed at us. "Got them no good outlaws for sure. Figured they were yours. Knew you'd want 'em back."

"An' we're ready to collect the re-ward." The son's eyes widened, while a smile split his wide face.

"Reward?" Driggs eyed us. He rubbed his chin. "Guess there's a sorta reward for these *pendejos.*" He glanced up and down the street. Not many people out and about. "Get 'em down, Bring 'em inside."

The old man gripped my ankle and pulled, dragging me over boxes. Since my arms were still shackled behind me, I couldn't defend myself. Eagan kicked at overturned boxes, but his journey out of the wagon wasn't easier than mine.

Driggs pointed to the open door and glared at me as I walked past. Eagan was behind me, followed by the two "helpful" citizens. The sheriff brought up the rear.

Eagan and I continued through the office and into the back room where the cells stood empty. At least I wouldn't have to share with a stranger. I'd have my own room…again.

Anger built up in my chest, which I knew would explode any second. What in the hell? How did all this happen? More importantly, what would happen next? Surely, he couldn't keep us in jail, especially when we tell the deputy and anybody else passing by, what we knew. And where was Deputy Randolph, anyway?

Driggs locked both cells, then the three of them stood back admiring their capture of us dastardly criminals. A good twenty seconds ticked by before the man pulled in air, nodded, and pointed toward the office.

"Looks like it's re-ward time, Officer." He walked back to Driggs's desk, the others following. "What's the offer? Two hundred? Each?"

"No, Pa." The son joined the others. "Saw a poster readin' *five* hundred. Each."

Pa nodded. "That's right. It *was* five hundred. Dead. Seven if'n alive." He placed both hands on the desk and leaned toward Driggs. "And they're both alive, thanks to us."

Fortunately, none of them had thought to close the door between the cells and office. My vision was clear. I watched Driggs sit behind his desk, the other two stand in front.

The sheriff sat for a beat, blinking, peering outside, raising his eyebrows. Finally, he rose, glanced toward us, sighed. "Tell you what. I'll make it a thousand each, if you'll take these *yahoos* out of town and shoot 'em. Kill 'em like rabid dogs. Bury the bodies where they'll never be found."

I sucked in all the breath I could hold and stared at Eagan. Holy Mother of God!

Junior whipped off his hat, slapped his thigh with it. "Hell, yeah, we'll do it." He turned to Pa. "Thousand each! Hell, Pa, we'll be richer'n Ol' Man Tilly, who owns all them cows. Richer'n...richer'n the *President*." He lowered his voice and put his hat over his heart. "Hell, Pa, richer'n God Almighty."

Pa's smile beamed around the room. "Right ye are,

son!" He tugged his hat back down and grew serious. "Sheriff, I don't hold to outright killin'. Ain't the proper way to do things." He pointed at us. "If'n you want 'em kilt, it'll have to be a fair fight."

"Fair?" Junior whined. "Ain't fair to us, Pa. What if'n they kill one of us? Or both? We ain't never gonna get that re-ward money."

"That's just the way it's gotta be, son. Like I told the sheriff here, I don't cotton to outright killin', 'less'n it's a snake or coyote. Them I kill outright." He turned to Driggs. "Give 'em a gun or knife and we'll do it." He stuck out a hand.

Driggs took time taking it. They shook.

"I'll need proof they're dead before you get your money." Driggs glanced back at us, spite written all over his face. Both eyes had narrowed.

Junior offered, "I know! We kin cut off a thumb 'r two. Bring it back. Like a trophy!" He looked from the sheriff to Pa.

Sighing, Driggs studied the top of his desk, then opened the middle drawer and extracted Eagan's deputy badge. The sheriff held it up. "Bring this back and I'll know they're *both* dead. This belongs to the younger one back there."

The old man leaned in close, studied it. "He's a lawman? Like you?"

"*Not* like me. He's a deputy from another county. Means nothing here."

He stood up straight, eyeing the sheriff. "Don't feel right, killin' a law dog." He rubbed his throat. "They hang folks for that."

"A thousand dollars, Pa." Junior tugged on his sleeve. "Just think, Pa. A *thousand*."

Driggs placed the badge in his hand. "I won't tell, if you don't."

He studied the badge, turning it side to side. He let out a loud sigh. "Well, all righty. You got yourself a deal." He slid Eagan's badge into a vest pocket, then ran a thick hand over his mouth. "If'n I'm a-gonna do all this, best have a drink 'fore I go."

"Pa?"

Did Junior always whine? Wasn't he grown enough not to? I wanted to slap him silly but, then again, he was the man quite likely to kill me. Now I really wanted to slap him.

Pa hooked a thumb in his pocket. "If'n I'm gonna get a drink, might be I can get an advance on my re-ward?"

From back here, it looked like Driggs had second thoughts about dealing with these men. He wagged his head, let out air, slumped his shoulders. He took time answering. "Here's the deal. These outlaws need to be gone about sundown. Streets should be empty by then. My deputy'll be getting back after that, and he doesn't need to know any of this." He leaned in close. "Get my meaning?"

He nodded.

Junior stared at us.

"Fine." Driggs dug around in his vest pocket, extracted four coins. "You come back drunk, either one of you, deal's off." He looked from man to man. "That clear?"

Both nodded.

* * *

SURPRISINGLY, I slept most of the afternoon. Eagan snored. My eyes opened to my stomach grumbling. It hadn't been fed in who knew how long and a deep voice in the outer office confused me. Not Driggs's, not the deputy's. Somebody else. Did I recognize it?

I sat up on the cot, arms still pinioned behind me. They had long ago turned numb. I listened harder. Yes, vaguely familiar. Based on the sun's rays, I had slept most of the afternoon. Probably an hour or so until sunset. Who was out there talking to Driggs? The two were partially out of my sight, the door halfway open. I listened hard.

"I'm telling you, you'll get your damn money, August. Got it safe and sound. Nobody knows where it is but me." Driggs moved behind his desk. Now I could see him fine. "Don't worry. It's all still there."

"Better be." A big man stood at the desk, his back to me. "Want my share first thing, tomorrow. All of it." He turned toward the small room where the safe sat. "It in there? Like you said?"

"Nah. I moved it. All but two thousand."

"Why?"

"I'm gonna have the two eyewitnesses eliminated. Tonight. Gonna cost us a thousand apiece, so a quarter of that'll come out of your share."

"What?" He turned to stare at us.

Bushy Beard! It *was* Bushy Beard, who'd helped rob the banks. I'd been right! "Eagan," I whispered. "Eagan, wake up."

"Hmmmh?" The gag muted his words.

"Shh." I moved as close as I could to the other cell. "Bushy Beard's out there and just confessed to robbing the banks." I cocked my head toward the other room. "Listen."

"Those fellas still back there?" Bushy Beard strode into our holding area, the door banging against the wall.

"All tied up, I see." He addressed Eagan. "Tried to escape, did ya?" He stood eye to eye with him. "What's wrong? Cat got your tongue?"

Eagan grunted what I knew were words Ma would never allow. In my mind I did the same.

Driggs stood behind Bushy Beard. "They'll be leaving soon."

The big man stood back, eyeing both of us. "Thousand each?"

The sheriff nodded.

"Hell," Bushy Beard said. "I'll do it for free. Keep my share of the money." He reached behind him. "Give me the keys and problem solved."

The front door opened and to my relief, in stepped Pa and Junior.

"Sheriff?" The old man called, then spotted him in with us. The two of them joined the others. "What in tarnation, Driggs? Who's he?"

"Never you mind." Driggs took Pa by the shoulders and pushed him toward the door. "Plan's changed. Don't need you anymore."

"What?" Pa and Junior spoke in unison.

"Why, Sheriff?" Junior whined again, louder this time. "Why?"

Driggs shrugged. "Plans change, that's why." He pointed at the door. "Time for you fellas to leave." He marched both men into the outer office. Bushy Beard stayed behind, sizing us up. "No, siree, Sheriff." Pa stood his ground. "We done shook on our bargain. If'n you wanna welch on our deal, then it'll cost ya."

Driggs marched from door to door, peering out at the darkening sky. He stopped, spun toward Pa. "I'll give you five hundred. No more. Keep your traps shut." He stuck out a hand. "And now you won't have to worry about killing a lawman. Deal?"

Pa looked at Junior, looked at us, Bushy Beard, then back to Driggs. He stuck out a hand. "Deal."

Driggs dug into a pocket, pulled out a handful of bills, counted, then stuffed them into Pa's outstretched hands. "Here. Not a word to a living soul." He waved one finger in his face. "No one. Got it?"

Pa made a show of counting out the money. Satisfied, he kissed the bills, folded them, and stuffed the bribe money into a vest pocket. "Let's go, Junior. Hope your mammy's got vittles cookin'."

I was never happier to see someone leave than I was then. But not so happy to see Bushy Beard and now knowing for sure that he was one of the robbers. And that he'd kill us for free. I thought back to Gertrude's Gasthause where he'd nearly strangled me. Strong. That man was bull strong. I wanted to rub my neck, but with my hands still bound, all I could do was swallow. Hard.

Driggs closed the outside door and joined us. He spoke to Bushy Beard. "Get rid of these two right now. Deputy's due any minute and he doesn't need to know about this. I'm sure Joe here will shout out the minute that door opens."

"Need to gag him, right now." Bushy Beard unwrapped the filthy neckerchief from around his own neck, held up a finger and motioned me to turn around.

When I refused, he grabbed my shoulder through the bars, jerked me against them, wrapped the foul, salty cloth around my mouth. God, I hated this and him equally. I grunted and growled to no avail. All I received was laughter.

"Want me to shoot 'em here, or take 'em into the

hills?" Bushy Beard waited for Driggs to find the cell key in his desk.

Driggs called out, "Too quiet tonight. People'll hear a gunshot." He returned with the key. "Take 'em up in the hills. Far out of town. Bury 'em deep."

Bushy Beard gripped Eagan's arm, pulling him hard. "You're a deputy, I hear?"

Eagan nodded.

"Killin' a lawman." Both eyebrows raised toward his hairline. "Powerful heap of trouble killin' a lawman, even if he is just a baby law dog."

"That a problem for you?" Driggs stuck the key in my cell door and waited.

Beard chuckled. "Nah. Always wanted to kill me a man of the law. It'll be fun." A smile split the greasy beard.

Driggs opened my cell, stuck a gun against my chest. "Do anything, Mr. Nolan, anything at all, and you'll watch your brother die first." He waggled the weapon toward the outer office. "Understand?"

Boy, did I. I nodded and waited for Eagan by the desk. Driggs opened the top desk drawer, fished through papers, then looked up.

"Damn! That jasper's got Eagan's badge. Gave it to him and forgot to get it back."

"Don't worry, Driggs. I'll get it."

I had no doubt August Huber would. I hated to think how, but then again, those two were willing to kill us. All right. No sympathy.

CHAPTER TWELVE

"WHAT'D WE NEED THE BADGE FOR ANYWAY?"
Bushy Beard frowned down at Driggs then over at Eagan.
"He don't need it where he's going."

"Don't you see...you German lummox? Need to bury
it with him. Somebody finds that badge, or if that fella
tries to sell it, that'll raise suspicions. Without it, looks
like Eagan just skedaddled from the area, maybe moved
down to Mexico. Him and his brother. Irresponsible kid.
Lawman, at that." Driggs stood to his full height. "Don't
want any loose ends."

I stood there studying the sheriff. He didn't fit the
robbers' images I remembered from the hold up in
Blanco Hill. So, I gathered he was the leader, an instiga-
tor, not a robber. Bushy Beard was the one who clobbered me. But who were the other two? I remembered
one was shorter and muscled, the other outlaw normal
size, but slim. Driggs had a belly on him and didn't move
easily. No, it definitely wasn't him.

So, who was it? Most importantly—where was the
money?

"Get goin', August." Driggs pointed outside, daylight dimming. "Deputy'll be back any minute."

Bushy Beard stepped back, reset his hat with his left hand, the right one holding a gun. "Now hold on, Driggs. You be in a mighty big hurry."

"Randolph doesn't know about this. Hate to have to kill him too, when he walks in."

Well, I'd be damned. I figured the deputy at least knew what was going on under his own nose. Maybe he wasn't as smart as he looked. Then again, he didn't look all that smart.

"You know," Bushy Beard snarled. "I ain't seen any of that money. Not one red cent. Thinking on it, I want my share right now, 'fore I kill these two." He glanced out the window and turned back to Driggs. "New deal. You go with us, and before I kill 'em, you give me my share. That way I know I'll get it."

"What? What're you talking about? I said I'd give everybody their share—you, Lib and Theo. You'll *all* get what's coming to you." Driggs feigned a look of pure innocence. "I *promise*."

I could see right through the lack of guilt and suddenly my entire body filled with hope. If we could get Driggs to locate the money, there was a chance, though a slight one at that. Eagan and I could overtake our captors. Or maybe they'd kill each other. "Wouldn't that be gran'" as Ma would say? We'd get the money and free ourselves. Then ride into each town returning life savings. I hadn't planned to be a hero, but recognition like that would be nice.

But who were Lib and Theo? Had we met them? Or seen them around town? Lib...odd name. Probably German. I ran it around in my head and came up with nothing.

"Well, I don't care 'bout nobody but me." Bushy Beard stuck a thumb against his sizable chest. "I want my money, tonight." He emphasized "tonight" by poking Driggs' chest.

Driggs recoiled at the touch. "Don't ever...*ever*...do that, again." His eyes narrowed and I swear he snarled, teeth showing.

"Just get me my cut and I'll never talk to you again."

"Fine." The sheriff stood, legs pushing back the chair.

The outer door squeaked opened, the hinges in need of oil. All heads turned. In stepped a man I'd never seen before. Or had I? Something about him was familiar. But what?

Closing the door behind him, he surveyed the quiet room. "What's all this, Driggs? August?" He inched closer. "Who're these two?" He looked us up and down, head to boots.

"None of your business, Lib." Driggs peered outside then turned back. "What d'you want?"

The man was medium build, late thirties, I guessed. A flat-brimmed hat shaded a round face. He narrowed his deep-set, moss-green eyes at me. And then I recognized him. Put a badge on him and this was Deputy Lionel Lieberman from Johnsonville. He was in on the heist? How could that be? What kind of man would rob his own town? His own friends?

Lib leaned in closer to Driggs. "I asked, 'who're these two'?" He spit as he spoke. "Don't give me none of this 'none-of-your-business' malarkey. I ain't splittin' the loot with nobody else."

August gripped Eagan's arm, tight. "They're just leavin', Lib. Leavin' for good." He chuckled and inched toward the door, Eagan in tow.

Driggs explained, his words rushed. "These two can

identify August and now us." He shrugged. "They need disposing of—right now, before my deputy comes back."

"Deputy...deputy." Lib studied Eagan, snapped his fingers. "That's where I seen you before. You're that deputy from Blanco Hill." He cocked his head. "Rode all the way over just to posse up. You and that other deputy, Tommy something. Couple others."

All hope to survive drained from my body and ran out through my toes. I stood weak in a puddle of despair. No way in hell we'd make it out alive now. Was that a sigh? Was it mine? It was.

Driggs opened the door and peered into the gray. "Gotta go. Now." His arms windmilled for us to get out. I dug in wanting to take as much time as possible in case a miracle happened, and we got rescued.

Like God himself would take time outta His day to come down and smite these men. I guessed stranger things had happened. I glanced up for lightning. There was only clear sky.

Although I was last out, yanked by Lib, I stood across from Eagan, while we gathered on the boardwalk in front of the office. Three horses were tied nearby, but there were now five of us. Would they make us walk? With our arms behind our backs? Gagged like we were, yelling out was no option. Would stumbling delay the inevitable? That held possibilities. No. We'd most likely be dragged behind the horse. More despair brought a quiver to my lower lip. Like a three-year-old denied dessert.

"Go get two more horses, Lib. Tell the stableman we're in a hurry. Town business." Driggs nodded west.

"Why can't August go?" Lib turned his back to the street, pulled his six-shooter. "I shoot better'n him, anyway. Let him go do it."

"'Cause I told *you*." Driggs's mouth drew into a tight line, his mustache hiding the top lip.

"*He* can go. I'm waitin' here."

"I don't wanna. I was here first." August pushed his gun barrel harder into Eagan's ribs. "An' I shoot better'n you, anyway."

Driggs's face turned red. "Hells, bells. *I'll* go." He glared at Lib and August. "Watch 'em. Shoot 'em if they move." The sheriff trotted up the boardwalk.

The four of us stood in a circle, Lib gripping my left upper arm so tightly I was sure he'd snap the bone. August had hold of Eagan's right upper arm. Both waved their revolvers like they were on a raid, willing to shoot anything that moved. But I knew they'd shoot us first, even if we didn't move.

Movement off in the distance made me turn. At the end of town, only a few blocks to the east, a man held up a torch, lighting the oil lantern hanging in front of a store. A soft, golden glow lit up the boardwalk. Maybe he'd get down close enough to us where I could holler out, or mumble out, for help. As slow as he was moving, it would be solid dark by the time he got close.

"Seen Theo around?" Lib raised one shoulder toward August, who was now busy finger-raking dried bits of dinner out of his beard.

Bushy Beard yanked at something tangled in the hair, then wiped it on his trousers. "Nah. Not since last week."

"Suppose he got his share already and lit out for Mexico?"

If I was in his boots, that's what I'd have done. I'd have hightailed it out of town so quickly, all anyone would see was my dust. Even at that, they'd have to use a spyglass to spot the back of me.

I studied Eagan. Dark circles under his eyes almost reached his chin. He'd aged ten years and, no doubt, wondered why he'd ever wanted to be a deputy. I had to wonder the same thing. What was the attraction? Not much money in it. The glamour? The prestige? Right. Like there was a ton of prestige, right now.

Boot steps on the boardwalk turned all our heads. The silhouette of a man striding our way, swaggering confidently, resembled Deputy Randolph. Could it be? While I didn't especially like the man, after all, he'd called us Irish "Micks," I was glad he was nearby.

Now half a block away, he stopped and stared. "What's going on here?" He walked faster toward us, calling out. "Who're you?"

Both guns clicked metal against metal. Half cock, or even full cock, I wasn't sure, but cocked meant business.

Randolph skidded to a stop when he reached us. "August Huber?" He frowned. "Deputy Liberman? What're you doing here?" His head swung from Eagan to me and back again. "Joe, why're you tied up, out here?"

Forgetting for a second I was gagged, I tried to warn him. To shoot first, ask questions later. Nothing I mumbled made sense.

August turned his gun on Randolph. "You're back early. Weren't supposed to see this."

"See what?"

"This." *Bang!* Flames burst from Bushy Beard's gun, striking the deputy's shoulder.

Randolph spun, grabbed, kneeled, then collapsed against the hitch rail. He slid to the dirt and lay still.

Was he dead? Severely wounded? Eagan and I grunted, hollering as best we could.

"You winged him, August. Told you I was a better shooter." Lib peered over at Randolph. "Hell, now he'll live to tell the world about us. Better shoot 'em again. Kill 'em this time. Or you want me to, since I hit what I aim at?"

Anger enveloping my body, I headbutted Bushy Beard. We *whumped* down two steps onto the street, me on top. Using the only weapon available, I smashed my head into his face. Again and again. Blood poured from his nose, across his face. He grunted, then like a bucking bronc, threw me onto my back and rolled to all fours. From my position, I could see Eagan and Lib fighting. Grunts from all of us filled the street.

I kicked up, missing anything vital, but managed to throw Bushy Beard off kilter. He rocked to one side and I rolled to my right, then kicked him hard in the chest. He somersaulted under a tied horse that pulled at the reins. The animal didn't like having a human underneath and pranced as best it could. The horse next to it did the same. Startled by the noise, the third horse whinnied, reared back, breaking the leather reins. Loose, it galloped off.

A hand gripped my ankle and pulled me under a horse. I kicked at the man with my free leg, but Bushy Beard grabbed that one too. Pinioned! Wriggling for all my life, I slammed into one of the horse's front legs. The horse stomped trying hard to miss me, but the hoof caught my upper right shoulder. Something cracked. My shoulder turned to fire, but I didn't think it was broken.

"Ahhhh!" Bushy Beard wailed, desperately rolling, holding his shin, attempting to avoid more hooves.

Praying the horse would behave, I scooted forward under the neck, then under the hitch rail. The horse continued dancing, not wanting to stomp someone again, but desperate to flee.

I lay against the bottom of the boardwalk, panting,

searching for Eagan. I spotted him lying face first on the boardwalk, Lib nearby on his back, out cold. I scrambled up the two steps, kneeled by Eagan.

"Eagan?" My word was garbled. I nudged him with my knee. "You all right?" Damn these tied hands. Damn this gag. I used my knee to push him over. He muttered and I sent a prayer upward.

"What the hell?" Driggs grabbed my hair, yanking me to my feet. "What the hell'd you do?" He spit as he hollered.

I kicked out, connecting with his shin. He repaid it with a punch to my jaw. I spun but kept my feet. Face throbbing, I headbutted him, like I'd done Bushy Beard. We both crashed to the boardwalk.

He pushed me off, pulled out his gun, stood, aimed it at Eagan. "He goes first. Right here."

Bang!

Driggs sailed backward, crashing onto his back. I hit the boardwalk, flattened out as best I could, then looked over my shoulder. A silhouette drew closer, running toward us.

I squinted. Nobody I knew would shoot the sheriff. Was it Bushy Beard? No chance. He was off in the dark somewhere, crying over his hurt leg.

"You all right?"

I squinted up into the darkness. Face bending over me looked familiar. I blinked twice, then the image focused. Tate! Great Mother of God, Tate was here! Questions flew through my brain, but right now, I needed Eagan to be all right.

While I struggled to sit, Tate kneeled by Eagan, who moaned. Tate cradled him, untied the gag. Eagan opened his eyes, and recoiled at the face in front of him. Finally, a smile stretched ear to ear—on both brothers.

* * *

THE THREE OF us spent that night in a hotel room. A real cotton mattress under me, a clean sheet on top, and my brothers' snoring relaxed me enough to sleep past the noon meal. My growling stomach brought me back to the world.

On my right, Eagan was still asleep. Across the narrow room, Tate sat in an overstuffed chair, newspaper in one hand, cup in the other. The aroma of fresh coffee hung in the air and I knew if I didn't get a cup of my own, I'd go crazy.

Tate put down the paper, chinned to me, and whispered. "Morning, Sunshine."

I nodded, pointed at the cup, and raised an eyebrow.

He held the paper higher, revealing a second cup on the side table. I slid out of bed, using my arms to push up. Both shoulders screamed pain, but I ignored them. For now. I was sure in a bit they'd loudly remind me of the indignity they'd been put through.

I padded over to Tate, sipped on the pure nectar, reveling in the moment. I downed the rest of the cup like I would die if I didn't guzzle it all.

And then it hit me. I didn't remember much after Tate showed up, saving our lives. What happened to Deputy Randolph? Driggs? Bushy Beard? Lib? All I was sure of—we were lucky to be alive. Damn lucky.

"What about Driggs? The rest of 'em?" I had to know, right now. Now that I remembered last night.

Before Tate could explain, Eagan stirred, threw off the sheet, and headed for a bucket placed in a discreet corner, a screen shielding it. He emerged looking like a bedraggled bear coming out of hibernation. His hair stuck out at odd angles, his eyes were swollen, bloodshot. He hobbled across the room and plopped down on the bed. He sat, rubbing his face, his chest, his wrists. Mine were sore and bruised too. But what hurt the most were the corners of my mouth. That damn gag had worn blisters.

"Now that you two beauty queens are awake, need to tell you about last night."

I sat in the other chair, concern filling my chest. "What happened last night? And why can't I remember much past you showing up, shooting Driggs?"

Tate wagged his head, scratched at his arm. "Neither of you were thinking clearly. Actually, not at all. Don't know why, but you were dazed. Like you'd been wounded too."

"So what about the others?" Eagan croaked and leaned against the bedpost.

"Driggs is dead. I killed him. Tommy'll make an official inquiry and be in charge of Fredericksburg until Deputy Randolph is able to resume duties."

"So, he's alive." I turned to Eagan. "Thought for sure he was dead."

Tate shrugged. "One tough bird, I guess."

"How about Lib...Deputy Lieberman?" I didn't want him dead. At least not until he told us where the money was hidden.

"Deputy Lieberman'll live, too." Tate pointed west. "They're both over at the doc's."

"We should go see them, right now." I was hoping Liberman would tell us where the money was.

"Better yet. How 'bout we go get something to eat?" Tate folded the newspaper. "They're not going anywhere, and I'm starved."

I patted the sides of my mouth, then my stomach. "Stomach wins! Three minutes." Finding clothes that weren't dirty, torn or stinking was impossible. No way would a café or restaurant let us in like this.

Tate shook his head, then tossed cotton under-drawers and a new shirt to each of us. "Got these this morning. Britches, you'll have to buy after we eat. No way your horse'll let either of you back in the saddle smelling like that." He waved toward the washstand. "Soap and water, and a razor'll make you look presentable again." He chuckled. "Not *good*, just presentable."

Questions again filled my head, but I knew we'd get the full story over grub.

Halfway to my sorely wanted meal, Eagan halted in front of the sheriff's office and eyed the building. "You know..." He lowered his voice and looked up and down Main, like a bunch of outlaws were about to attack. "If I'm not mistaken, there's no law in town."

"Just you." Tate pointed toward the office. "You're in charge, 'til Tommy or Sheriff Wagner show up."

I wasn't sure how to handle this turn of events. What *would* happen with just Eagan behind the desk? What about if someone decided to rob a store right now?

"Best we go inside, check around, then lock up." Eagan stuck out his chest a bit, which brought a smile to my mouth. He certainly took his oath seriously.

We opened the squeaky door, checked in the back— empty cells. The safe—closed and locked. Papers on the desk still in disarray. Looked like no one had bothered to come inside recently.

I was fumbling with the safe's lock, hoping I had the magic touch, when a voice I didn't recognize got my attention. I stepped into the main office. Eagan sat behind the desk, Tate at the door, holding the knob. A middle-aged man, possibly a businessman, based on his clean cotton trousers and striped shirt, bowler perched on freshly cut hair, stood looking down at Eagan.

The man glanced at me, then returned to studying Eagan. "Like I was saying, hadn't seen Driggs or Randolph out today, making their usual rounds. Thought I'd come in and check."

"Glad you did, Mr...." Eagan stood and extended a hand.

"Gatwick. Ernest Gatwick. I run the mercantile down the street."

"Deputy Eagan Nolan from Blanco Hill. Please to meet you. I'll be here until we get another officer in. Should be later, today."

Gatwick cocked his head, stepped back one step, frowned at Eagan. "You a deputy, you say? Awful young to be a lawman." He studied Eagan closer. "Don't see a badge." He swung his head toward Tate and then me. "You deputies, too?"

"No, sir." I answered before Tate would say something he shouldn't.

"Where's the sheriff?" Gatwick stepped toward the cells. "He back there?"

Eagan followed. "No, sir. Both Sheriff Driggs and Deputy Randolph are unavailable. And will be for a few days. I'm filling in while they're away."

I was impressed with my brother's clear thinking and ability to speak so well off the cuff.

"Well, where'd they go to?"

"Not at liberty to say, right off." Eagan raised one shoulder. "Sorry."

"Fine." He eyed Eagan again. "Sounds like a mystery. But still don't see a badge."

Eagan shrugged. "Got stolen couple days ago. I aim to get it back tomorrow." He added, "When the officer from

Blanco Hill comes today, you can ask him about me." He nodded toward the door. "Thank you for stopping by."

Gatwick sighed loudly, returned the nod, and left. We relaxed into a puddle of smiles.

"Can we go eat now?" Tate waved us outside.

Faces shaven and washed, hair combed, armpits scrubbed, new shirts buttoned and tucked in, we entered the Gentle Dixie Café, up the street near the east end of Main. The six people at various tables stopped conversations, forks held mid-air, and stared. We took seats near the back, with tipped hats we regarded the other diners, then ignored them.

We ordered coffee first, then bacon, eggs, toast, and a ham sandwich for Eagan. Pie would come later over at Hilda's bakery. If she had any left. I mightily hoped she did.

While we waited, Tate studied his cup. "Good thing you had that telegram sent. We'd never have found you."

Over breakfast, Tate filled in gaps from last night. He held up a hand, put down his fork. He lowered his voice and glanced at the other patrons. "Never expected any of this."

We hadn't either.

"Need to go see Lieberman and Randolph soon's we eat." Eagan finished his first cup of coffee. "Hope they're awake."

Eagan and I related cave stories, being rescued, then almost killed by our rescuers. We ended up explaining why we were on the boardwalk when Tate had found us. But questions still lingered.

Silence surrounded the table until Tate let out a stream of air. "You're two lucky sum-a-bucks."

I couldn't argue with him on that account.

"I'll tell Tommy to lock up Liberman soon's he can.

Liberman shot Randolph. Almost point blank." Memories, flashes of pure panic took over, my hands shook. Damn, that was close last night. I held my cup, coffee sloshing over the rim. I fought down horror. "What about Bushy Beard? Real name August Huber."

"Don't know who that is. Saw only four when the fighting was all over."

We sat quietly, chewing, sipping, thinking.

Stomach finally full, but knowing there was room for pie, I finished my coffee. "Wish Driggs didn't die."

Two sets of eyes stared at me, one shamrock green, the other light copper. I played with the fork, pointing it west. "He knew where the money's at. Said they were going to get it before killing us. That's what Bushy Beard insisted on."

"Yeah," Eagan nodded. "Him and Lib. But there's a third man, name of Theo. Must've been the short robber."

Tate dropped a bill and coins onto the table, while Eagan took one last sip of his second cup of coffee. We stood and walked into fresh air. I stretched my arms overhead. The shoulders ached, my arms almost refusing to reach all the way up. But with encouragement, they straightened. I'd examined the half-moon bruise on my right shoulder that morning. That horse could've broken bones quite easily. If I knew which horse it was, I'd give him extra grain.

From here, it was either go see Hilda and thank her for sending the telegram, or see what money was in the sheriff's safe. Or even check in with the doc to see how Randolph and Lieberman were doing. Possibly, a nap was also in order. All sounded reasonable.

We stood on the boardwalk, toothpicks in mouth,

although I had to take mine out, as my mouth was way too sore. Eagan spit his away also.

Tate glanced at the sun. "Tommy won't be here for another hour or two, at least. Let's go see the deputies, ask around about this Theo fella, then check out the safe. I'm curious where the money is at."

I guessed a nap wasn't happening, but that was all right. Even though I was exhausted, I had to get the money back. Had to. Three towns—and Da—depended on me. Us. The three of us. I brought my sore shoulders back and eyed the two. The Nolan brothers were ridin' together again.

CHAPTER THIRTEEN

DOC REPORTED DEPUTIES RANDOLPH AND Lieberman would live to fight another day. Doc was a much younger fella than I'd expected. I figured a town doctor would be an old, grizzled type with white hair hitting the ear, a bit bent over, cantankerous. But this one looked to be on the short side of thirty. Long, dark hair pulled back, wrapped with a leather band. Round, jovial dark blue eyes, set off with round spectacles. That part I'd expected. Didn't all doctors wear glasses?

Trying to talk with the wounded proved pointless. Both were under laudanum's effects, Lieberman mumbling, while Randolph was out cold.

The four of us stood in the outer office, me rubbing my shoulder, Eagan massaging his head, and Tate nodding.

"Thank you again, Doc, for what you did for me earlier this summer." Tate pointed to his shoulder.

Doc extended a hand. "Yep. That bullet was down deep, but you were lucky it didn't hit anything major."

I remembered Tate saying he'd been shot around nearby, and by Driggs, no less. So, no question, it was only right that my brother killed him. Kind of had it coming.

"We'll stop by tomorrow." Tate headed for the door. "Don't let Lieberman go anywhere. He's under arrest. My brother here's a deputy."

Doc frowned, then extended a tentative hand. "Deputy."

Tate explained. "From Blanco Hill. There's a sheriff and maybe another deputy from there who'll be showing up soon. They'll stay until somebody from Fredericksburg can step in."

"Good to know." Doc thumbed toward Lieberman. "I'll be sure to keep him sedated." Doc walked us to the door. "See you tomorrow."

I assumed Driggs was at the undertakers, and I had no desire to go there. Nothing to say or do. Didn't want to see him. But I wished there was some way in the afterlife, he could come back and tell us where he'd hidden the money. I realized a smile had crept onto my face, because the corners of my mouth hurt and my lips cracked.

"Joe?" Tate stopped me on the boardwalk. "What's so funny?"

I relayed my images of Driggs' ghost pointing toward the hidey hole. He'd mutter how much each town lost and say how sorry he was for stealing it in the first place. And who exactly this Theo was.

"That kind of thinking calls for...pie." Tate pointed toward Hilda's. As we walked, we discussed what the ghost would be wearing. A bedsheet or his going-to-church clothes? Would he have the money with him? I envisioned bills sticking out from under his hat and jutting from his pockets. Could he actually form real words or merely moan and rattle his chains?

We arrived at Hilda's snickering. It had been a long time and laughing felt good. The bakery was still open, but the variety and number of pastries in the glass showcase was limited. Still, they all looked delightful. And the smell! The aroma of freshly baked anything sent my heart racing. My mouth watered and without thinking, I licked my raw lips. I grimaced despite my joy.

Hilda floated around the counter, giving us cursory hugs, an odd thing for a woman to do to men she barely knew. Then I reconsidered. She obviously knew Tate well. I wondered what had happened to their relationship, but right now I couldn't decide if I was more enamored with the baked goods or the woman who baked them.

She stood taller than most women, but still much shorter than my six foot one height. Closer to Tate's age than mine, that put her in her early twenties. Not a problem in my mind. And she was pretty. *Real* pretty. Large blue eyes peeked at me from under impossibly long eyelashes. Her ivory complexion showed off a sensual mouth that laughed easily.

Absolutely, I'd like to get to know her better. A *lot* better.

Tate and Hilda were deep in conversation, but I caught bits and pieces. "*Danke,*" and "*mein vater,*" must be German for father. She blushed some, then turned to me.

"Joe, I am happy we could get *dein* brother to come when he did. I did not want you...killed." She glanced at Eagan busily choosing a morsel. "Or Eagan."

"Me, neither." I looked at Tate then at Hilda. "I'm not sure how much longer I'll be in town. May I escort you to supper tonight? Just the two of us?"

Was that a frown on Tate's face? Probably. But I'd done the asking and he'd have to settle for Eagan as a dinner partner.

Hilda nodded, a tiny giggle erupting. "I'd be delighted to, Joe." She glanced at Tate, but not for his approval. "I close at five. How about right after that?"

"Perfect." Butterflies danced in my stomach. Looked like I was ready to court again. Or was I? Well, this would be more of a "thank you" meal than anything romantic. But still and all...

Taking our time looking over the baked chunks of heaven, at long last I chose a blueberry strudel, Eagan a lemon scone, and Tate bought an entire pie. Chokecherry.

Tate handed over coins as we turned to leave. I remembered another piece of the bank robbery puzzle. I asked Hilda. "Do you know a man named Theo?" I held up a hand shoulder high. "Short?"

She cocked her pretty head to one side. "*Nein*. But I'll watch out."

We checked with the hotel clerk, a restaurant clerk, Mr. Gatwick at the mercantile, anywhere somebody might frequent. The answer was always the same. Nope. Nobody like that.

Frustrated, we sat in chairs on the boardwalk in front of the mercantile and ate our pastries. My strudel was like biting into a cloud of blueberries. Light, fluffy, the right amount of sugar. I wanted at least ten more but, with supper fast approaching, figured I'd let this tidbit sit in my stomach and make it smile.

Eagan downed his scone in three bites, a grin plastered on his face, now sprinkled with crumbs. He closed his eyes and tilted his bruised face toward the afternoon sun. Today wasn't as warm as the previous weeks, which meant fall was approaching. My favorite season. But it wasn't here quite yet.

Tate used his hands to scoop out parts of the pie. I leaned across Eagan and snagged a glob. The chokecherries were tart with a tinge of sweetness. A lot like Ma made. A mouthful went down like nectar. My eyes closed like I'd died and gone to heaven. I reveled in the moment.

"Well, if it ain't the scourge of Blanco Hill, sittin' right outside in full view of God and His creations, stuffin' their faces with...what? Pie?"

I opened my eyes to see Deputy Tommy O'Sullivan relaxing on his horse. He had one leg hooked around the saddle horn, an arm resting on his thigh. Tate stood, pie in hand, walked down the two steps and over to our friend. "Want some?"

"Got a spoon?"

Tate shook his head. "We're using what God gave us." He held up a messy hand.

"Thanks, but no. God also gave us eating utensils."

"Too bad. It's real tasty." Tate licked his fingers.

I reached up and shook hands with Tommy. Relieved to see him, I fought a smile creeping up my face. "'Bout time you showed up." Waving my arm up and down Main, I tried to sound concerned. "Crowds've been something fierce. Already had three shootings and we got, what...? Five?" I turned to my brothers for confirmation. They nodded. "*Five* outlaws in jail."

"Turns out...the Nolan Brothers are a force to be reckoned with." Eagan pushed up from the chair. "Got everything under control."

Tommy regarded each of us, his eyes narrowing, mouth tightening. "Uh-huh." He chinned at Eagan. "Where's your badge, *deputy*?"

"Seems he needed money. Sold it to the first man he saw." I worked at keeping a straight face.

All eyes turned to Eagan. He held out both hands palm up and shrugged.

Tommy settled his rear in the saddle, shook his head. "If you all aren't a sorry lot to look at." One shoulder raised. "But I'm damn glad to see you."

Eagan shaded his eyes, his hat lost in the past couple of days. "Let's go back to the sheriff's office. Talk this out." He patted a pocket. "I have the key."

Inside the office, we explained the complicated demise of Sheriff Driggs. Tommy's eyebrows raised his hairline but didn't interrupt until we were done. He responded by looking at each of us, one at a time. He nodded. "Sounds like he had it coming."

We pushed papers around again, re-checked drawers, even overturned the rotten mattresses in the cells. Nothing. All eyes turned to the side room which held the safe. Too small for all of us to squeeze into, that left Eagan and Tommy to twirl the combination dial. Tate and I stood shoulder to shoulder in the doorway, peering over their backs, hoping against hope the iron door would spring open and we'd take a gander at towering stacks of bills.

The outer door slammed open and I jumped, spun, crashing back into Tate.

"Who the hell are you and what're you doing here?" A man, bowler atop a round head, rounded belly straining his shirt, short legs—much too short for the weight they carried—stood in the doorway, hands fisted on his hips. "What d'you think you're doing? Where's Driggs?"

Hands out at my sides, I didn't want him attempting to shoot me. And, although I didn't see a weapon, I stood stock still, but my mind was reeling. "I...we..."

"Who all's back there?" He marched toward the supply room, bulling past the desk and me. He pushed aside Tate at the door jamb and squeezed into the room.

Tommy and Eagan stopped, turned, and stared at the man. Tommy recovered first.

"Can I help you, sir?"

"Who're you and where's Driggs?" He grabbed Tommy's shoulder and pulled. "What're you doing with the safe?" The tubby man looked around like he was desperate for a club, a weapon of some sort.

Tommy and Eagan stood, both towering over the man. Tommy kept his voice soft. "I'm Deputy Tommy O'Sullivan from Blanco Hill and this's Deputy Eagan Nolan." Tommy pointed at his badge and Eagan's hand went up toward where his badge should be.

"Where's Driggs? Randolph?" The man stood, one hand on a hip.

"I'm sorry, sir." Tommy edged toward the door. "Didn't catch your name."

"You're really a deputy? Blanco Hill you say?"

"Yes, sir. Deputy Nolan and I both are." Tommy had backed the man into the front office now. Tate, Eagan, and I joined them. "These gentlemen"—he nodded to Tate and me—"are posse members. Duly sworn."

Well, that was a lie, sort of. A half one, at least. I'd been sworn in a few days ago, but I didn't think Tate had been. It didn't matter, though.

The man, face turning from red cheeks to pink cheeks now, stuck out a hand and blew out a sigh. "Name's Jessup Bauder. Fredericksburg mayor." He surveyed us four, the inside of the office, even peeked toward the cells. "Where's the sheriff? I heard gunshots last night, but, well, I didn't investigate right then, as I should have." His gaze cast downward.

I wondered what he'd been doing that was more important than investigating gunshots, but then thought about my wife. If I was busy loving her, I wouldn't interrupt that for anything. Hell, I probably wouldn't even have heard a ruckus outside my house. Frieda's face refused to materialize. Was I forgetting what she looked like? What she sounded like? Alarm overtook me, my hands shook.

Tate reached over and gripped my shoulder, nodded, like he completely understood my thoughts. I nodded back and forced myself to put away my feelings and concentrate on the moment at hand. Tommy had seated the mayor in a solid wooden chair in front of the desk, and he had taken the one behind.

Tommy explained in detail, then added. "And sir, looks like Deputy Randolph will be up and about in, I'd say, a week. One of us," he nodded to Eagan, "will be here until you get another sheriff. I'm sorry he was killed."

Mayor Bauder studied the floor, the desk, his hands. "What a shame. First a bank robbery, now shootings and one death." He looked at me. "What's this world coming to?"

I probably shouldn't have said anything, but frustration and confusion surrounded me. "Bank robbery. We believe Driggs was involved in the robberies. All three of them. Blanco Hill, Johnsonville, and here."

"Involved? How?"

I shared as much information as I thought necessary. "The same three men held up the banks." I held my hand slightly above my head. "First one was August Huber. He admitted to it last night."

"Hum." Bauder frowned. "Don't know him."

I felt the need to remind him. "We believe he is Gertrude's brother, of Gertrude's Gasthause."

"No!" He frowned. "She has a brother?"

"Yes, sir, she does. The other two men—"

"One is Deputy Lionel Lieberman, from Johnsonville." Eagan jumped in. "The third man is a mystery. Short, don't think he said a word. I also don't know if he fired his gun, but he had one." He nodded toward me. "My brother, here, is an eyewitness to the first robbery."

We waited for the mayor to make a proclamation, a declaration, or anything audible. Instead, he sat, hands folded, eyes on his lap. We shifted our weight. I eyed the door to the safe, wondering when we'd get back to opening it up. Two of us cleared our throats.

Bauder looked up then stood. "So much to do. Need to inform the town counsel. Plan a funeral. Go see Randolph…"

"Find the money." Eagan spoke for all of us.

"Of course, yes. Find the money. This town's in serious trouble without it." The mayor started for the door, then turned back. "You have my full support, gentlemen. Thank you for intervening when you're so needed." With that, he strode onto the porch, reset his bowler, pushed his shoulders back, and marched down the two steps to the street.

Eagan and Tommy again kneeled in front of the safe, massaging the dial, back and forth. Tommy kept his ear glued to the heavy metal door. Eagan, eyes closed, had his head as close as possible. Turn…turn…pull on the handle. Wouldn't budge. They tried again and again.

I sat at the desk, quietly shuffling papers, looking for a clue, any clue as to where he secreted the money. While I searched, I thought about the mayor. He was short. Short enough to have been one of the outlaws. I found Tate stretched out on my old cot, his eyes closed but I knew he wasn't asleep. I tapped the bottom of his boot, pointed outside.

We stood on the porch and discussed my thoughts about the mayor. We kept our voices low. "Could he be the third robber? Matches the description."

Tate surveyed the street and the few people passing by, including three men on horseback and one wagon loaded with children and boxes of supplies. "Might be." He screwed up his face. "Seemed awfully surprised. I don't think it was him though. Just didn't feel like it."

"Afraid you'd say that." I shrugged. "Had the same feeling too." Hopelessness sat on my chest, making it hard to breathe. Maybe we should simply give up and face facts. The towns were in serious trouble.

"Hey, brother." Tate nudged my shoulder. "Don't you have a supper to go to?"

I perked up but immediately regretted it. "Probably should cancel. Don't feel like talking to a girl right now."

He gripped both of my shoulders, turned me facing him. "Let me tell you one thing I've learned, younger brother." His gaze bore into my soul. "Don't let one moment pass you by. You'll never, *ever*, get it back. But then, you already know that. Doncha?"

I hung my head. "I do."

"Hilda's a great gal. You know, we almost got married."

"You did? With Hilda?"

Tate nodded, glanced toward her bakery. "Until her da found out I was going under another name, had been in prison, and then jail here." He raised one shoulder. "Apparently, I wasn't suitable husband material."

Husband. I was suitable. I'd been a good husband until...

Tate shook my shoulders, hard. "You gotta move on. Frieda's gone. And I'm so sorry for that. I truly am. But you've done your grieving. Now move on. And Hilda will be a good supper companion. I know from experience."

Should I ask a truly personal question, or leave it be? I bit my lower lip, sore as it was.

"I know that look, Joe. I know what you're not asking." He let out a sigh and wagged his head. "No. There was no taking our courtship to the highest level. I was willing, but I couldn't ask her. She's a good girl. I respect her."

He was right. As usual. I thought back to the countless hours we'd spent at home, either in our beds when we were supposed to be asleep, out on the porch where most of our secrets were shared, or down by the stream in the moonlight. He always listened to my thoughts and feelings, and usually had something to say about them. We argued, like all brothers do. But now that we were grown, there was a different bond.

"What're you standing around for?" Tate turned me toward the hotel. "Go get pretty. Hilda deserves pretty." He shoved, gently.

I took three steps, then stopped. "Wait." I stuck out a hand. "Got some dollars I can borrow?"

* * *

I MET Hilda at her shop and helped her lock up. Smells of pastries grumbled my stomach until it was embarrassing. We strolled up the street headed for the Hills Restaurant, highly recommended by her. I hoped it wasn't too expensive. Tate had loaned me all the cash he had—

at least that's what he'd claimed—and at that, it was less than ten dollars.

But that would hopefully buy a nice glass of wine for her, a beer for me, and hopefully, dessert. The Hills sat at the edge of town, an easy walk from her store. Along the way, we did small talk: the weather, bruises on my face, her pastry sales. All fine and good. Respectable.

The restaurant, nice enough looking from the outside, was spacious inside. Aromas of cooking steaks, biscuits and other blissful smells mingled well. My stomach gurgled and grumbled like it had never been fed. We were directed toward the middle of the room, joining at least fifteen other patrons at various tables. A family of four sat on one side, while three men, dressed well, occupied a large table, others scattered about.

Remembering my manners, I pulled out her chair and held it while she sat. I took the one across from her. A safe distance, but intimate enough. A young waitress handed us real paper menus. Usually, the fare was written on a chalkboard. Part of me knew we were in a classy place, the other half panicked I didn't have enough money. I'd wait to see what she ordered, then choose mine accordingly.

A quick scan of the menu brought a grin to my sore cheeks. Prices were reasonable. Hallelujah. I was hungry and didn't want to sit here watching her eat while I chewed on the menu.

I ordered a glass of white wine for her, a locally brewed beer for me. She requested the roasted chicken and I chose trout. I did quick mental math and realized we could even have dessert. Or a second glass of wine and beer. Just not both.

She sipped her wine. "*Vater* and I decided to open my shop after *Mutter* died. Five years, now." A wide smile took up most of her pink-cheeked face. "She always loved the pastries. The strudel, cherry, was her favorite. So, *Vater* and I chose making a bakery."

"I'm glad you did." My beer glass sat nearly full. "I love any kind of pastry."

Hilda laughed. Out loud. Then patted the side of her mouth with a cloth napkin. "I know you do. Like Seamus. Uh...Tate. I knew him as Seamus O'Brien." Her laughter softened as she leaned forward. "Did you know your brother was going to rob me when I first met him?"

"He what?" That was the first I'd heard any of that.

She put a dainty finger to her lips. "Don't tell him. He doesn't know I know." Her gaze trailed across the room then landed back on me. "He was hungry. Came in to rob me and probably eat a scone. Or six. But he is such a nice man, he didn't. Promised he would come back when he could pay for something."

We put our conversation on hold while the server slid a plate of crispy, brown chicken in front of Hilda. My trout looked to be cooked to perfection. We clinked glasses to toast such a momentous occasion. The next few minutes passed with small talk over our mouths full of succulent food. The fish flaked off the bones nicely. Hilda's face relaxed more and more with each bite.

Most of the meal gone, I resumed the important topic. "So Tate considered robbing you? Sounded like him. But you two went out after that?"

She smiled, a wide, sensuous grin. "We did. He's charming. As you know."

"Not always charming with me. He can be rowdy." I studied my beer. Right amount of hops and bitters. Maybe Blanco Hill would open a brewery. My thoughts returned to Tate. "What happened, if you don't mind my asking."

Hilda leaned back, her plate now filled with a small pile of chicken bones. "He didn't talk about his past life much. He *did* mention he had brothers, though. When *Vater* and I found out his lies, I chose not to see him again." She picked up her glass, studied it. "I *did* like him, though. He was charming."

"Tate? Still with the charming? We talking about the same man, here?"

Her smile brought sparkle to her eyes. "You remind me a lot of him. I feel like I've known you forever. You're easy to be around."

"You are too." Not ready to go down that path, I put my fork on my plate, on top of the fish skeleton. The potatoes and greens long gone. I changed topics, but only a little. "Tate's complicated, I guess. But he's doing fine as a cowboy. Ranch hand. Gets paid surprisingly well too."

I told her about my stint at the telegrapher's office and eventually admitted that I'd been married. "But only briefly." I hung my head. "She died in childbirth" That needed to be said if I was ever going out with Hilda again.

Hearing those words come out of my mouth shocked me. *Died in childbirth*. That said so much, and yet, with only three words, my entire world had shattered.

She reached across the table, put her hand on my forearm. "I am so sorry. So very sorry." She frowned. "You are so young for that kind of pain."

I nodded. And then, Tate's words circled me. *Move on.* Others had said the same thing. I sat up straight, threw my shoulders back and forced a slight smile. "I am. But

I'm here with a beautiful, young woman tonight. And so very glad."

Surprisingly, I felt better. Like a boulder had lifted. Maybe I really was ready to move on. Although my belly was full, my load felt lighter. I was finally, truly, relaxed.

We passed the next half hour in pleasant conversation and a superb dessert. A slice of cheesecake, which we shared. She declined a second glass of wine, so I declined another beer, although I was ready for one. My life had changed. I felt it. I knew it.

I walked her to her house, a light shining in the front window. Her da was most likely waiting up. We stepped onto the porch, and I hated to see our evening end. But we both had work tomorrow and needed what sleep we could get.

I held open the screen door, then slowly shut it when she moved within inches of me. My arms slid around her, and I pulled her close. She smelled like a combination of strudel, cinnamon, clove, and a hint of fried chicken. Knowing I shouldn't, I couldn't stop myself.

Our lips met. Hers soft, full, tantalizing. Mine sore, needy. Hungry.

CHAPTER FOURTEEN

I TIPTOED INTO THE ROOM, ONLY TO DISCOVER it empty. Disappointed, I'd been looking forward to sharing part of my evening with my brothers—not the kissing part, but how terrific she was. I slipped out of my vest and shirt and as I was hanging them on a hook, my family entered, smelling suspiciously of more than one beer.

As we readied for bed, we shared our evening. We'd all had a good time—me with Hilda, then Eagan and Tate at the Texas Tumbler, enjoying saloon grub of ham, gravy, a biscuit and at least two beers each. They'd visited with many customers, but no one knew anything about August Huber or those who did hadn't seen him around recently. No word about a short fella, named Theo or otherwise. Confused and concerned, I decided to save more worries for tomorrow and sank back onto the mattress, enjoying the peace it brought.

Eagan's and Tate's voices woke me. Sunlight streamed through the smudgy window, urging me to get up. I didn't want to. My entire body groaned at the thought, but my brain insisted it behave. They were already up and dressed, which meant I'd be left behind if I didn't get going. I yanked off the sheet, threw feet on the floor and wished I could fall back into bed.

"What say we check in with Tommy, go grab breakfast, then see if Randolph is awake?" Tate threaded his arms through his vest. "We can go from there."

"I'll probably need to spell Tommy for a few hours." Eagan smoothed his hair, giving one last look in the mirror. "I'm sure he didn't get any sleep last night."

I elbowed Eagan, took his place in front of the mirror, and checked my face for anything that shouldn't be there. Satisfied I looked presentable, in case I ran into Hilda, especially, I nodded. "Let's go."

Tommy reported an uneventful night. No gun fire, no rowdy, drunken men needing to sleep it off. Nothing of any consequence. "I took advantage of the empty cot back there," he pointed to my old cell, "and slept for a couple hours."

"Not nearly as comfortable as the hotel's bed." I couldn't help myself. "Probably more creepy-crawlies in yours too."

Tommy mock-scratched his chest, then turned serious. "Think I'll go with you to breakfast. Then need to find this Bushy Beard, August Huber. I'll arrest him. Maybe he'll tell us who the short fella is."

Tommy locked the office, and the four of us headed up Main in search of food. Three doors up stood the café where I'd gone with Deputy Randolph that one time where I met his girl. I wondered if *she* would be there. Ida, I believed her name was.

We seated ourselves and a young man appeared at our table. Based on his smooth chin and cheeks, a bobbing Adam's apple, body thin as a sapling, I took him for barely fourteen.

"*Guten Morgen. Kaffee?*"

All of us nodding, he rushed off. We planned the rest of the day. Tommy and Eagan would search for Huber, while Tate and I would check in on the two patients. Of course, the priority was recovering the money. We'd been unable to open the safe last night. Our hopes rested on Randolph remembering the combination.

Hot, strong coffee topped off a full plate of eggs, bacon, fried potatoes, and flapjacks. Enough food to feed a small army—or four tired men, who needed sleep and food. My shoulders fired off each time I picked up a fork or cup. The bruise on my shoulder now throbbed as it turned deeper purple. Just like Eagan's, my wrists were scabbed over from the ropes and iron, but violet and deep red bruises looked like bracelets. Despite the bright colors, everything hurt.

Except my lips. They fairly danced with the memory. I sighed and touched my mouth.

Eagan shoulder bumped me. "Got a sappy look on your face there, brother. You not telling us something?"

"Nothing you need to know."

Tate held up his cup to me. "Here's to you and moving on."

I nodded and most likely blushed, as my face heated. "Thanks. I am. I have."

I was afraid they'd start teasing me, but we drained our cups, paid the fare, and walked outside into a warm day, turquoise skies dotted with obscenely white clouds. I hurt all over, and yet, I was happy. Was it because of Hilda? Absolutely. And Tate. And Eagan. And Tommy. My life had changed and somehow, I was no longer willing simply to sit behind a high desk receiving and sending coded messages. Day after boring day. No, I wanted to be doing this, whatever *this* was. Out in the world chasing bad men. Or at least helping good ones.

We stood in front of the sheriff's office, where we divided. Eagan and Tommy headed back the way we'd come, citing the mayor's office as first stop. Tate and I aimed for the doc's.

The lobby was empty, but a woman, drying her hands on a towel, rushed in when we closed the door.

"Ma'am, we're here to see your two patients. The deputies." I hoped Lieberman was still there.

"And you are…?"

"Joe and Tate Nolan. We were involved in the…scuffle…from the other night." I'm not sure why I was hesitant to call it a shooting. Since she was a nurse, I was sure she'd seen and heard gunshots and the damage they do.

Tate peered behind her at the hall. "We're duly sworn posse members. Deputy O'Sullivan, who's now in charge of Fredericksburg, asked us to check on those two."

She stepped back and pointed. "Of course. Right this way. Doc's in with Randolph now."

We followed her down a short hall, stopping at the second door on the right. Doc looked up from where he sat next to the deputy. "Doing better. Think he'll live."

Shoulders relaxing, I smiled. "Good to know."

"Got an idea when he'll be up and about? Able to get back to work?"

"Why don't you ask him?" Doc stood.

The deputy raised a hand, turned to us. "Good to see ya." Although his words were weak, soft, there was a strength behind them. He'd be all right soon enough, I was sure of it.

Tate leaned in the doorway, while I sat where Doc had

been. I studied Randolph. Ugly bruising on his face reminded me of Eagan's. Both looked like they'd been horse-dragged through town, boot spur caught in a stirrup.

"How're you feeling?" I hoped I sounded sincere, because I really was. "Deputy O'Sullivan from Blanco Hill and Eagan, who, if you remember, is a Blanco Hill deputy, are watching over the town 'til you're up and running again."

"Good."

I wasn't sure what that responded to but felt the need to explain further. "The mayor will be putting together a funeral for Driggs. Should be soon."

"Good."

Although he was quite groggy, from the laudanum I assumed, I had to ask. Fingers crossed he'd answer. "Deputy, what's the combination to the safe? We think Driggs stored some of the banks' money in there."

He frowned at me, up at Doc standing behind me, then over at Tate. "There was money in there. A lot of it. Took most of it. Don't know where."

Just what I figured. "Combination? You remember it?"

"Six...twenty-three...two." He paused. "I think." Randolph shut his eyes and rubbed his right shoulder, heavily bandaged.

Doc touched my shoulder. "Needs to rest."

"One more question. For both of you." I looked up at Doc. "Either of you know a fella, first name Theo? Short?"

Doc frowned. Randolph rolled his head back and forth. I stood. "Thank you both, anyway. If you remember him, let me know. We're sure he's the third bank robber."

"How about Deputy Lieberman?" Tate asked. "How's he doing?"

"Still out cold." Doc walked us to the door. "He's not going anywhere."

Tate and I thanked the doctor again, promising to return tomorrow. We stepped into a warm, but not-too-hot-yet morning. On our way back to the office, we discussed how to disperse the money, if indeed there was any in the safe. How to find this ghost, Theo. And where the heck was Huber? The nurse had reported no one with a broken leg, especially a man with a full beard, coming in for help.

Two mystery men.

Tate and I swung up onto the sheriff's office porch. I stuck my hand into the vest pocket, only to remember Tommy had the office key.

Bang! A bullet whizzed past my ear and slammed into the doorframe. Tate and I ducked, hit the wooden planking. Splayed out face down, I covered my head with my arms.

"What the hell?" Tate rolled toward me, where I was jammed up against the bottom of the door. I turned over and started to sit.

Bang!

Fire seared my forehead. I fell back, grabbing at the pain.

Bang!

"Joe?" Tate hollered at me, but sounded more like he was in a tin can. The words echoed.

"Fine!" I lied, yelling back exactly the same moment a third bullet whizzed past my head. I curled into a ball. If I could have gotten to my feet, I would probably have been able to spot the shooter.

"Stay down! Stay still!" Tate's tin-canny words

whirled around my head. In fact, the whole world whirled, turned gray.

What was it with me and my head? First, I got walloped in the telegraph office, then recently at the bank hold up, and now this. Something sticky rolled down over my eye, onto my cheek, then chin. It dripped onto my vest. I swiped at the red goo over my eye but, instead of clearing my sight, simply smudged it. I could barely make out Tate, not two feet away.

Silence. We waited. Breathed. And waited, some more.

Not sure how long I lay, coiled up like a newborn lizard. Tate stretched his legs. Nothing. No bullets raining on us, no nothing. He rolled to his left side and touched my shoulder. "Joe?"

I opened the eye that wasn't glued shut.

"You all right?"

Since this was the second time he'd asked, I supposed I didn't look like it. I didn't answer. I wasn't sure if I *was* all right. My head again throbbed, the place where the bullet grazed me was still on fire. Fact was, my entire body shook.

Tate crawled up onto his knees and scooted closer. "Let's get you insid—"

Bang! A bullet tore off Tate's boot heel.

He threw his body on top of mine. "Ow, dammit! Ow!" He whispered in my ear, "What the hell?"

Another bullet ricocheted off a porch post, sending bits of wood over my head. Splinters clattered to the porch floor. In my echoey ear, I heard voices shouting in the distance. No way could I tell who they were, what they said, or where the voices came from. Or how many. All I knew was Tate still lay on top of me, and I found breathing hard.

I pushed, hoping he'd roll off. But he pressed down and now I couldn't breathe at all. Using what strength I had, I pushed again. This time, he moved enough for me to suck in precious air.

He then eased off for me to straighten my legs. Would there be a sixth gunshot? Would this one find its way into my chest? Or head? Tate's body? Could we get inside before the shooter reloaded?

Tate gripped my arm to where I could sit, leaning back against the closed door. Kneeling in front of me, he searched left and right along the street, across the street, even on top of buildings, looking for the shooter. My brother's image was fuzzy, red, and faint. I swiped at blood coating my face, wiping most of it out of my eye.

Heavy bootsteps on the wooden porch. Eagan slid to a stop next to Tate and kneeled by me. I looked up at Tommy, standing over my body. He fumbled in his vest for the key, while shouting, "How are you doing?" I didn't answer over all the other words pouring over me.

The door banged open, I sailed backward. Tommy stepped over me, grabbed my arms and pulled me inside, while Tate and Eagan stepped around me, then slammed the door shut.

More words. Lots of words. Most I made out. "What the hell?" and again, "Are you all right?" and "Who d'you think?" flew around the room bouncing off the walls and echoing. Still lying on the floor in front of the desk, I draped my arms over my head, trying to shut out the noise now causing even my brain to throb. Something about "Doc" and "over there" and then I let the others be in control. I'd simply lie there until…well, until I didn't.

Eyes closed, I blocked out the world until I felt myself being hoisted. Someone had slid their arms under mine, and someone else had grabbed my ankles. I swung side to side—gently—until my body rested on my old cot mattress. In jail again. I wanted to laugh, but suddenly, this morning's breakfast decided to find a new residence other than my stomach.

I rolled to my side and threw up all over the floor. Three, four heaves later, I felt much better. I lay back, eyes able to focus on Tommy, leaning against Eagan's cell bars.

Tommy, arms folded across his chest, regarded me. "Make enemies easily, I see." He nodded toward the outside door. "Doc's on his way. Tate's hobbling over to get him. Part of his boot heel got blown off." A grin pushed up his mustache.

I waved an arm and used all the strength I had to push up with the other one. "No need. I'm grand."

"I'm sure you are, but I want Doc to tell me." Tommy unfolded his arms and moved closer to me. "Any idea who the shooter was?"

Despite the pounding and throbbing in my head, I considered. "Can't be Driggs. Not Lieberman. Not Hilda or her da." I hoped he realized I wasn't serious about the last two. I looked at Tommy. "Gotta be Bushy Beard. Theo, maybe. Those two make sense."

"Or maybe the two fellas Driggs was gonna hire to kill you and Eagan. They've still got his badge, I'm guessing."

Well, hell. I hadn't thought of those two. And they wouldn't necessarily know Driggs was dead. They also made sense. All right. So at least *four* men were gunning for me. What the hell had I gotten into? Here I was, a meek telegraph operator, asked to do something simple like join a posse. Now here I was, black and blue, shot to pieces, and sore all over. And now, another damn pounding head. I looked over at a fuzzy Tommy. "Guess I'm lucky."

Eagan walked in, bucket and cloth in hand. He kneeled next to me and glared at the mess I'd made.

"Sorry." My world spun again. Probably too much thinking. But at least I wasn't shaking like I'd been earlier. I couldn't look at what Eagan was mopping up. My stomach flopped over, so I closed my eyes, hoping I wouldn't cause another mess.

The outer door squeaked open and in walked Tate, followed by the doc. All four crowded around me, hovering like angels of death. Was I dead? No, my head hurt too much to be dead.

Doc cleaned my face. So much blood! The rag had gone from white to dark red. He parted my hair and peered at the bullet's path. He poked and prodded, until the world turned gray, again. He sat back then patted my shoulder.

"You're lucky, Joe. Damn lucky. Another half inch..." He shook his head.

"He gonna be all right?" Tate stood at the foot of the cot.

Doc opened his black bag, extracted a roll of white gauze along with a small bottle of dark liquid. "Be fine in a day or two." He looked me in the eyes. "Rest. Stay here where it's safe. Don't try to go dancing at Gertrude's tonight. Ya hear?"

"Yes, sir. No dancing."

Doc swabbed me with something straight from Hell, I was sure. My tender scalp stung and burned, hurting like it was trying frantically to get away. I struggled not to bolt out of the cell and dunk my head into the nearest horse trough. I gripped the sides of the mattress, instead.

Throbbing eased in a couple of minutes.

He wrapped my head, then handed Tate a small bottle of laudanum. "Just when needed. It's full of hops, you know."

"I've had experience with this stuff, Doc. I know exactly how to use it." Tate tapped the bottom of my foot with the bottle. "And how *not* to use it."

* * *

I TOOK Doc's instructions to heart. I lay back on the hard mattress, while the others stood or sat nearby, discussing the day's events. I listened and offered suggestions, occasionally. I realized I'd slept when I looked where Tommy had just been standing, only to find him coming in through the front door. No one else was back here with me.

"Eagan?" More confused than concerned, I wondered what I'd missed in their planning to find the shooter. If there had been any more. What about the money. And last, how they had managed to rob banks without anybody truly knowing. "Eagan?" Had my question been loud enough?

Eagan appeared by my cell. "Have a nice nap?"

I ran my tongue over dry lips. "Water?"

He nodded and disappeared into the office. Instead of Eagan, Tate, glass in hand, stepped into the cell, put the glass on the floor and helped me sit. I hated needing help. Why was it always me? It took both hands to grip the glass. The water went down smoothly, snuffing out raw spots in my throat.

I handed Tate the glass. "Did we get the money?"

Both eyebrows raised, which, for Tate, was always a good sign. I relaxed. "We did. Took three tries, but finally got it open."

"And?" He was taking way too long.

"Found close to two thousand in there." He shrugged. "But that was all. And no clue to where the rest might be."

"Damn." My sore shoulders sunk. "What're we gonna do with that? Think Lieberman knows where the rest is at?"

"Maybe." Tate sat on the edge of the cot. "Listen. I talked to Doc on the walk over here, and he said Lieberman's still out cold. Might be in what he calls a coma. There's a chance he'll never wake up."

"What?" I'd never heard of this coma thing.

"Yeah." Tate shrugged. "Says he thinks when the deputy fell back, he hit his head in such a way it caused his brain to swell. May take days, weeks, or even years to wake up."

"Years? Well, hell." My head pounded and I rubbed. "Got any laudanum left? Head's killing me."

He leaned back, sighed, regarded me, then nodded. "I'll be honest. I'd rather give you whiskey. That okay?" He eased to his feet. "Not as addictive as the other."

That was fine. I remembered him earlier this spring being addlepated by laudanum. He wasn't himself. From what I was told, it took him long, agonizing days to kick the habit. I didn't want that to happen to me. I nodded. "Whiskey, then. A big bottle."

A soft chuckle rolled from Tate as he disappeared and I swear it couldn't have been fifteen seconds, when he sat on my cot again, glass of whiskey in hand. "Sorry it took so long. Looked like Driggs didn't keep any in the office." He pointed behind him. "Had to go over to Gertude's. Picked up two bottles, so we'll have some on hand."

Since I was still sitting up, I had no trouble handling

the whiskey. Like the water, it went down smooth, tickling my throat as it passed. "Where is everybody?" The office was way too

quiet.

Eyeing my half-full glass, Tate took a sip, then returned it. "Both off doing deputy things. Over to see about Driggs's funeral, down to the mayor's office to get his take on the shooting. Then go see if Gertrude will tell them where her brother is. He's got answers we need."

A second swallow was even better than the first. Warm tingles spread throughout my body and even the pain in my head eased up.

Tate looked up through the single window. "Tonight, thought we'd move you to the hotel, under cover of darkness. Meanwhile, you and me'll stay right here. Keep the door locked."

"Why'd he shoot at me?" I'd thought about this often, when I wasn't sleeping. "I'm not a lawman, nobody special."

Tate patted my leg and stood. "Must be your pretty face." He chuckled and backed out of the cell.

CHAPTER FIFTEEN

DEEP VOICES WOKE ME. I RECOGNIZED BOTH MY brothers' and Tommy's. Still groggy, but feeling totally useless and restless, I managed to sit up on the edge of the cot. Once the world stopped spinning, I found my feet. Air filled my lungs and I swore I felt blood running through my veins. Definitely good to stand.

I wobbled over and leaned against the doorjamb. Tommy sat behind the desk, Tate in a chair in front of him, Eagan in another chair at the side. All talking stopped when I appeared.

"What'd I miss?" Were my words as slurred as they sounded to me?

Eagan bolted out of his chair, rushed over, gripped my arm and led me to his chair. I sank into the still-warm seat. Before any questions could be uttered, I held up a hand. "Don't ask. I'm fine, thank you." I eyed each man. "Appreciate the concern, I do. But we got bad guys to catch and money to recover...unless you already have."

All heads shook. Tommy studied a stubby pencil in his hand. He'd been writing something on a piece of paper and I craned to read it. Nothing but chicken scratch.

"Feels like we've hit a dead end." Tommy tossed the pencil to the desk. "Nobody's heard of this Theo. Nobody knows where Bushy Beard went to. Nobody knows who took a potshot at you. Hell, nobody saw nothin' and nobody knows nothin'."

"Yeah. Everybody's heard what's going on, but nobody knows anything." Eagan folded his arms across his chest, while he leaned against the front door. "What's going on around here? Feels like the whole town's in on it—whatever *it* is."

Tate leaned back, crossed an ankle over a knee. He played with the new boot heal. "Maybe Eagan's right." He nodded at him. "Maybe some citizens are out to rob the rest of 'em. At least that's true for Johnsonville, what with Deputy Lieberman being one of the outlaws."

I snapped my fingers. "And with Driggs in on it here, maybe other higher ups in each town are in on relieving people of their hard-earned money."

"Which questions our own sheriff back in Blanco Hill." Tommy picked up the pencil and scribbled. "Suppose he's in on it? Or the mayor?"

"Would certainly explain why Sheriff Wagner's been gone so much." Eagan glanced east. "Unless he really is in love."

Tommy chuckled. "Oh, he's in love, all right. All lathered up about her. All he talks about. Wish they'd get hitched, so he'd quit being so windy about her."

The doorknob rattled, followed by a gentle knock. Eagan jumped, then unlocked the door, opening it only a couple of inches. He peered out, then stepped back to allow Hilda enough room to enter. The large sack in her hand emitted a mouth-watering aroma. Strudel? Scones? Some of both?

Tate immediately offered her his seat, and held it for her while she settled.

"I've brought enough for everyone." She smiled at us all but seemed to beam at me. "And even a couple extras. But you've got to share."

Tommy opened the bag and about melted on to the desk. We all breathed in heaven. He peered into the bag. "Looks like scones and tarts. Thank you, Hilda. How'd you know we needed this?"

She smiled. "You've been working hard and, with Joe injured, thought you would enjoy a pastry."

Confusion knocked on my brain. "Wait. How'd you know I was shot?" I took the scone Eagan handed me. Looked like berries inside.

Hilda's caring gaze at me, her eyes soft, mouth even softer, made me swallow. I probably blinked a million times and my heart seemed to beat a bit faster.

She raised a shoulder. "Everybody knows. It's all over town." She confessed. "Plus, Eagan and Tommy told me." Hilda attempted to hide a grin. "I stopped by earlier, but you were...asleep."

How embarrassing. She came by and saw me sleeping? "Ah." I'm sure my single word was muddled, especially with scone in my mouth. "I'm fine, though."

Hilda turned in her seat to address Tate, standing behind her. "Did you find the shooter? Whoever tried to kill him?"

I'd been thinking about that. Later, we'd need to examine the holes where the other bullets hit the building and porch. Maybe, just maybe, we could figure out where the shots came from.

The others wagged their heads while they ate. I'd

finished my scone and was hoping for a second, seeing as
how I was special, since I was hurt and all. But Tommy
rolled down the top and set it at the other edge of the
desk, far out of my reach.

Tate moved around to stand near Tommy. "We're at a
loss. Can't find Bushy Beard...August Huber. Can't find
this Theo. Can't—"

"Maybe I can help." Hilda sat up straight. "See, I
know August's sister, Gertrude, who owns—"

"We know. Been there a time or two." Tommy
nodded.

"Anyway," Hilda continued. "She owns a business as I
do too. It is rare for women to own businesses by them-
selves. Usually, it is the husband who owns it and the
wife works it."

I had to admit, I thought that's what everyone did,
including Hilda.

"But with Gertrude, and Bertha, and me, we are the
only women business owners. We have to stick together,
so I know them well." She stopped and thought. "Oh,
and *die Schulmeisterin,* the school mistress, Anna O'Shea.
While she's not actually in business for herself, she does
have some say in the running of the town."

Four women and probably twenty or more men
running things. I considered. Was that the way in most
towns?

"Who's Bertha?" Tommy scribbled her name.

Hilda smiled. "*Eine wunderbare frau.* A wonderful
woman. She owns the millinery shop, *der Hutmacher
handwerk,* on the next street over. Has for years." She
reached up and patted her dark blue halo hat—Ma had
one similar, only in green. The blue set off Hilda's eyes
and fair complexion. "This is one of hers."

"Beautiful." I wasn't talking about the hat.

"If you'd like, I can stop by Gertrude's and ask if she has seen August. Maybe he is at her place, what with his leg broken." Hilda eased to her feet, bringing the rest of us with her.

"That would be a major help, ma'am." Tommy stuck out a hand. "And thank you for the treats. We'll save the rest for later."

"I'll let you know what I find out as soon as I can." Hilda glanced through the front window. "She should be at the saloon about now."

She gave me a breath-taking hug, whispering, "Feel better, *mein lieber*."

Eagan locked the door as she shut it.

Cheeks on fire, I turned from the closed door only to find three sets of eyes boring holes into me. My gaze searched the floor, the walls, the ceiling, trying desperately to avoid questions. They didn't say anything. They didn't have to.

I sat harder than I'd intended. My head jarred and the room grayed. I fought down the pain, while quietly struggling to follow the conversation. I was done being an invalid. Done being a victim. Done being hurt. I vowed, right then and there, I'd find whoever shot me, shot at Tate, hid the money, robbed the banks.

They could run, but dammit, they couldn't hide forever. Could they?

* * *

EAGAN AND TOMMY decided to ask the bank president and manager more questions. It had been over a week since it had been robbed and maybe, quite possibly, the bank staff would remember some overlooked details.

That left Tate and me to mind the store, so to

speak. This time, Tommy left the key with Tate. The two of us sat in the office, staring at the stack of bills. We each counted—twice. There sat one thousand, nine hundred, and eleven dollars. Almost two thousand. Enough to hie down to Mexico and live *la vida loca*, as I'd heard it called. The crazy life. Hell, I was living a crazy life now—for free. Guess I didn't need one in Spanish.

Tate occupied the official chair behind the desk, leaned back. "Know what I'd do if this was mine?"

I could guess, but it wouldn't be nice. "What?"

"I'd buy me some land. Raise cattle and kids." A smile slid up one side of his face, pushing up his thick, freshly cut mustache. "Maybe have a wife, too." He nodded. "Yep. Suits me right down to the ground."

"Never thought of you as the settlin' down type." I eyed the money again. "Figured you for a man about town, dancing with every single woman you could find. And then with a few who weren't so single."

"Done my fair share of that, little brother." Tate stared out the window. "But my time on Carmichael's ranch, gettin' to know Mr. C and his wife, well, reckon I've grown a bit."

"Grown a lot."

Tate addressed the window and then me. "Mr. C told me I'm like his son. Same age and size. But the son went wild. Got himself killed in a hold up." He pointed at his shirt. "Fact is, this is one of his. Mrs. C outfitted me real good."

I was truly surprised. Looked like we both had done some growing.

Tate raised both eyebrows until reaching close to his hairline. "There's more. Mr. C.'s gonna will it to me. I'm to run the ranch when he can't, anymore. There's no blood relative to leave the ranch to and he wants me to have it." He wagged his head. "Can you beat that?"

"Beat that? Hell, Tate, I ain't never heard of such a thing." I was sure my smile lit up the room. "I'm happy for you. Now I'll quit worrying that you're gonna end up like those shabby, homeless Rebs. Sitting on the street, asking for handouts."

"Not a chance." Tate stood, stretching his arms over his head. "Gotta worry about you, now. We've been sittin' here trying to figure out why you? If anything, Eagan would have been a better choice to get shot."

"Thanks." I wasn't sure how to take that. I didn't want to be a target and sure as hell didn't want anybody else to be. "Ideas on the shooter?"

Tate opened the door, stepped onto the porch. "Maybe we can get clues out here. I know the shots came from where Eagan and Tommy were. That direction."

I knelt in the doorway, glancing left and right. Only a few people out and about, one couple, arm in arm, walking away. No nefarious looking rats skulking around. On the door itself, directly over my head, if I remembered right, was a three-inch long gouge, obviously made from a bullet. "Here."

Tate ran a finger along the scar and nodded. "Damn lucky."

We inspected the post, finding where the wood had been sheared off. Couple more bullet holes, then a bullet embedded in the wall. Tate dug it out, held it up. "Forty-five." He looked closer. "Nah. More like fifty." He wagged his head. "Enough to do real damage."

"Yeah. All the way down to dead." Holding onto the door jamb, I eased up, happy to realize I stood without swaying. "Now, all we have to do, is find someone carrying a fifty." Like locating the shooter would be easy.

That was the bullet caliber of choice. Many men used rifles that size.

Tate followed me inside, then closed and locked the door. I lowered myself into the chair by the desk, while Tate took his old seat behind it. We sat silently for a minute. I contemplated why me? And what would we have for supper? My stomach grumbled, complaining. I'd had breakfast but lost it all. Now it was time to eat. However, we couldn't simply walk up to the café. We'd have to wait for the others. Even then, they wanted to wait until dark, so I could slip up to the hotel.

What if the shooter was waiting for us there? Would he kill everybody? Or just me? And truly, was it me he wanted? Too many questions. I rubbed my head.

We waited not too patiently. Tate darkened a mustache of a man on a wanted poster. I leaned back and thought about my future. I was ready to court again, but not ready to go back to being a telegrapher. Even though I'd been shot and nearly killed, captured and nearly killed —I was seeing a pattern here—still, it was better than working in a safe office, away from the action. But did I want to be a lawman?

Light tapping on the door broke the reverence. Tate jumped up before I could scoot back. He parted the window curtains, sighed, then unlocked the door. In walked Hilda. Just the person I wanted to see.

She took the chair next to mine. "Wanted you to know. I went over to the Gasthause a few minutes ago. No Gertrude." Hilda shrugged. "The bartender hasn't seen her all day. And he doesn't have any idea where she might be. He says she is usually quite punctual. Just not today."

"Where does she live?" Tate picked up the pencil again, poised over paper.

She pointed north. "About three miles out of town, there's a road. Miller's Creek Road." She looked at me then back to Tate. "Follow that a mile, take the left fork and her *haus* is right there."

Way out of town. In the hills. Good hiding place. "So, you've been there?" I hated for Hilda to drive all that way. Alone, I assumed.

"*Ja.* I have been there two, three times. We meet there sometimes. Away from the men."

"What about August?" Tate leaned forward. "Does he live there?"

"*Nein.* Nobody knows really where he lives. He does not come to town often."

Hmmm. Too many questions and I felt silly sitting there with gauze wrapped around my head. I was fine. Head hurt only when I breathed, and mostly I ignored the pain. I fumbled with the knot, untied the binding, and unwound the gauze. I folded it where dried blood made the white a dark red.

I held up my hand and stopped Tate from arguing. He swallowed his words, which made me smile. I was done being pitiful.

"I must be getting back to the store. *Vater* is alone there now." Hilda stood, her dark blue blouse, ruffles cascading down the front, accentuated her small waist. How could someone who baked all day keep such a fine figure?

Tate and I opened the door for her and I received another hug. This one a bit tighter than earlier. We waved and I watched her cross the street, disappearing into a small crowd.

I turned to Tate. "I can't simply sit here, waiting to be killed." I searched for my hat, then remembered I didn't have one, the original lost somewhere in the past few days.

"What d'you propose?"

Tate wasn't going to agree, but I couldn't just sit. "Riding out to see Gertrude. I need fresh air and it's away from town. Probably won't get shot at."

He did exactly what I thought he'd do. Opened his mouth to object, but I pulled a shotgun out of the rack by the door. "Am I going alone?" I checked to see if it was loaded and picked up two boxes of shells.

We left a note saying where we were going and why. Since Tate had the only key, we decided to keep the door unlocked, but the cash securely stashed in the safe. Tomorrow, we'd figure out what to do with it.

The road ran over hills, down gullies, across flats, past a grove of pecan trees. We took the left fork and walked our horses toward a house, sitting off the road. We pulled rein a quarter mile off and sat studying the place. Made of slump rock halfway up, then wood to the pitched roof. From out here on the road, the house looked large enough to have four rooms, maybe more. A barn, big enough for two horses and maybe a small carriage, sat off to the right. Chickens roamed freely, clucking as they pecked at small bugs in the yard.

Should we go right up to the door and knock? Should we scout around the perimeter, hoping to avoid anyone seeing us?

"Wonder who's home?" I glanced at Tate, who continued staring at the house.

We sat another half minute. Tate sighed. "Well, hell. Didn't ride all the way out here just to turn around and go back." He pointed right. "Let's check out the barn. See if anyone's home."

Before he could change his mind and head back for town, I gigged my horse into a fast walk. We gave the barn a wide berth, finding a stand of Texas oak nearby. We tied our mounts, then hurried to what little protection the barn offered.

I pressed my ear against the back of the barn. No sounds. No horses whinnying, no nothing. Tate on my heels, I tiptoed around to the front, slid open the barn door, and peered into dark gray. The open door allowed in enough light to reveal no horse, no buggy inside. We stepped in and quickly surveyed the barn. Hay was piled in one corner, and an empty stall took up a third of the room. I bent to pick up a sack of oats when, *Boom!* Out popped a striped devil, hissing and growling. I jumped aside. The creature bolted past my leg and out the door.

I stood frozen, sack in hand. My heart pounded and all breathing stopped. What the hell was that? I put down the sack and looked at the door. A cat. A damn feral barn cat.

I breathed in and out once, twice. Heart at long last beating normally, I relaxed. I must have leaped ten feet high, when I was sure Lucifer himself had me. I glanced at Tate.

Holding onto the stall's railing, he laughed, quietly, although now and then a chuckle would erupt. He pointed at me, whispering. "Should've seen your face. Should've seen…jumped this high." Tate held a hand over his head. "This high. You wet yourself?"

"Ha. Ha." I saw nothing funny about it. I had to admit to myself being startled by a cat was comical. I kept my voice low. "Nothing here. Let's check the house."

We closed the barn door, scurried across the yard to the side of the house. I couldn't hear a thing through the rock, but standing on tiptoes I could see through a window. Mostly I spotted a ceiling. I whispered, "Let's go around back. Probably a door back there."

Tate nodded and sneaked off in search of said door. I crouched as low as possible, matched

his boot prints. I glanced all around, hoping, praying the shooter hadn't followed us. So far, so good.

The back door was unlocked. The door hinges, sorely in need of oil, screeched and squawked as Tate pushed it open. I knelt. Instinctively, my arms covered my head, my eyes squeezed shut and my breathing stopped. I waited. And waited.

"Psst. You comin'?"

Still crouching, I stepped into the house which, even from back here, smelled of old beer and rotten apples. My stomach threatened to give a heave ho, but I forced my mind onto other things. I followed him from this back room full of crates and who knew what, past a wooden box labeled *whiskey* and into a narrow hallway.

We stopped, listening for signs of life. Nothing. Goosebumps raised on my arms. This place was eerie. Empty. Creepy. I stood straighter and walked close enough to Tate I felt safer, but far enough away to check what he missed.

A bedroom on the right contained a bed, two nightstands, a wardrobe full of dresses, a wash stand complete with water and mirror, and a wooden chest at the foot of the bed. I opened the chest, just in case someone was hiding there, or the money was in there. I pushed aside a knitted blanket only to discover a white dress. A closer look and it could have been a wedding dress. A wedding dress? Gertrude? Guess it was possible. Had she actually used it? Was she married?

I closed the lid, took one last look, and met Tate in the front room. "Kitchen's clear," he whispered.

"Bedroom's clear, too," I whispered back.

Tate nodded to his left. "I'll check the other bedroom and meet you out front."

"Fine." I stepped toward the tufted sofa.

Bang. I jumped. Not a gun shot. I looked at Tate.

"Back door!" We spoke in unison.

We bolted through the house, slammed open the door just in time to see a dark figure disappear into the trees. He, assuming it was a he, had a good head start, but I was determined to find who that was. Surely, it was August. Without a word, we took off after him. Once we hit the trees, Tate pointed right as we ran. I veered a bit that way while he continued straight.

Ten minutes, maybe fifteen later, I had to stop. I bent over, desperately sucking in all the air in the world. Heart pounding in my chest and throat, I briefly wondered if Tate was doing the same.

Footsteps crackling dried leaves behind me, I spun. Whoever it was, caught me, as my knees buckled and the world turned black.

"Too much, too soon." Tate's words brought me back.

I looked up at him squatting by me. "Dammit to hell." I hated being weak. Hurt. Frail. "You find him?" I rolled onto my side and pushed up. I was shaking but sitting.

Tate wagged his head. "Disappeared." He stood, gripped my upper arm. "Let's get you up and back to the hotel. You've had enough excitement for one day."

And quite the day it'd been. We walked back toward the horses, Tate still gripping my arm. I wanted to make him quit helping, but I had to admit, I wasn't so sure I could make it on my own.

Halfway there, we were in the middle of the field,

when a buggy in the driveway stopped. A woman pulled up a shotgun and aimed it directly at us.

"Who are you? What you vant?" She cocked the weapon. "Hands up!"

Based on the German accent, I figured this was Gertrude. Then I vaguely remembered her from the saloon. She looked different here. Maybe because things in my view all swayed.

"Ma'am." Tate sounded sure of himself, confident. "We came to see you. Went looking around. Hope you don't mind."

"I *do* mind. Dis is my property." She leaned forward. "Who are you?"

CHAPTER SIXTEEN

"Tate Nolan, ma'am." Tate's arms reached sky high. "This's my brother, Joe."

I nodded, afraid to move.

"So?"

"Mind if we put our hands down?" He cocked his head toward me. "He's not feeling well and I think he might black out." When she didn't respond, he continued. "We came to see you. Ma'am."

She lowered the shotgun. We lowered our arms. Tate gripped mine again.

Birds chirped, chickens *bawk, bawk, bawked,* and the horse stamped its foot. Somewhere in the distance, a goat bleated. Gertrude lowered the gun, returning it to the buggy's seat. She picked up the reins and flicked them.

"Come inside."

Familiar odors of rotting apples and beer permeated everything in the front room—sofa, chair, braided rug— everything. I fought down a roiling stomach, while we stood just inside the doorway. Gertrude leaned her shotgun against the wall by the door, close enough to grab within seconds. She untied her bonnet, tugged at a few errant strands of hair, and tossed her hat onto the tufted cushion. She eyed us, the shotgun, then back to us. Point taken.

Gertrude also made no effort to treat us as guests. I considered. If I'd found two strangers lurking around my property, I probably wouldn't make them feel comfortable, nor treat them like long-lost friends, either. She had every right to be rude.

"I busy. Vhat you vant?" She stared at Tate like he'd spit on her or something equally drastic.

He cleared his throat. "Well, ma'am." He glanced at me like I was going to do the speaking. Or had the answers. "We're looking for your brother, August Huber. Understand he stays here sometimes."

"Vhat you vant wit him?" Her harsh voice grew louder.

How to tell this woman, shotgun at the ready, that her brother was wanted for armed robbery of three banks? And we're not even duly sworn lawmen. Simply posse members. Not sure if we had a legal right to arrest him without a deputy. Maybe we couldn't even bring him in.

Tate again glanced at me. I offered no help. His voice was low, but resolute. "Ma'am, as I'm sure you know, there have been three bank robberies, recently."

"Ja. I know. So?" She picked up the shotgun and cradled it like a baby.

"Well, ma'am." Tate warbled. "Eyewitnesses have put him at the scene of all three crimes." He took a breath. "He's wanted for questioning."

"Vhat?" Gertrude stepped closer to us. "Vhat you say about him?"

I figured I should say something, instead of stand there like a deaf-mute. "He needs to turn himself in. Sheriff has some questions for him. That's all."

She pointed the shotgun at us. Instinctively, I moved away from Tate. From this range, she'd definitely get one of us, but she couldn't get us both. She hollered. "Get out. *Mein* brudder not do dose tings. He's a gut boy."

"Where is he now, ma'am?" Tate stepped back, against the door. "Can we just talk to him?"

She shrugged. "Not here. Does not live here. I have not seen him." She cocked the shotgun. "I said get out."

We didn't have to be told a third time. Tate yanked open the door. We flew down the steps and into the yard, run-walking to our horses. After swinging up into the saddles, we glanced back at the house. As I figured, she was now on the porch, shotgun pointed our way. From this distance, surely, she couldn't hit us. Probably.

While we didn't exactly gallop away, we also didn't waste much time getting back on the road. I spotted town in the distance and pulled rein. Sun was still up, and I wasn't crazy about the idea of riding into town right now. It seemed I had a target painted on my back. No way was I looking forward to being shot at, again.

But...I'd ridden *out* of town with no problem. Maybe the shooter was done. Maybe he had made his point. Whatever that was. I looked over at Tate, who sat regarding the sky.

"Couple more hours 'til full dark." Tate changed his gaze to include me. "Wanna stay here and I'll go in, tell Tommy and Eagan what we found? Or you wanna chance it and go on in now?"

"I'm not much in favor of getting shot again, but I'm

thinking it's probably safe enough, now." Gobs of doubt took over. I eyed him. "Suppose?"

He shrugged. "Only one way to find out."

Great. I was afraid he'd say that. "Let's try it. Head for the livery." I gave my horse a gentle nudge and, like she understood, walked quickly, yet quietly, to the stable.

"So far, so good." I unsaddled the horse, nodded to the stableman, nodded to Tate. "Now. The hard part."

I took a deep breath, a long look up and down the street, then stepped out into a light breeze. Cool air mingled with the dust it brought. Tate and I chose an alley to scamper up, until we made it to the rear of the office. No back door, so we would be forced to go through the front. Rounding the corner of the alley and then getting onto the street was nerve-racking, but we got up the steps to the porch. No gunfire. No near misses.

I opened the door, rushed inside, Tate right behind. He slammed it.

Tommy jumped up from his chair. "My god. There you are. 'Bout ready to go searching for you."

"No need. Safe and sound." I cast around for Eagan. "Where's—"

"Privy." Tommy shrugged. "Every couple hours." He returned to his chair. "Find anything interesting?"

Before we could give a full report, the door swung open and Eagan walked in. I jumped, then immediately felt a bit embarrassed. Guessed I was more nervy than I'd thought. Tate and I took seats in the office, crowding into a room comfortably fit for no more than three. As usual, Eagan stood by the door.

We relayed our adventure, including seeing someone bolt into the woods. Gertrude's shotgun brought *"oohs."*

The others asked questions, some of which we could answer.

"Maybe Hilda knows something about Gertrude that would be useful." Eagan raised one shoulder. "She's already been helpful in telling us where she lives."

I started to offer to take her to supper again, but two things stopped me. First, if I got shot at again, she'd be in danger. Couldn't let that happen. And second, I had only three dollars of Tate's ten, left. Not enough for a proper supper.

Tommy and Eagan shared what they'd learned at the bank, which was nothing.

"We talked to every employee, including the bank president, and...*nada*." Tommy slammed the pencil he'd been playing with onto the desk. "What the *hell* is going on, around here?"

We sat, silently. Snorts, exasperated breathing, scooting around in chairs.

The door squeaked open again. Eagan, standing next to it, jumped back. Tommy reached for the revolver on his hip. Tate stood but I froze. I blinked hard at the young woman, who walked in and looked at each of us.

Tommy, first to recover, nodded at her. "Ma'am?" He pointed to Tate's now-empty chair. "Have a seat. How can I help you?"

She studied each of us in turn, ending on Tommy. "Gentlemen." A light grin flitted on her face. "I'm the schoolmarm, Anna O'Shea."

"Oh, yes ma'am. We've heard of you. I'm Deputy O'Sullivan." He introduced the rest of us, then took his own chair. Tommy pointed again at Tate's chair. "Please, have a seat."

About my age, Anna O'Shea was slim, shorter than Ma, who came up barely past my shoulders, and wore a light brown skirt and top. Her hair, a tad lighter than walnut, was pulled back into a loose bun. A black hat with ribbons trailing off the back framed her face, perfectly. She was pretty. Not Hilda pretty, but handsome enough. Her brown eyes were too deep set and lips too thin for my liking.

I startled myself. Eyeing women again. Too soon after Frieda? No. Like Tate said, time to move on. Frieda would want me to.

Miss O'Shea took a breath. "I have a student, who seems to be missing."

We sat taller. Tate picked up the pencil. "Missing, ma'am?"

"Well, he hasn't been in class for several days. Wasn't there again, today. This afternoon, after school, I stopped by his house and his father told me he's been sick." She glanced over at Eagan. "But I don't believe him. Something about how he said it made me suspicious."

"You think your student's gone? From town?" Eagan asked the obvious.

She wagged her head. "Maybe. I don't think he's been happy at home." She paused. "I'd hate to think he ran away." She continued. "See, his mother died about a year ago and his father doesn't pay him much attention. Always busy at work. At least that's what I've been told."

Made sense to me. I'd probably do the same. Then I rethought. Probably not. I asked what I thought was the next obvious question. "What's his name, ma'am?"

"Theodophulus Bauder. Goes by Theo." She turned her brown eyes on me. "The mayor's son."

We sucked in air. All of us men. Great Jesus! That had to be the Theo we were looking for. Had to be. It all made sense. Should we tell her what we suspected? Was she in on the robbery? Seemed like half the town was.

But then again, if she was, why'd she'd come report this to the law?

Tommy recovered first. "How tall's Theo?" He scribbled on a half sheet.

"Tall? A couple inches above me and I'm five-three." She held a hand up slightly over her head. "About this tall. But he's built like a Hereford bull. Shoulders this wide." She spread her arms out at her sides. "Muscles straining his shirts, strong as an ox."

Exactly the height I recollected. What little of it I remembered. But he was a big boy in many ways.

Tate asked the next obvious question. "Does he have friends around here he might be staying with?"

Duh. Why didn't I think to ask that? We waited while she thought.

She nodded. "Why yes. Yes, he does, I believe." She looked at Tate. "An older man. And by that I mean probably late twenties, early thirties. Name's Huber. August Huber." Her face lit up. "He's Gertrude Huber's youngest brother. Gertrude owns—"

"The Gasthause." Tommy's smile split his face. "We know. One last question. Do you know where this Huber lives?"

Her shoulders slumped. "I don't. But not in town, I do know that." She rose and addressed the four of us. "Please find him. Theo's a nice boy and I don't want harm to come to him."

"We'll do our best." Tommy crossed the room and held the door for her. "Ma'am, Miss O'Shea. You've been a big help. Thank you for stopping by."

From the window, I watched her make her way down the street and briefly wondered where she lived. I could ask Hilda if I cared enough. But this schoolmarm had given us the final piece of the puzzle.

We sat around the desk tossing out ideas, theories, and plans. We questioned information, motives and connections. The most important question was posed by Eagan. "When's supper?"

That threw us into new rounds of questioning. Do we *all* go over to the café or do I go to the hotel and wait for them to bring me supper? Whatever the decision, all I knew was that I was hungry. About now, my old boots were looking kind of tasty.

Tommy held up a hand. We quieted. "Here's what we're doing. You two," he pointed at Tate and me, "go back to the hotel. Eagan and I'll bring supper along."

We nodded and stepped outside, onto the porch. Tommy locked the door, and we headed up to the hotel and café. Before we'd gotten half a block, town mayor Jessup Bauder, flagged us down.

"Sorry to bother you." He focused on Tommy. "But… well…it's kinda embarrassing yet concerning."

"What is, Mr. Mayor?" Tommy frowned.

He regarded us, like he was changing his mind, then blurted out, "My rifle's missing."

My chest filled with worry and something close to panic. Like my head was on a swivel, I looked around the town. Up and down Main, on roofs, everywhere a shooter might be.

Tommy kept his voice even. "What do you mean, 'missing'? Like somebody broke in and took it? From your office or your home?"

Bauder sighed, rubbed a soft hand across his mustached face. "Home. I have a fifty-caliber Sharps that I used in the war. Has sentimental value to me." He straightened his shoulders. "And now, somebody's stolen it!"

I briefly wondered how an instrument of killing could

have sentimental value, but maybe it saved his life, back then.

Tate pointed over his shoulder toward the sheriff's office. "As I'm sure you know, somebody shot at us this morning." He paused. "Forty-five, maybe fifty caliber."

"Could have been your rifle, Mr. Bauder." Eagan glanced behind him at the office.

It was all starting to come together. I hated myself for asking, but my head throbbed, reminding me of what a close call I'd had. "Where was your son this morning? About breakfast time?"

We all stared at the man. He grunted, cleared his throat, looked toward his office, then toward the school. "He would've been on his way to school, of course. Just like every day."

"Sir." Tommy stood taller. "The schoolteacher came by this afternoon, said your son's been absent for days. You told her he'd been sick. Now, which is it?"

The mayor puffed himself up to full height, bringing his hat up a tad past my chin.

"I came here, to you," Bauder spit out his words like a declaration of war, "to report a stolen weapon." He moved up close to Tommy. "*Not* to be questioned about my son." He reset his hat, spun on his heels and marched down the street.

We watched him go, then realized we were out in the open, all with targets on our backs. "Let's go." Tommy nodded toward the perceived safety of our room.

Tommy and Eagan veered off to the café, while Tate and I hurried to the hotel. Tate unlocked the door, stepped in, and froze. I about ran into his back. I peered over his shoulder. What few clothes we had were strewn all over. The single drawer in a side table left open. Water from the bowl and pitcher was sloshed onto the floor.

Beds lay in piles of sheets, pillows ripped apart and both mattresses sliced open, cotton batting spread all over the room.

"Tornado do this?" I whispered.

"Just in our room?" Tate whispered back.

I slipped around him and stood in the middle of the room. There wasn't a thing left untouched. Not a thing. Even my old, stinky shirt had been ripped into shreds.

Now thawed, Tate helped me push aside what was left of the room. He closed the table drawer. "You see my saddlebag? I set it over there." He pointed to what was left of the wingback chair.

I kicked aside bits and pieces of detritus, but nothing that looked like a leather saddlebag. "Sorry. No. What'd it have in it?"

Tate leaned against the door. "Let's see. Ammo. But it's thirty-sixes. Clean socks. Couple tins of meat. My favorite shirt." He turned sheepish eyes on me. "In case Hilda and I went out." He cleared his throat. "But it's obvious you two are better suited for each other."

"Damn right, big brother." I pretended to glare at him. "You had your chance. She's not mine yet, but maybe someday…"

"Someday." Tate nodded at me. "Let's tell the hotel manager what happened up here."

"So we don't get charged for damages." I considered the lack of substantial funds in my pocket.

"Exactly." Tate walked out. "Maybe somebody saw something."

Within five minutes, the manager and the two of us, along with Tommy and Eagan, a shallow box of food in hand, squeezed into what was left of our room.

"This is an absolute disaster," the manager whined. "Why would anybody do such a thing?" He turned his stare from the room to me. His eyes narrowed. "You have a drunken party? Decided to get wild? You and your hooligan?"

Tommy handed me the box then pointed to his badge. "No sir, not hooligans. I'm deputy sheriff from Blanco Hill." He nodded toward Eagan. "This here's another deputy from there. And these two," he indicated Tate and me, "are duly sworn posse members. We're all men of the law."

"We would never destroy property, sir." I thought I'd state the obvious.

The manager, his eyes wide eyes, glared at us. "Then who did?"

* * *

THE FOUR OF us took our food down to the lobby, found a round table and a couple of wingback chairs, where we could eat. The manager was none too happy having us eat there, but we were hungry and the staff was working on finding us another room. Before we made much of a dent in our supper, the clerk showed us to our room, this one at the far end of the hall, on the right side. The window overlooked the back of the hotel, where two privies stood. It wasn't the best view, but at least this room had two beds complete with mattresses and pillows that weren't torn apart.

There was a good chance the hotel manager would ask for damages and I wouldn't blame him. But we didn't do it. If the town had any money left, surely, they'd pay. We briefly wondered if the mayor would pony up expenses but thought better of asking him ourselves. Best let the hotel owners argue over who pays.

Mouths full of ham sandwiches, we discussed who

could have ransacked our room. Theories ran wild, but soon it became obvious. Someone who thought we had the money.

Eagan finished his meal, brushed crumbs from his fledgling mustache. "All right, I'll say it. Theo did this. Maybe with help from Bushy Beard."

Tate nodded. "Too bad nobody at the front desk saw anybody who didn't belong here."

"But the big question now, is where are they? At least Theo." Tommy wadded the sandwich wrapper. "If August is as bad hurt as you think, then he wouldn't be able to hobble up and down the stairs, quietly. He would have been noticed."

"So, just Theo." Eagan balled a fist. "I'd like to paddle that boy."

"We all would." I swallowed the last of the sandwich, wishing for more.

We sat for a bit, letting our modest meal quiet our complaining stomachs. Tommy stood, stretched. "I've been thinking." He regarded us. "That poker game down at the Texas Tumbler. How does all that play into the bank being robbed? Or does it? We know Driggs was holed up in that back room for hours. But who else was with him? Do we know?"

I shook my head. "Barkeep refused to say."

"Well, he doesn't know me. Maybe I'll go over, ask around." He unpinned his badge and placed it on the table. He pulled coins and one bill out of his vest pocket. "Feel like playing poker, tonight."

"I'll go with you." Tate stood. "Doesn't know me, either." He stuck out a hand toward me. "Think you've got my money."

I was afraid he'd ask. I dug around and extracted the

three dollars and fifty cents I had left and handed it to him.

"This is all? Nothing else?" Tate's words were tinged with false outrage. "What'd you buy her for supper? The entire cow?"

I shrugged. "Courtin's expensive." I forced a wide smile. "Thanks for the loan. I'll pay you back."

"Probably never." Tate made a show of jamming the money into a pocket. "Don't wait up."

* * *

I MADE as much noise as I dared, hoping to wake Tommy and Tate. I had no idea when they'd come in last night. Apparently, I'd slept like the dead. I shuddered at that thought. But this morning I closed the door a bit loudly on my way down to the privy, then rattled the door handle on my way back in. The sound of three men slumbering, one lightly snoring, filled the small room. I plopped into the chair, tapped my boots on the floor, shifted my weight, stood, washed my face and cleared my throat, at least twice.

"That you, Joe?" Eagan mumbled, his tousled hair appearing above the sheet, followed by the rest of his head.

"Sun's up." I pointed at the window over his head. "Let's go."

"Shhhh…"

I wasn't sure who said that, but there were outlaws to catch and money to be retrieved. All of a sudden, I felt a need to get back home. Did I even have a job anymore? I wasn't sure how long I'd been gone, but long enough that more than likely, I'd been replaced. Permanently. Which in many ways was fine with me. That would give me a boot in the rear to go find a different job.

And what about Da and the store? How was he getting on with barely any income? With what I assumed were fewer customers, did he need Eagan's help?

I studied my face in the shaving mirror. My dark blue eyes, blue enough to be summertime blueberries, were circled in red, like someone had taken a red-colored pencil and outlined them. Bruises on my cheeks highlighted the black under my left eye. I had one of every color on my face. The blisters in the corners of my mouth had shrunk into dark pink circles. The gouge taken out of my forehead and scalp were flaming red. Yep. Every color, and each one hurt.

Eagan padded out the door, closing it softly. I reclosed it a bit harder. Tate turned onto his side and Tommy muttered an oath. I sat, fidgeted and stood again when Eagan came back in.

"Think we'd be all right getting breakfast?" I watched Eagan slip on his new shirt. "We'll leave a note for them to join us."

"Don't like sitting here, waiting for somebody to burst in and shoot us." Eagan buttoned his trousers. "Let's go eat. I'm starving."

We left a note, closed the door quietly, moved downstairs as if we were stalking a mouse. Nobody in the lobby, not even the clerk. Wasn't it his job to man the desk? No wonder somebody entered our room unseen.

Eagan and I made it safely to the café, ordered from the same young man as the day before. He'd gotten taller and skinnier since then, if that was even possible. He greeted us like family, his smile lighting up the café.

"Over dere, Mister Deputy." He pointed. "*Am besten* table." He waited for us to sit. "*Kaffe?*"

We nodded. I searched my brain for what little German I knew. *Am besten. Am besten.* Was he seating us someplace to get shot easily? I snapped my fingers. "Best."

"Are we celebrities, you think?" Eagan frowned at me. "Why all the fancy treatment?"

I pointed at him. "Gotta be your pretty face. Sure isn't mine."

We were into our second cup of coffee and halfway through flapjacks, eggs and bacon when Tate and Tommy ambled in. They sat with us, ordered same as what we had and, for all the world, looked like they'd just survived a stampede. Eyes burning red, both in need of a shave, rumpled shirts, they slumped into chairs.

"Good morning." I regarded each and hoped I hid the grin. "A bit too much partying?"

Tate slurped half a cup of coffee in one swallow, then eyed us over the rim. "Seems Driggs was there most days. Playing poker with…get this…"

Eagan and I leaned in close.

Tommy jumped in. "That deputy from John-sonville—"

"And the mayor."

"This mayor?" I pointed to my plate like that was where Bauder lived.

Tate and Tommy nodded.

I threw myself back against the chair. "Holy mother of—"

"That's not all." Tate glanced at Tommy, both with cups in hand. "Seems our very own Blanco Hill Sheriff Wagner has joined in a time or two."

Eagan let his fork clattered to the plate. "Now let me get this straight. Driggs, Wagner, Lieberman, Bauder…all played poker together. Often. Right?"

They nodded.

"But that doesn't mean they robbed the banks." I hated to be the voice of reason, but it all seemed to me pure coincidence. "There's no evidence about Sheriff Wagner. Or did we miss something?"

"And how did you get all this information?" Eagan surveyed the room. Two tables occupied, each with a well-dressed man and woman. Nobody resembling an outlaw. "The barkeep spill the beans? Was he drunk? Or'd you two buy him off?"

Tommy raised a shoulder. "Guess it was my charm."

"Or…" Tate wagged his head. "Meeting a fella who enjoys a good game of poker, beer and cigars. Says he played with 'em, on occasion." He shoved a forkful of scrambled eggs into his mouth, spoke over it. "He'd heard about the bank holdups, of course. Apparently, he travels through on business."

Tommy spoke over his coffee cup. "Some sort of freight company owner. Said he'd sat in sometimes for hours. Thought something a bit "off" with Driggs and Lieberman but couldn't put his finger on it."

I sat back and considered. It was all coming into focus.

"Was that bartender there last night?" Eagan drug a fork across his empty plate. He glanced toward the kitchen.

"Night off, apparently." Tate's eyes softened. "Lovely, young bartender, instead. Curly hair. Easy on the eyes."

I finished everything on my plate, even the flapjack crumbs and listened to my stomach thank me for sending sustenance its way. If it could, it would purr. "So," I downed the final bit of coffee. "How does playing poker together make them bank robbers?"

I thought the question was another of my obvious

ones, but three sets of eyes stared at me, each one blinking rapidly. "I mean...what's the connection? Obviously, they knew each other, but how'd they manage to rob a bank, while playing poker? Or did they?"

Tommy pushed back his chair and eased to his feet. There was no spring in his step this morning.

"Let's take this up at the office. Someplace not so public." Tommy fished into a vest pocket, extracted coins and his badge. The coins he tossed onto the table, the badge he pinned on.

The young man appeared at our table, scraped up the coins. *"Danke euch."*

I stood, pushed in my chair, then turned to the boy now picking up our dishes. "Excuse me." I waited for him to stop and look at me. "Do you by chance know Theo Bauder, the mayor's son?" I figured them to be about the same age and this town was small enough that all the children would know each other.

He nodded. *"Ja, das tue ich."*

"I'm an old friend of his da's," I lied. "He tells me Theo's been sick. Has to miss school." I studied the youngster's face, now hinting at something to be hidden. "I'm hoping it's nothing serious. Would you know?"

His gaze flicked from me to the door, where my party was waiting, back to me. It swept across the table. Reluctantly, he shook his head. *"Nien.* I don't know. Sorry."

"Well, thanks anyway." I wished I had extra coin to give him. Sure looked like he could use it. "Hope he feels better."

He ducked his head, muttered something.

I leaned closer. "What?"

"You are new lawmen. *Danke."* He whisked around and scurried away, leaving me trying to figure out why he would say what he did.

I joined everyone on the boardwalk and relayed my lack of information. "Although, he looked like he knew something, he wouldn't say." I shrugged. "And he thanked me for being new law in town. Guess that's why we got the royal treatment."

As we headed for the sheriff's office, I glanced over my shoulder more than once. No glint of a rifle through an upper-story window, no cocking of a weapon echoing off the buildings, nothing but a horse and wagon in the street, a woman heading toward a meat market. Nothing hinting at danger.

We made it safely inside, where we took our usual places. Tommy listed what we knew.

"Driggs is dead. I understand there's to be a simple funeral, later this afternoon."

"We're not going, are we?" Tate's face was set firm in concern.

"One of us should." Tommy pushed back a hank of hair on his forehead. "Guess that'd be me."

"Next, we need to find Theo Bauder and August Huber." Tate leaned back in his chair, reached for the ceiling and stretched. "Question is... where do we start?"

"Think Miss O'Shea would let us talk to her students? Maybe they'd know something." Eagan rubbed his scarred wrists. "Maybe at recess?"

His rubbing made mine itch. I scratched at the few scabs left. Although I had been bound with iron, my wrists were rubbed raw. I couldn't imagine how painful Eagan's were, being lassoed with rope.

"Good idea." Tate sat up taller, like energy had entered his body. "How 'bout you and I go, in about an hour? That way, Tommy and Joe can stay here, where's it safe."

"While I don't enjoy being shot at, I don't like hiding." I thumbed behind me. "If it *was* Theo who shot at us, then he's probably hanging out with August. I'll go see if Gertrude's behind the bar. If so, that'll mean August and Theo are probably at her house."

"You know, little brother." Tate half turned in his seat. "Sometimes you do good thinking." He slapped at my leg. "But only sometimes."

CHAPTER SEVENTEEN

WE SAT IN THE OFFICE FOR ANOTHER HOUR, talking stories, sharing what-ifs, and generally philosophizing about life. The more we talked, the more I realized it was time for me to move on. Not only with the Frieda phase of my life, but with my job choice. I'd thought earlier about not going back as a telegrapher and now I was certain. Maybe being lawman wasn't my life's goal, but working outside, with the whole town, was in my future.

Was Hilda in my future as well? I'd like to get to know her better. That was a given.

Tate opened the door and the sound of children playing outside rolled down the street. He smiled. "I remember those days. Nothing better than recess." He turned to Eagan. "Let's go."

That was my cue to head over to the *Gausthause*. Would a beer be too much? It was still early, but I hadn't had one last night. Halfway to the street, I remembered. I had no money. Not one coin. Not enough even to buy a beer.

Shoulders slumped, I pushed open the door and behind the bar, there stood Gertrude, beer mug in one hand, white towel in the other. She glanced up at me, silhouetted in the doorway, then growled.

"Vhat you vant?"

Startled, I struggled not to stutter. "Uh...just looking for my friends, ma'am." I swiveled my head right to left, even though I expected to see only strangers. "No. No friends in here."

She set the mug on the counter harder than necessary and reached under the bar for what I assumed was a shotgun. I backed to the door just as she brought it out. Yep. Something from before the war. Could've been a German gun. Whatever kind it was, it was damn big. I didn't wait to find out more. I backed into the street and stood to my right.

Safe, so far. I breathed deeply, waiting for my heart to quit pounding. At least one question was answered. She was not at her house. But right now, I needed...pastry. Something sweet. Something baked. Something from Hilda.

My trek down the street was swift and, again, nobody shot at me. Maybe that had been a one-time deal. I hoped so.

Hilda beamed at me when I opened the door. A woman was choosing what looked to be the best tarts in the store and, instantly, I was jealous. I wanted those. But then, I glanced at the cherry strudel. Oh, yeah. There it was. Bliss.

I shoved a hand into my vest pocket. Empty. I'd forgotten. Again. I held the door open and nodded to the lady as she smugly walked out, then turned to Hilda.

"It's so good to see you!" We spoke in unison. Then

laughed. She came around the counter and gave me a quick, floury hug.

She pointed to my head, her long fingers brushing the top. "How is your head? Looks painful."

"It's better, now that I'm with you." Hell, even to me that sounded corny.

Hilda laughed. A deep, from-the-heart, laugh. Her wide smile brought sparkles to her eyes. Was she laughing at me? Suddenly, I wanted to take it back. All of it. Every humiliating word.

I studied the wooden floor, my brain telling me to turn around, leave, and never come back. Da would say I was an *amhlán*. A fool. I was. Stupid, stupid, stupid. I stepped back, ready to turn and run.

Hilda shoulder bumped me. "Why are you going? You just got here."

Too embarrassed to even speak, I cocked my head toward the door.

"Please. Do not go, yet." She flashed that heart-stopping smile. "You vant a strudel?"

The little boy inside me jumped up and down, cheering. The grown man outside simply nodded. "I do, if you won't hate me." I wagged my head. "Didn't mean to say something stupid."

She froze halfway to the counter, then turned. "Stupid? I love vhat you talk. Say. You are funny."

All right. So, I wasn't a total dolt. She flashed that dazzling smile as she handed me the cherry strudel. Even the air seemed to be holding its breath as our hands met. I wanted to sweep her up into my arms and never let go. What was it about her that made my heart pound, my palms sweat, my throat go dry? She was special, I'd give her that. So very special.

"Are you going to eat, or stare at it?" Hilda's cherubic voice brought me back to the here and now.

I couldn't help myself. I leaned into and kissed her. Hard. My free hand slid behind her, bringing the beauty right up to me. She pressed against me in all the right places. Her lips—peppermint and cinnamon. Her breath —peaches and cream. Her arms around me—pure ecstasy.

With the other hand, I reached behind her and slid the strudel onto the counter. Like a dance, she leaned with me, doing an awkward sort of waltz, then back as we straightened to continue kissing. My hand slid up and down her back, stroking this sensual creature. The other hand desperately wanted to slide farther down her body, but my brain insisted I be a gentleman.

She held on to me like I was the lifeline she'd been waiting for. Maybe I was, but I didn't spend any time thinking about that.

The bell above the door tinkled. We jumped apart. I smoothed my mustache and she, her dress. Hilda, cheeks glowing red, greeted two middle-aged women, who eyed me up and down like I was a mouth-watering pastry. Their eyes widened and one's eyebrows rose. Sly smiles appeared on both faces. My own face turned warm, then hot. Hilda rushed around the counter and stood behind the display.

While the women discussed the selection, Hilda patted her hair back into place and eyeballed me to the strudel still on the counter's edge. "Do not forget your pastry, Mr. Nolan. I have a table over there, if you would care to sit." She pointed to the corner.

For the first time, I noticed a small, round table with two chairs. "That'll be perfect." Just like you, I thought. I took my strudel to the table and sat, watching her discuss her wares. So proud of her work. And she had every right to be. It was all delicious. Like herself.

About the time I finished my delight, the customers chose two tarts and two strudels. They paid, then stopped at the door, and regarded me like I was for sale too. I stared back, totally confused as to why they were so interested in me. It wasn't like I was somebody famous, or wealthy, or anything special. Reluctantly, one pulled the door open, and both stepped outside, stopping to stare through the window.

Hilda sat with me while we chuckled. She shrugged. "They have not seen you before. Guess they wanted you, as well as my pastries."

Wiping what I hoped were crumbs from my mustache, I smiled. "I want you more than the sweets, but I really like those too."

Standing, she wiped her hands on the apron. "I have to finish today's baking. You vant to come to supper, tonight? *Mein vater* cooks *gud*."

"Your da?" Meeting him this early in our courtship seemed a bit rushed, but if that gave me another opportunity to see her, I'd chance it. "How does he feel about the Irish?" I wasn't about to walk into another den of Gael haters. I'd learned that the hard way. Frieda's family barely tolerated me, as it was. And they had absolutely no love for us Catholics.

She laughed. Another deep laugh. Her hands flapped. "Silly. He loves the *Gaeilge*. *Mein mutter*, Dairíne Walsh was from Galway. Came over the same year *mein vater* did."

Whew! So that made Hilda half Irish. Easing to my feet, I held her by the waist and kissed her gently, this time. "I'd be delighted to come to supper. What time?"

She thought. "Let us say six." Hilda flapped her

hands, again, this time toward the door. "Now shoo. I have work."

I wanted to kiss her again, hug her until my arms turned numb. Instead, I nodded and moved for the door, my legs complaining I leave. "See you tonight."

Evidently, I'd walked up the street, my boots loudly *thunking* atop the wooden boardwalk, but I didn't realize I was doing it until two women passed by, stopped and glared at me. I found myself in the office, Tommy still seated behind the desk, two men I didn't recognize standing in front.

Both stood rigid, their backs erect. One pointed an angry finger at Tommy, the other man scrubbed his own face with a stiff hand. The man with the finger noticed me, and cut short what he'd been saying.

Tommy, looking angry and relieved at the same moment, nodded at me. "Fellas, this's a duly sworn posse member from Blanco Hill. He's here to help capture the bank robbers."

"Joe Nolan," the pointing finger man said. "Yeah, we know." He glared at me. "So?"

The other man, taller than the rest of us, fisted his hand, the other occupied with his hat. "I'll ask again, *Deputy*." His words were filled with contempt and disdain. "What are you doing about getting our money back? We...the town...can't go on like this."

"Hell, business's at a standstill." The first man used his pointed finger to pound the desk. "This town'll dry up and die if something isn't done. Now!"

"Right now!" The other man, a watch chain hanging across his ribs and ending in a vest pocket, hooked his thumbs into his waistband. "We're tired of waiting. I've telegraphed the marshal over in Austin. Asked him to send *real* lawmen to take over."

With that, I figured Tommy would leap to his feet and curse. Instead, he eased out of his chair, crossed his arms over his chest. He raised his chin and lowered his voice. His words came out calmly but, behind them, I detected something close to rage. "Gentlemen. I told you when you walked in, we're doing all we can. Yes, investigation takes time. But we're making progress."

Afraid this would go to blows, I decided to jump in, even if my help wasn't called for. "We already know who the robbers are." I looked from man to man. "And we know two of them are hurt."

"And we're fairly sure we know their hangout." Tommy threw back his shoulders. "Just a matter of time now and they'll be in jail."

"Hells, bells, *Deputy*. That's all well and good, but where...the...*hell*...is the money?" The taller man moved in closer to Tommy. He shook a stiff finger at the cells. "Having the bandits in jail doesn't pay the bills."

The other man pointed too. "Fact is, it costs money to house outlaws." He let out a breath. "Hell, I say shoot 'em, when you find 'em. Save the town money it doesn't have."

"Gentlemen." I waved toward the door. "Another day or two, this'll all be over. As Deputy O'Sullivan said, we're doing everything we can. I'd say by this time tomorrow, we'll have men arrested and, hopefully, money back in the bank." I was talking out of the top of my hat, if I had one, but the bravado seemed to pacify them. A bit.

Both turned to me. The older of the two narrowed his eyes. "Let's hope you do, Sonny. Otherwise, there's gonna be hell to pay." He took a step, then turned. "And a new sheriff in town."

They smashed hats onto their heads, threw open the door and slammed it behind them.

The quiet they left behind almost made me laugh. Almost. It was like they'd sucked out all the energy in the room. Still, their angry words echoed in my head. "That wasn't an idle threat, was it?" I took Tate's usual seat, while Tommy eased down.

"Don't think so. But it'll take a while to get a marshal here." Tommy picked up the pencil, again. "Those're businessmen. I don't blame them for being frustrated."

I considered Blanco Hill. Da and his meat market. Mr. Whelan and his telegraph business. Even Ma with her piecemeal sewing. How were they all managing? Had anybody moved away yet? I hoped not.

"What'd you find out at the Gasthause?" Tommy scribbled on a wanted poster, currently his favorite pastime.

"Gertrude's there, so the house should be empty."

"And Hilda? How's she today?" Tommy glanced up at me, a sly grin pushing up his mustache.

"How'd…?"

He shrugged.

"She's wonderful. Invited me to supper, tonight. Her da's cooking."

Tommy held up the pencil. "Her pa? Men cook?"

"Apparently. And he likes us Irish. Says her ma was from Galway."

"Lucky you." He softly whistled. "She's a keeper, Joe."

As we waited for Eagan and Tate, I shared my thoughts about leaving the safety of the telegrapher's desk and moving on to something more exciting. Or at least, different.

"You know…" Tommy shrugged. "Even if they send a marshal, Fredericksburg's gonna need a sheriff and deputy. Maybe you should consider doing that, moving here."

Before I could say no, he continued. "Only three hours from your folks and five minutes from Hilda." Tommy chuckled. "Sounds like a good deal, to me."

I hadn't really considered moving to this town, but why not? I needed a place of my own. Living with the folks again was fine, for now. But having been married and out on my own, I realized the freedom I'd had. I'd definitely give his suggestion some thought.

I settled into the chair, plotting and planning my new life. Tommy busied himself with searching through all the desk drawers, then inspecting each of the four rifles in the rack on the wall.

At last Eagan came in, Tate right behind. Eagan took Tommy's chair and Tate leaned against the wall.

"Not much new." Tate's mouth turned down, as did his gaze. "Miss O'Shea wouldn't let us talk to the children, not without their parents' permission."

Tommy turned, last rifle in hand. "Guess that's only proper. But we need to ride. Joe says Gertrude's at the saloon right now."

Three of us got to our feet and adjusted our gun belts. Tommy handed each of us a rifle and a handful of bullets. "All loaded. Hope we don't have to use 'em."

* * *

NOBODY SPOKE much on the ride out to Gertrude's. Now that we knew the way, it didn't take long until we spotted the well-kept house across the field. Tying up in the same grove we'd used earlier, we re-checked our rifles and, if the others were like me, took deep breaths to steady nerves. I sure as hell didn't want anyone hurt, much less dead. Especially any one of us.

We stood hidden in the safety of the trees, using their shadows to cloak our presence. I narrowed my eyes, hoping for a better view. No movement except the chickens in the yard, clucking and scratching. A goat sauntered through the hens, scattering them. Up on the porch, a big yellow dog lay in the sun. More than likely asleep. Would he raise an alarm?

We'd have to circle around to the back. Hard to do since all of the trees had been removed from near the house. There was nothing but low scrub at least forty feet in every direction. No smaller trees to break up the space. And still we stood, looking, thinking, planning.

Tommy checked his rifle for the fifth time, this morning. "How about this? Tate, you and Joe head around to the left. Eagan and I'll head right. Let's try the back door first."

I nodded without speaking, realizing no words would come over my pounding heart. Was this it? We'd catch the two remaining robbers? They'd tell us where the money is hidden? We'd recover it, pass it out to the respective towns? And then go home, back to our lives?

Was resolution this close at hand? Why not?

Gaze fixated on the house, I followed Tate through the trees, until we reached the edge of the grove. Nowhere to go now, except out in the open. Mentally, I pulled up my britches, set my invisible hat on straight, pulled in air, glanced at Tate, then ran. Into the open. Across the field.

Bark! Bark! That old dog scampered around the side, now running alongside me. Was he expecting me to throw a stick? I ran full out and so did the dog. He wasn't growling. Maybe he thought we were playing.

I heard more than saw Tate run behind me. I zigzagged across plowed up ground, which tried to trip me up if I wasn't careful. Twice, I stumbled but managed to keep my feet. I reached the house, then plastered myself against the wall. Seconds later, Tate did the same. We, the dog, Tate, and me stood panting on each side of the door.

We waited at least a full minute. The dog lay at my feet, looking up like I should feed him, throw a stick, or something. He blinked, closed his eyes.

Do we go in? Wait for the others? They'd had a longer track to navigate than we had, and weren't here, yet. I leaned around the corner and spotted both Tommy and Eagan, despite his pronounced limp, loping toward us.

Bang! Smoke spiraled from the trees behind us.

Both men fell to the ground, arms covering their heads.

"Think they're hit?" I hollered to Tate.

Tate pointed. "Look. They're moving." He dropped to a knee and aimed his rifle toward the smoke and fired.

A returning blast sent another single strand of smoke from the shadows. The bullet pinged against the house, raining down chunks from the wood siding. We both ducked and I sent a quick prayer upward. Tate probably did, too.

I pulled in a deep breath, aimed, and fired toward the smoke. Crouching, Tommy and Eagan duck-ran toward us. Bullets kicked up dirt at their feet, while a couple hit directly above my head. They bolted across the field, Eagan outdistancing Tommy.

They came sliding in, where Tate and I crouched. We scurried to the side of the house, farthest away from the attacker. My heart planted itself in my throat as I asked, "Do we go inside? Maybe August is in there."

Tommy shook his head. "I'm not liking that idea. We go inside, we're sitting ducks. Whoever's out there"—he pointed to the stand of trees—"probably Theo, is gonna disappear, if we don't go right now and catch him."

I peeked around the corner. Nobody running across the field at us. Just the dog still on the back porch. He raised up to look at me.

Tate cocked his head. "How 'bout two of us go inside, see what we can see." He shoulder bumped me. "We'll be fine. Catch up with you in a few, Tommy."

Uh, wait! Is what I wanted to say. But he'd already dashed to the back door. I followed, about falling over the dog. The door squeaked open and Tate flung himself inside, rolling to a wall. I did the same. No shots rang out. No bootsteps running our way. No…nothing.

So far, so good. I eased my way up until I sat. We both got to our feet, rifles clutched in hand. We tiptoed through the house, peering into both bedrooms, the kitchen and front room. Nothing out of order, nothing indicating a man—or men—had been present. In fact, it was too quiet, as if the house itself was watching. I shuddered.

I waited in the front room, while Tate took a longer look in the kitchen. Feeling a tad foolish with nothing to discover, I stepped to the kitchen. "Let's go. Nothing here."

Bang! A bullet shattered the doorframe, sending wooden shards into my face. *Bang!* Closer this time, it slammed into the table at Tate's hip.

Tate fell to his knees, grabbing his face. "Ow! Ow! Splinter in my eye! Ow!"

I swung around knowing I'd see August or Theo

standing there, rifle aimed at my heart. Just an empty space.

He'd been close. Way too close. I rushed to Tate and kneeled beside him. "Look at me. Let me see."

Blood trickled down his right cheek, his eye swollen. He clawed at it, but I slapped his hand away.

"What happened?" Eagan slid next to Tate. "Your eye?"

We both nodded. Tate scooted back and forth, batting at his face. He mumbled, then clambered up to his feet. "Get it out! Get it out! Ow!" Tears streamed down his cheeks.

Tommy bent below the window. "I'm going after him." He bolted from the kitchen, across the front room and slammed the door. He shouted curses at the dog.

I grabbed both of Tate's shoulders, held him steady. "Calm down. Calm down. You'll hurt yourself, you keep trying to rub it."

Eagan and I each held down an arm and moved in close. I examined his puffed red eye. In the outside corner, a splinter poked out. Didn't look like it had pierced the eyeball.

"I see one." I hoped my voice was low and calm. "Eagan, you see any more?"

Eagan turned Tate's face toward the single window. "Just that one."

"Get it out! Get it out!" Tate fought against my grip, almost ripping his arm free.

I held Tate's face. "Look at me. Take a deep breath. Deep." I breathed in and out with him. "Like that." I paused, then continued. "From what we can tell, there's a splinter next to your eye, not in it. That's the good news."

I did a quick survey of the kitchen. No whiskey bottle

sat on the counter. Nothing handy that would help with the pain.

"Bad news, Tate." I looked directly into his eyes. "We can get it out, but it's gonna hurt like a son-of-a—"

"Just get it out." Tate shook.

I leaned in nose-to-nose with Tate and hollered at Eagan. "Hold him tight." I grasped the splinter and pulled.

"Ow! Ow!"

Eagan released him, found a towel near the wash basin and held it to Tate's face.

Bang! Not a gunshot this time. We all ducked, expecting a bullet to lodge into

something—or someone—but the sound wasn't quite right. What was it?

Another door? "Back door. I'm going." Without waiting for discussion, I took off, rushing through the house and then outside. I swear I couldn't have been possibly twenty seconds behind whoever it was, probably Theo. Yet, when I got outside, I saw no one, no one running, no one kneeling to shoot, no *body*.

I peered at where I'd seen a figure, yesterday. Again, I didn't spot any movement, but that didn't necessarily guarantee they weren't there. I ran faster than I thought possible, across the open field. I cursed whoever had decided to plow furrows almost up to the door. I ran along one channel and then across the dirt mounds keeping my stride short.

When I hit the trees, I slowed, then stopped. I pulled in air and held it, listening for running footsteps, heavy breathing other than mine, twigs crunching under feet. Nope. Nothing. How was that even possible?

I crept farther into the grove, head down, eyes searching for that one clue. I needed only one. And then, there it was. A fresh boot print in the dirt between two trees. A couple feet farther, another print. Finally! I was on his heels and I vowed I'd catch him.

I followed what few tracks I could find for a quarter mile north of Gertrude's house. I'd been gradually walking up hill. And now, from where I stood on top, I spotted a roof in the distance, trees shading most of it.

I spent half a minute catching my breath, deciding whether to return to the house and bring everyone back, or simply keep going. I was so close to the outlaw I focused on capturing him or them. Hopefully, I'd retrieve the money as well. I'd go on alone. It would be faster. Besides, Tommy was out here somewhere.

I sneaked down the hill, using trees and scant bushes for cover. A one-room line shack sat backed into a hill. There was only one way in and one way out. I lay in the dead leaves, surveying the shanty, looking for a road, a path in and out. To the right, a faint outline of a trail meandered off. Obviously, wasn't used often.

Reality hit me. I needed backup. Had Tommy gone back to the house? Together, surely the four of us could take two men—actually a boy and an injured man. I scooted back as quietly as possible, got to my knees, then stood. I turned and bumped into Deputy Lionel Lieberman.

CHAPTER EIGHTEEN

LIEBERMAN POKED A SHOTGUN INTO MY CHEST, the metal barrels pressing sharp against my breastbone. I raised my hands, then realized my rifle was lying at my feet. No way to defend myself. I wasn't really good at fist fighting but could hold my own when necessary. However, the pressure against my chest erased any ideas of pugilism as an option.

Questions bombarded me. I had to ask. My voice scratchy. "Why aren't you at the doc's?" Either he'd made a quick recovery, or he'd killed the doc and nurse to escape.

"Oh, I wasn't quite as sick as everyone thought. Just got a tiny bump on the noggin." He pushed the barrel harder into my ribs. "I'm good at play actin'. Don't ya agree?"

I did, but wasn't about to bolster his already over-filled ego. I decided to change tactics. "What're you doing here?"

"That's my question to you. Don't you and your brothers know when to turn tail and run home?"

"We vowed to bring in three bank robbers." Pride was busy overriding any fear I'd had. I was mad, outraged. I'd spent way too long chasing these weasels. It was time for them to be arrested. Time to find that money. "What the hell gave you the right to rob people of their hard-earned money?" To my surprise—and his—I pushed the shotgun aside, spun a pointed finger. "Hands behind your back. I'm arresting you."

"Arresting *me*?" Lieb reached out and grabbed my finger, bent it up. "I have the gun. And arrestin' ain't gonna happen today." He looked down at the shack. "Hell, ain't *never* gonna happen." He released my sore finger, shoved me back with the shotgun. "Get goin'."

I turned, making my way down the hill, all the while feeling the shotgun barrel jammed into my spine. We arrived at the shack and the door opened. Out stepped August Huber, blood-stained bandage wrapped around his lower left leg and a dark-haired kid, a bit out of breath and cheeks red from running, looked to be around fourteen. August carried a handgun and the kid held a Sharps rifle at the ready.

"You get just this one?" the kid hollered at Lieb.

"So far." Lieb shoved me closer to the others. "Expect the rest to be right behind."

The kid stepped back. "Bring 'im in."

August held open the door and watched every move I made, making me feel more like a specimen than a prisoner.

Prisoner. There was that word again. Twice now, I'd been held prisoner. Recently. I'd need to rethink this wanting to be a lawman idea. But first, I needed to get out of this. Alive.

The four of us squeezed into the one-room shack, most of the area being taken up by a table with three chairs, a cot, blanket strewn at the foot, potbelly stove and wooden box of various supplies. By the door stood an arsenal of weapons. I counted three shotguns, four rifles, two double-rig gun belts with two revolvers per belt, various boxes of ammo and what might be a spyglass. They'd certainly be ready if another war broke out.

Lieberman clutched my shoulder and pushed me to the table. I plunked hard into a chair. He grabbed my still-sore arms, yanked them behind me, then tied each wrist to a chair rung. If I decided to run, I'd have to bring my seat with me. While he trussed, I regarded a saddlebag on the table. Sure looked like Tate's, the one stolen from the hotel room. That sealed it. Theo or August, or both, had destroyed our room.

Most pressing, I had to warn the others about the trap these three were setting. Holler out? Try to get away? Feign death? Maybe if I distracted them, I'd figure something out.

I started with who I assumed was Theo. I aimed my questions at him. "Your da know you're here? He knows you're involved in the bank robberies? Ain't you a tad young to be an outlaw?"

Theo about jumped over the table. He grabbed me by the front of my shirt, yanked me within an inch of his face. "What d'you know about anything? Shut up. Just shut the hell up!" He blew out onions and I couldn't tell what else. "What the hell d'you know? Just shut yer stinkin' gob!"

"Want me to kill him now, Theo?" August leveled a pistol at me. "He needs killin'."

Theo shoved me back against the chair. "Yeah, he does." He leaned in close again. His moss-green eyes daggered holes into me. If he could kill me like that, he would. Hell, I'd be so full of pits and dips, I'd be a sieve. "No killin'. Not right yet, though. Need 'im to get the money and the rest." He straightened. "Then we kill 'em all."

Goose bumps stampeded up my back. I couldn't let that happen. Talking my way out of this situation wasn't going to work. I'd have to fight. My nerves sparked rage, muscles tightened, my resolve gelled. I'd get out of here alive and so would my brothers and Tommy. Or I'd die trying.

I didn't have long to wait. Maybe twenty minutes. I'd fidgeted in the chair, tugged at the bindings, but couldn't get loose.

Lieb cracked open the door and looked up the hill. He eased it closed, then whispered, "Up there. I see three of 'em." He turned back to us. "Those ol' boy's gotta be dumber'n steers at butcherin' time."

August hobbled to the window, next to the door. He peered out. "I see that deputy, Tommy something." He pointed. "Right up there. Thinks we can't see him."

Theo whooped softly. "We gonna kill us some stinkin' lawmen. Today. Right now!" He paced wall to door and back. "They'll be sorry. Real, damn sorry." He stopped at my side, leaned down, again close to my face. "You'll be the first to die, *Joe*. Yeah. Real dead. Just like your wife."

"You son-of-a-bitch!" I raged against the ropes. "Leave her out of this!"

Theo stood back and laughed. A loud, throaty laugh, obviously loving every second of this adventure. He bounced on the balls of his feet and pointed a finger in my face. "*You're* the reason she died, *Joe*. *You* caused her death. *You*—"

"You! In there!" Tommy's voice echoed in the room. "Come out! Hands up!"

Theo rushed to the door, stuck his head out. "We got Joe in here with us. He ain't goin' nowhere. You gotta come in and get 'im!"

Silence. Was I breathing? My chest rose and fell, so apparently, I remained alive. What were they waiting for? Were they positioning themselves around the cabin? Going back to town for reinforcements that didn't exist? What the hell was taking so long?

Lieb opened the door, stood next to the jamb, and peered out.

Bang! A bullet tore a hole into the door directly above the deputy's head. He ducked, slammed it and rushed to the opposite side of the room. "Holy Mother of..." He regarded August and Theo standing on either side of me. "That was close."

Theo swiped a dirty hand across his face, where peach fuzz of a beard lightly shadowed his face. "Not close enough." He slid a Bowie knife from his boot, cut the ropes around my wrists, and hauled me to my feet. While he was considerably shorter than me, maybe a foot or so, he made up for the lack of height with his wide shoulders and passion. Yes, he was insane. And danger-ously so.

Holding the knife against my throat, Theo moved to where his chest was plastered against my back. As one, we opened the door and marched outside. Lieb and August stood in the open doorway, daring my boys to shoot.

With the blade crammed against my skin, this was a nightmare I'd never, ever dreamed of. My knees threat-ened to buckle and my stomach promised to bring up everything I'd eaten in the past month. I tried not to tremble but my hands shook, anyway. Hard. Pulling in a deep chestful of air, I fought grayness. I could not, would not pass out. Never. Not like this.

And then, like a quick, hot touch of the devil running through him, Theo slid the blade an inch or two across my neck. He called out. "See? See what I can do?" He held up the bloody knife. "There's more. Lots more." Before I could blink, he returned the blade to my neck, pressing harder this time.

Stinging panic overtook me. I vowed not to die like this. Not with a knife slicing at my throat.

Out of the corner of an eye, I spotted my brothers hunkered down behind a large bush. Tommy had to be close by. Part of me was overjoyed to see them, knowing they'd do everything to save me. The rest of me didn't want them anywhere around, in case Crazy Theo and his two *amigos* got to shooting. And they would. It was only a matter of time. A short time, at that.

Theo held me tighter, his nerves at full stretch. I couldn't be closer to him and yet, his breathing was calm, his heart impossible to feel over mine. We were one.

"Let him go, Theo." Tommy stepped from the left, opposite my brothers. He pointed a rifle at Theo, cocked it, loudly. "Drop the knife and let him go."

"Or what?"

"I shoot you." Tommy's voice hardened. "You want that?"

Theo and I backed against the cabin's wall. As short as he was, the only person getting shot, here, would be me. I knew Tommy didn't want that, but then again...

"What I want," Theo's words turned soft, like he was talking to a kitten. "What I want is the money." He peeked out from around me. "You can have him, if you'll just give me the money. All of it."

"We don't have it." Tommy held up the gun, aiming directly at me.

"Liar!" Theo screamed. "You're all liars!"

Nerves stretched taut, heart pounding in my throat, hands shaking, I stomped Theo's instep with as much force as I could muster.

"Cripes!"

The knife dipped and, in that instant, I jerked up both of my feet, slid from his embrace and hit the ground.

Bang! Tommy fired. Theo spun and rushed inside. I rolled toward Tommy.

A strong hand grabbed my leg and pulled be backward. I careened back into the cabin, knocking into the doorframe as I went. The door slammed behind me. August seized my arm and threw me across the room. I somersaulted into the potbelly stove, knocking it over. Soot flew into my eyes. They burned.

I crab walked backward and bumped into the wall. Two pairs of eyes and two angry faces glared at me. August kicked out, catching me in the stomach. I groaned, held my gut, and curled. Lieb put a boot into my leg so hard I was afraid he'd broken it.

"I'm hit! I'm hit!" Theo screamed.

More kicks, curses and a fist. Then the assault ended. I lay there, jammed against the wall, gasping for air. For my life.

Words flew around the room, but none made real sense. As I pulled in enough air to breathe, August and Lieb laid Theo on top of the table, pulled up his shirt and peered at a bloody mess.

Good. He was finally getting a taste of what he'd wrought. He'd brought all this on himself. Would they blame me? Of course, they would. I lay still, hoping they'd forget I was there. I'd wait for a chance to escape.

Then I noticed Theo's Sharps rifle, his da's pride and joy, laying forgotten on the floor across the room. He'd obviously tossed it there when he was helped to the table. Was there a chance he'd forget it?

While they fussed over Theo, I lay thinking about the situation. Obviously, these three didn't have the money or know where it was hidden. The three outside knew who all was in here, but they didn't know where the money was, either. Most importantly, how would I get out of this mess? Was I able to stand and run? Something iron tasting coated the inside of my mouth. I touched it. Blood. Probably loose teeth. I could run with loose teeth. My stomach gave a heave ho and up came pink. I figured that wasn't good. I had to get out of here.

I scooted around and pushed myself up to sitting, back against the wall. I gripped my stomach, although my chest hurt like Lucifer's fire. I couldn't hold everything that hurt at once.

"Get that rag over there." Lieb pointed to a box across the room. "Should stop the bleeding."

August rummaged through a wooden box and came up with a used towel. Lieb folded it and mashed it against Theo's side.

"It hurts," Theo whined.

"Bullet wounds usually do." Lieb put Theo's hand on the bandage. "Press down. I'll find a wrap."

August held up an old shirt, also from the box, ripped it in strips. "This'll do, Lieb."

Lieb wrapped the fabric around Theo. "Damn lucky. Bullet nicked you is all. You'll heal up by tomorrow." He tied the ends and stood back. "See? Told you that worthless deputy's no good. Can't hit what he's aiming at."

And with that, all eyes turned on me. If I could have melted into the wooden wall, I would have. Instead, I brought my achy shoulders back, lifted my chin feeling the slice in my throat open. I decided to try a new tactic. Maybe no one would get killed this way. "Seems to me none of us know where the money is." I looked from Theo to Lieb to August. "We"—I cocked my head toward the door—"have no idea where to look. It's not in the sheriff's safe." I wasn't about to tell them we'd found almost two thousand dollars.

"He's lying." Theo held his side and slid off the table, Lieb holding an arm. "They're all lying. Bet they got the money, and now just want to get us."

"Well, son, if we—"

"Don't ever call me 'son'! I ain't your son!" Theo kicked my thigh, the impact sending me onto my side.

Theo clutched his wound, bent over. Lieb and August, gripping each arm, helped him to the cot. He sat and glared.

I righted myself. "So, if *you* don't know and *we* don't know, maybe we call a truce. Put our heads together, figure this out."

"And then you'll take all the money and *we* go to jail." August marched to me, kicked at my leg. "I ain't going to jail," he hissed into my face. He glanced at Lieb. "Not again."

Lieb took a chair at the table, where he could see all of us. "I joined up with Driggs to make some money. Deputy's salary's piss poor. Don't make enough to feed myself." He swung his gaze to include us all. "Ain't goin' back to that. When I get my share, I'm moving down to Meh-he-co. Grab me a *señorita* or two, maybe three. Drink fine mescal and have myself a glorious, ol' time."

"What I'm gonna do"—August gazed at the ceiling—"is take me and my sister back to Germany. Still got family there." He nodded at Theo. "Yep. That's what I aim to do."

"You've both got only hair under those hats. Driggs was the only one knowin' where all that money we stole is. And he ain't exactly talkin'." Theo jerked and held his ribs tighter. "And if those yahoos out there don't know, Joe's right. If we're gonna see any money, we gotta figure this out. Together."

I blew out a sigh, more of necessity than relief. "Did Driggs even hint at where he hid it?"

Three heads wagged.

Since we were into sharing, I asked a question I figured might get me killed. "What was with Driggs and those poker games? Can't make the connection."

Lieb stared at me. I steeled my muscles for a fight.

"Damn, you're dumber'n you look, Joe. Figured between you three brothers, one of you might have a half a brain under your hair." Lieb held up a hand like he had cards in them. "Couple of us'd go out through the window, rob the bank, come back like we'd been there all along." He grabbed the front of my shirt, pulled me nose to nose. "You're dumb. Real dumb. Surprised you can even pull breath, you're so woodenheaded."

I had to admit that was a good ploy. Using the cover of a marathon poker game as decoy. Why hadn't I thought of that? I opened my mouth for more questions, but the door creaked open. A ball of something giving off a stomach-turning stink sailed into the room, hit the floor. Smoke erupted from it. The door slammed shut. Within seconds, it opened again, a second smoking ball flying in. Immediately, smoke filled the cabin.

Coughing, eyes watering, I sat still, hopefully forgotten.

"What's going on?"

"I can't see!"

Everyone coughed. Cursed. Coughed and cursed some more. Including me. I slid back against the wall, drew up my knees, covered everything I could with my arms. Still I coughed, my eyes watering.

"Can't breathe." August's voice.

"Grab a rifle." Theo.

"Can't breathe." August ripped open the door, bolted outside. Lieb staggered out behind him.

Theo pulled a pistol from his gun belt and stuck it against my side. "I ain't goin' to jail and I ain't dyin'. If I do, you're goin' with me." He yanked me up to my feet. I stood wobbling, hoping I could find my way to the door.

We staggered through the darkness. I plowed into the table and fell over the chair. Tears and snot streamed down my face. I coughed, bringing up nothing but smoke. We careened to the door and entered a world of fresh air. I sucked in what I could.

"Got your boy here, lawman." Theo moved the gun from my chest to my head. He coughed. "Wanna see him alive ever again, you three back off. Take Lieb and August if you want to, but me and Joe here, we're leavin'. Don't try to stop us. I'll kill him quicker'n you can say kiss my ass."

"Joe?" Tate hollered at me. "You all right?"

"One move. One." Theo cocked the weapon. "He's a dead man." He eyed Tommy to Tate to Eagan. "I got nothin' to lose. I'll shoot and won't miss."

He'd pull the trigger; I had no doubt about that. In fact, I was surprised he hadn't done so yet.

I wanted to shake my head but, before I could do even that, Theo and I sidestepped left toward the far side of the cabin. Tears streamed down my sore cheeks; my vision watery at best. I coughed and sneezed, as I stepped with Theo around the side of the cabin. We stumbled toward a small lean-to, which looked like it served as a makeshift barn.

Three horses, already saddled, stood in the scant shade the roof provided.

Theo loosened his grip on my arm, lowered the gun. "Do or say one thing...*one*...thing wrong and I'll fill you full of holes." He glared at me. "Understand?"

I nodded.

"Good. Get on. Let's ride."

"Where we going?"

He jammed the barrel into my gut.

I swung up onto a black, nudged her out of the area. Theo took my reins and off we went, like the devil was on our tail. And he was.

I held onto the saddle horn, though I didn't really need to. There was something reassuring about gripping the leather knob. We rode up the hill, ducking under tree limbs, winding around bushes and emerged from the trees onto the hilltop. From there, peering across the tops of trees, I could see maybe thirty miles in all directions.

Would this be the time to chance an escape? I considered the possibilities. That gun was not cocked now, but still in Theo's hand. I could fall off the horse and dislodge him from the saddle. No, he'd shoot me, no doubt.

We hadn't stopped on the way up like I thought we might. The horses were a bit winded from the climb, but we kept going, this time downward.

We picked our way down the steeper part of the hill, then a bit faster near the bottom. From there, we rode hell-bent for leather, west. Skirting tree groves, stands of thick bushes, I spotted patches of flat brown to our south. We were paralleling the road! And where exactly would our route take us? The river wasn't far. Maybe we were heading for New Mexico and eventually Mexico.

The hard riding jarred my head, my ribs, my entire body. How Theo managed to continue in the saddle and stay upright, was impressive. His bullet wound must be bleeding badly, about now. I figured any moment he'd keel over. But no, he sat up straight, glanced at me occasionally and kept going.

An hour of hard riding brought us to the Pedernales River. The rolling brown water and its gurling soothed my nerves, a bit. But only a bit. I expected any minute to be lying in a heap on the ground, dead. If not dead, certainly dying. Or maybe dying and wishing I was dead.

Theo pulled rein, sat watching it for a moment, then allowed the horses to drink. As much as I needed water myself, I wasn't about to ask. If he was thirsty, he'd dismount and maybe, just maybe, let me have a get off. My rear certainly needed one and my entire body demanded rest.

Using the moment, I studied the area. Hill off to my right looked familiar, as did a stand of oaks farther west. I recognized all this from riding with Driggs a few days ago. What felt like years ago.

My back and head demanded a get down and sip of water. "Any chance I can step down to the river, take a drink?"

Theo held his side, glared at me. "Think you've got it made, don't ya? Think ya can have anythin' ya want, don't ya?" He winced, eyes narrowing. "You got money. A job. Brothers. A pa, a ma, too. You got it all."

Do I dare say anything back? Would he whip out his gun and shoot me, because he could? And could I jump out of the saddle, tackle him to the ground? He was younger and shorter than me, but injured. He might be easier to take.

Letting go of his side, he eased around, feeling for what should be a rolled blanket with his Sharps inside, tied against his saddle. Nothing. "Damn! Must've left Pa's gun at the cabin! Dammit!" He pulled the gun out of its holster and aimed it at me. We sat at the river, horses enjoying a good drink. Still we sat, side by side, neither of us moving. I didn't dare even flinch, for fear he'd shoot. I focused on his face, now showing a mishmash of fear, pain, and anger. Mainly anger.

One side of his mouth pulled up into a sneer. "I ain't dumb enough to think one of them boys ain't followin' us. Maybe two of 'em. Hell, for all I know, all three." He glanced behind us down the road. "But 'long as I got you, they won't dare shoot me."

My head throbbed and my throat went desert dry. "Where—"

"Told you! Shut up!"

That damn pistol of his cocked again. The forty-five barrel now resembled a cannon. I pushed down panic, knowing to keep a clear head, even though it was pounding. I'd simply have to keep riding. As would Theo.

Without water for ourselves, we continued our trip west. We rode at least an hour, maybe two, all the while listening for hoofbeats behind us. Would it be Tommy or Tate following? Undoubtedly at least one. Logically, I figured, Tommy would be following, while Tate and Eagan took the two outlaws to jail. Eagan, being a sworn deputy, had as much right to lock them up as Tommy did. I had trouble realizing my baby brother could do something like that. He'd grown up before my eyes and I hadn't truly noticed until now.

Miles later, the river left the bed and made its own

path down an embankment. Definitely looking familiar now, I realized the cave we'd been held in was near here. Was that where we were headed?

Theo pulled back on the reins, taking us to a walk. We continued close to another mile, then went down the embankment to the river at least thirty feet below the road. Sure enough, dug into the embankment, between the river and road, was the cave, smaller than I remembered.

We pulled up at the mouth. Theo studied the area, looking east, west, then up toward the road and finally at the river. Satisfied, he dismounted and nodded for me to do the same. Once my boots hit the ground, I couldn't decide between getting water or trying to tackle Theo. Unfortunately, my horse was between us. Jumping my captor would be hard.

I pointed at the river. Theo pulled his gun, wagged it toward the water. He followed me step by step, watching as I drank out of cupped hands. The nectar flowed down my throat. Three swallows later, Theo poked my back.

"Enough." He tilted his head toward the dreaded cave. "In there."

CHAPTER NINETEEN

EXACTLY AS I'D REMEMBERED, THE CAVE WAS small and dark though it wasn't pitch black. Daylight poked its head inside. I could sort of make out where I was, but falling over rocks and such was still easy. Gun pressed against my backbone, I moved slowly, carefully, hoping to do nothing to offend young Crazy Theo. From what I'd seen, he had a hair-trigger temper and no maturity to tamp it down, when needed.

"Stop." Theo poked hard. "Hands behind you."

Great. I'd been thinking that at some point soon, I'd be able to overpower him. But now not so much with hands tied. He jerked my arms behind me and, within seconds, my wrists were lassoed. Again. Maybe he wouldn't gag me.

He pushed me forward and I lurched over a rock. Fortunately, I kept my feet, which kept me from plowing headfirst into the rock wall. I turned and slid all the way down to the dirt floor. With hands behind me, I couldn't lean comfortably but, all in all, I couldn't complain. I was still alive and that counted for a lot.

Theo brought in the two horses, making the cave crowded and stinky. Horse sweat was not the best odor and, combined with mine, made me cough. The animals stood still for a minute or two adjusting to the dimness, then pawed at the ground. No food in here—for them or us.

And then I remembered. I was supposed to go to Hilda's for supper tonight. I glanced outside. Probably right about now. No way could I get a message to her. Well, she'd either forgive me or forget me. I hated to let her and her da down, but I was tied up at the moment—quite literally.

My stomach gurgled. I frowned at the part of my body that constantly complained. Was I always hungry? Seemed like I was.

Theo stepped outside and took a quick peek around. I watched him from where I sat. Nodding, he came back in, squatted next to me. "Do or say one thing, loser. *One* thing and I'll shoot you. Not bad enough to kill you, you understand. But it'll hurt like a son-of-a-bitch. You'll beg me to finish you off. To end the pain."

Great. If he wanted me to shiver, he succeeded. Goosebumps ran up and down my arms. He meant every word. I wondered where this anger came from, but then thought about his ma's dying and his da's job. Home life wasn't the best.

I nodded at him.

Theo settled back against the rock wall. He played with the gun, aiming it at the horses, then me, then his own head. Laughing, chortling. He attempted to twirl it on his finger but managed only to drop the weapon. If I hadn't been tied, I would've dove for it, but no way could I like this.

I had a ton of questions but chose to stay silent.

Maybe he'd explain why we came here. But for now, I'd stay quiet with my head full of thoughts.

We sat like that for a good half hour, watching the cave darken by the moment. I needed to find a tree to relieve myself, but did I dare ask? The longer we stayed quiet, the worse my need became. I scooted around just a little.

"Need to relieve myself. Mind if I go outside?" I didn't have to invite him to accompany me, I knew he would. "It's urgent."

He sat looking at me, then holding his side, scrambled to his feet. Gun pointed at me, he waggled it toward the cave's mouth. "One minute. And I'm watching."

I pushed up to my knees, then managed to stand. I stood at the cave's entrance and got my business done. Sweet relief. I surveyed the trees and bushes, the world turning a dark gray. No rescue would happen tonight. I resigned myself to spending yet another night tied up.

It would be a long night.

* * *

THEO LOOKED like a sweet little boy as he lay curled up sleeping. Tousled brown hair hung in his eyes, his snores soft. If I hadn't known better, I'd think he was an angel. But I did know.

I'd spent the night tossing and turning. This morning, I sat back to the hard wall and considered escape. If I ever got back to Blanco Hill, I'd spend a week at home resting and letting Ma dote on me. I'd sleep, take a bath, sleep some more, scrub my hair and face until both shone. Ma would fix me her delicious Irish stew and bake a pie—maybe two. She'd roast pork chops from Da's shop, and I'd eat until I couldn't stuff anymore in my face. After a nap, I'd go eat more.

Theo roused, rolled over and glared at me. I shrugged. Still here.

He pulled up his shirt and inspected the bullet crease. No blood seeping. From my point of view, the wound resembled more of a bad scratch. He'd definitely live. He unwound the bandage, stood and tucked in his shirt.

We made our way outside, this time a bit farther away from the cave.

Done, Theo stared into the treetops. "Used to come here when I was a kid."

I wanted to tell him he was still a kid and then reconsidered. He wasn't a kid anymore. Not now.

"My parents and me. They'd bring picnic food and I'd bring some friends. We'd play pirates. We'd use that cave like it was our ship. Had lots of sticks as our swords." Theo trailed off, lost in thought. He looked down and sighed.

The Theo I knew reappeared. He gritted his teeth and glanced back at the cave. "Gotta be in there." He narrowed his eyes at me. "Let's dig."

"Why d'you think it's buried there?"

Theo bit down on his lower lip. "Driggs and me came out here a time or two, to scout out the area." He pushed me up to the cave's mouth.

I studied the floor except where the horses still stood, still saddled. "So, you think he buried the money some place in here?"

He grabbed my shoulder, whipped me around, pointed the gun in my face. "Dammit, Joe. You're stupider 'n that horse, over there. And that's pretty stupid." He pushed me backward. "Get diggin'."

Nothing but rock walls and dirt floors covered with

rocks. Corners were hard to see. I ventured a suggestion. "Best move the horses. Maybe they're standing on it."

He eyed me like I'd insulted his ma. "That's what you want, ain't it? You want these horses to be outside when your friends come to get you. They'll see these critters and know we're in here." He waved the gun. "That's what you want. I'll be dead and you'll be rich."

I thought about trying a more sane conversation with him. I shouldn't but couldn't help it. "Money's not yours, Theo. Belongs to the good people of three towns. It's theirs."

He spun around, eyes glowing. I backed away.

"Don't care who it belonged to. Mine now! All mine! And, dammit, I'm gonna have it."

My shoulders rose and I waited for him to calm. I spoke softly. "The horses?"

His gaze flitted around the gray room. He moved in close to me. "I'll take 'em out. For now."

I nodded.

"Get down on your knees, face the wall. Back there." He cocked his head toward the rear of the cave. "Don't move."

I did as requested. No telling if he'd shoot me just because I moved the wrong way.

The horses clip-clopped out and I chanced a peek over my shoulder. He led them out of sight and I quickly turned my nose back to the wall.

Within a minute, he bent over me, untied my hands. My shoulders relaxed while I rubbed the wrists. Still on my knees, I turned around, looked up at him. "If we find that money..." I knew not to speak. "You're gonna kill me. Aren't you?"

He stood back and thought. "Maybe not right off. I can use you."

That was a piece of information I could use. Good news, I thought. "How so?"

Theo pushed me down to all fours. "First off. Gonna kill my pa. That's where you come in."

"Kill?" All my inner warnings went off at once. "Why kill your da? What'd he do to deserve being killed?"

"He needs it. All his fault. Yeah. You're gonna do it." His eyebrows narrowed, like I'd asked the stupidest question. "Then I'm takin' all that money down to Mexico. I speak enough *Español* to get by. I'm gonna buy me some women, whiskey, and fun."

"But—"

"Dig."

Asking for a stick to help dig with would be too much. "Can't see the corners. How 'bout you light a fire, so we can see better?" I nodded toward the ring of rocks outlining a campfire.

"So you want them to find us just that much easier?" He jabbed a pointed finger next to me. "I said 'dig'!"

I started with areas that looked like the dirt was freshly dug. Three spots looked to hold promise, but after going down a foot or so and finding nothing, I was ready to give up. Besides, the skin on my fingers and hands was about gone, nails broken and ragged. What skin I still had was dark brown from the dirt.

"Try here." Theo pointed his gun to where the horses had been. He stepped back as I grunted to my feet, arched my sore back and rubbed it.

I took a moment to peek outside. The sun stood well overhead, wispy white clouds lingering, as if waiting for more to join the party. Shadows lengthened. Was it midafternoon all ready? Would we ever find the money? His theory of Driggs burying it here was sound. But wouldn't a place closer to town be better?

As I started digging again, I had to ask. It might get me killed, but I had to know. When I'd asked yesterday, I got no answer. The question had been eating at me all day. "Why kill your da? What'd he ever do to deserve death?"

"Killed my ma."

"Your ma?" I'm sure I stuttered.

He turned sad, yet angry, eyes on me. "They said it happens sometimes, but not *my* ma." He took a deep breath. "She was gonna have a baby. I was gonna have a brother." He shrugged. "Maybe sister. But she died, while havin' that baby. If Pa hadn't left her alone to go to some, what he said was an important meetin' in Austin, he would've been here. With us. With Ma. But he wasn't."

Part of me wanted to tell him it wasn't his da's fault, but it wouldn't do any good, coming from me. I knew how he felt, though. I'd blamed myself for Frieda's death. But in the end, I realized it was a tragedy that I didn't cause.

I let out a long sigh. "It's easy to blame that sort of heartbreak on somebody." I looked at Theo. "That's how my wife died. The one you made fun of?"

Instead of being belligerent, he simply nodded.

"Nothing I could do to save her. And I held her in my arms. I was right there and yet…"

"Shut up! What d'you know?" Theo kicked at an old campfire rock. Then a second. They rolled against the wall. "He could've saved her!" He picked up two more and threw them outside.

Cursing, acting out his rage, he threw the ring of rocks outside until nothing but burned twigs and soot lay in a circle. He kicked at the ash. "What was so damn important in Austin? Huh? He should've been with Ma!"

He kicked down a few inches, black covering his boot toe. "Hell, he *made* her have a baby!"

I stood out of his way, watching this man-child succumb to all-consuming grief. Would this be the chance to take him down? He continued ranting and raving, cursing and blaspheming, tears streaming down his face.

He kicked what was left of the ashes, scattering them around the cave. Suddenly quiet, he turned on me, grabbed my arm, yanked me to my knees. "Dig here."

"In the ashes?"

"Dig, damn you!"

Theo was back. At this rate, I'd eventually dig up the entire cave. He snorted up snot, whacked my back to get me going and swiped an arm across his nose and mouth. "Dig!"

My fingers scraped soot, twigs and leaf remnants until I couldn't feel my hands anymore. At least a foot down now, I was ready to rebel, tell Theo I was done. Go ahead and shoot me. That I wasn't going to grub around in the cave anymore.

And then I hit metal. That *tink* echoed in the small space. I looked up at Theo, whose red eyes widened. He dropped to his knees and we both dug furiously. Could it be? I was as excited as Theo.

Dirt and soot flew over our shoulders, around our knees, until we uncovered the bottom of a tin pail. Like frantic dogs, we dug around the can and then down at least a foot. Sure enough, an inverted pail.

I leaned back, my entire body complaining at being bent over for so long. But my curiosity propelled me to return digging. Theo snorted, grunted, snorted. Working both sides of the canister, we rocked it back and forth, loosening the dirt. And then, like a tooth coming loose, the bucket moved!

Theo shoved me aside. "Get away!"

I sat back hard, my blackened hands tapping on the ground.

He wriggled the pail, rocked it back and forth and then pulled up. We stared into the hole. Cash. Money. Bills. Some banded with string, some loose. Stacks of money sat there. Coins.

My mouth dropped open. Never in a million years would I have thought to look there. Brilliant. That was a brilliant hiding place.

Theo grabbed the bucket, tossed the money into it. A maniacal smile stretched ear to ear and then some. He held up a handful. "Here it is! All mine! I'm rich!" He turned to me. "Rich!" He threw bills over his head, watched them float to the floor.

He froze, then turned to me kneeling beside him. His eyes roamed over my face like they were searching for more than money. The spark fluttered out and he jumped to his feet, brandishing the weapon. "Up. Hands behind your back."

Not again. My body wasn't going to take much more abuse. Well, it'd have to, simply in order to survive. There was no use arguing with him. Theo was an insane teenager and logic wouldn't work, right now. With creaking knees and aching muscles, I stood and endured yet more leather tying my wrists together. My shoulders complained. My wrists complained. But my mouth didn't. I wouldn't waste my words.

"You." Theo turned me around and pushed. "Over there. Nose against the wall."

It reminded me of the times as a kid I was in trouble at home. Ma was not a hitter, so spankings weren't dealt out as punishment. Hers was worse. Much worse. Holy hell! To a hyperactive boy, having to stand with my nose against the wall was torture of the first order. I'd stand an hour or two and, somehow, *somehow* she'd know when I moved. That would get me another half hour. I'd almost prefer the swats.

"Whoo hoo," and "I'm rich!" echoed off the walls. Apparently, he wasn't afraid that somebody riding by, like possibly Tommy and my brothers, would hear him. He celebrated neither serenely nor quietly. And I wasn't about to suggest he tone it down. No, if they heard him, they'd come. And that would be a good thing.

As I stood there, I considered the brilliance of hiding the money under a campfire. Who'd have thought to look there? Certainly not me. I grimaced, remembering Eagan and I had used those very rocks to saw through the ropes around our ankles. So close, yet…

I waited, standing, wondering how deep of a hole? Was there a second pail? And then I realized yet another brilliant move. Driggs buried the money, inverted the bucket far enough down, so that when the soil was heated from the fire, the paper wouldn't get hot enough to burn. The soil and tin insulated the cash. Doggone brilliant.

My legs began to spasm. Tired of standing, tired of kneeling, tired of digging, just plain tired. I closed my eyes and leaned my forehead against the wall. Could I sleep standing up? Maybe.

Theo grabbed my left arm and tugged. "Let's go." He held up a bucket stuffed with cash. I noticed bills sticking out of his vest pockets, under his gun belt, under his hat. Probably had some in his boots too.

We made our way down to the river, where the horses lounged, drinking, standing in the shade. Theo pushed me up onto the black I'd ridden yesterday, kept the reins in his hands and shoved the money into saddlebags. Filling his completely, he then filled the bags on my horse as well. I had no idea how much money was there, but I spotted mostly twenties and fifties. Indeed, he was rich.

Theo, patted his side once more, swung up into his saddle, glared at me. "One wrong move..."

I nodded. "I know."

He kicked his bay and off we went through the trees, following the river. Heading west, I wondered if my brothers would find me. Figuring they should've been here by now, disappointment slumped my shoulders. Surely, they were out looking.

And then dark thoughts hit me. Maybe Lieb and August had managed to get the drop on Tommy, Eagan, and Tate. What if my brothers were lying wounded somewhere? What if Tommy went for help, instead of searching for me? What if they were all dead?

I shouldn't think like that, but it was a logical conclusion as to why they weren't here yet. Then again, they didn't know where we were going. Hell, I didn't even know until we got here. How would they know?

I squinted into the setting sun. If my calculations were correct, we had a little over an hour of daylight left before darkness again covered our world. We'd need to stop and make camp. Or would we?

I had to ask. "Where're we headed?"

"Mexico." Theo eyed me like I might have other ideas. "Now shut up and ride!"

* * *

WE MADE camp under a stand of stately Texas oaks, the Pedernales River a stone's throw away. Theo reluctantly untied my hands. He followed me to the water. I splashed my face, then rubbed off dirt, grime and soot. Damn, it was cold but felt great. No amount of gentle scrubbing helped my hands. They remained splotchy gray, the skin scabbing up, no fingernails. All raging sore. I couldn't hold even a stick.

Painfully, I unsaddled my horse, let him drink, then hobbled him with the other near grass. That would have to do for tonight. As for us—we had water at the river, but nothing in the saddlebags except money. And there was nowhere around here to buy food. I envied the horses. At least they got supper.

Now that I was a bit cleaner, exhaustion hit. My eyes refused to stay open. I spread out the saddle blanket near a tree and lay on it. Would Theo forget I wasn't bound, that my hands were free? As tired as I was, I was no threat to him, now. Maybe tomorrow after several hours of sleep.

I closed my eyes only to be startled by Theo grabbing my left arm, jerking it out to the side. I rolled and he gripped my other arm. Using a long piece of latigo, he bound my wrists then tied the end to a small tree. I tugged. Nice and secure. I wasn't going anywhere, except to sleep.

But sleep wouldn't come. The half-moon and stars provided enough light to watch Theo move around the campsite and sit cross-legged, cradle both saddlebags like beloved puppies. He faced the river, now burbling its way toward Mexico. Just like us.

CHAPTER TWENTY

A BOOT INTO MY SIDE STARTLED ME AWAKE. I stared up into Theo's sneering face, lack of sleep etched around his eyes. Early morning sunbathed him in a halo.

"Get up. We're ridin'."

While he was untying my hands, I thought about my captor's mental state. Now that he had the money he had decided, apparently, to skip killing his da and continue on down to Mexico. He didn't need me any longer. Why hadn't he threatened me, last night? Why was I still alive?

I settled the blanket onto my horse's back, despite raw, now swollen hands. I then hefted the saddle into place. I cinched it tight, then, looked over at Theo. Was it my imagination or had he matured ten years overnight? With shoulders pulled back, he stood taller. He even walked with an air of confidence, his chin tilted up just a notch.

And then it hit me. Why the hell was I putting up with this crazy kid? I was strong enough to take him down. I was maybe six, seven years older and definitely in good, physical shape. Well, except for my head and overall sore body. What kind of weapons did I have? No gun. No knife. No ropes. No…nothing. Just me.

Theo stood behind me, latigo in hand. "Mount up."

I turned and met his gaze. "No."

"No?" His arms flapped at his side. "What d'you mean 'no'? Get on, let's ride." He grabbed for my wrist.

I pulled away. "I said no. Not going with you."

He pushed me hard enough that I backed into the horse. He grabbed my wrist again. "We're goin' to Mexico. You and me."

I shook my head. I didn't want to hit him, but I clenched my fists just in case. He'd made the serious mistake of not tying my hands sooner. Now, I planned to use them. "I'm not going. You'll kill me, anyway. Why ride all the way down there, first?"

"Kill you? Hell, I'm not gonna kill you." He flicked the cord around one wrist. "I'm gonna sell you down there. I hear Anglo slaves sell for a fortune."

With my free hand, I hauled back and slugged him square in the side of the head. He gripped my wrist tighter, shook his head, but I managed to push him backward. He let go of the leather, wobbled a couple steps but rebounded with a hard right jab to my stomach.

I doubled over. He pulled his gun and clobbered me on the back of my head. I gripped my knees, and stars circled the world. But I righted myself and, before he could shoot, I knocked the weapon out of his hand. It sailed yards down to the riverbank.

"Son-of-a…" Theo bent over and headbutted me, hurling me under the horse. He grabbed my leg and pulled, dragging me over dirt and rocks.

I rolled as he kicked into my side. Hard. The blow choked off my breath. I gasped. Colors exploded.

I grabbed a shallow breath, then leaped into action like a wildcat. Launching myself to my feet, I used all the dredged-up anger and frustration from the past couple of weeks. I attacked with everything I had. We thudded to the ground, rolled and punched. His stout body was hard, quick and dangerous.

Like a puma poised to strike, he came up onto all fours, glared. Growling, claws out, he pounced on top of me. The bloodlust was at a fever pitch.

He raked deep into my skin. Blinding white streaks of pain took my breath. My cheeks and chest burned like Lucifer's fire. I brought my feet under him and kicked up. Theo sailed over me *whomping* to the ground.

I stumbled toward the gun, the river about to carry it away. Thundering footsteps behind me. I couldn't move out of the way in time. We crashed into the cold water and the sharp rocks underneath.

I went under, face first, struggling up, sporting sharp gravel in my cheek. I flipped over and he pounded my face. I deflected, punching where I could.

He mounted my chest, holding onto my shirt like I was a bucking bronc. He pushed my face under water, and held it there. I wriggled and thrashed, desperate to breathe. I found a rock, and used it to clobber his shoulder.

Theo slumped enough for me to pull my head into air, gulp, then push him over. We somersaulted back and forth, taking turns trying to drown the other. On the bottom for the third time, Theo again held my head under water. I found a bigger rock, smashed it against the side of his head.

He went limp, slid off me, and landed on his back in

the river. I coughed, choked, then pulled in buckets of glorious air.

On hands and knees, I towed Theo to the water's edge but I couldn't drag us completely out of the river. I simply didn't have the strength. I flopped onto my belly on the muddy bank and gasped like a fish out of water.

CHAPTER TWENTY-ONE

STRONG, DESPERATE HANDS CLUTCHED MY shoulder, rolling me onto my back. I refused to open my eyes. That was too much work. *Way* too much effort.

"Christ Almighty! Is he dead?"

Other hands shook me. "No. He's breathing. See? Just out cold."

"Sure looks dead."

I recognized the voices but couldn't quite place them. Men. Concerned men.

"This one dead?" This voice a bit farther away. Must be kneeling by Theo.

"Don't think so."

"Let's get them out of the water. Joe's half drowned."

So, they know my name. More hands slipped under my shoulders and drug me up the bank and across the dirt. Someone knelt beside me. I heard hard breathing. "Joe? Joe!" A hand patted my scratched cheek a couple times, then slapped it.

I swatted at the hand and opened my eyes. Tate looked down at me, eyes brimming with worry. I thought

I grinned, but maybe not. It was hard to tell with the aches, mud, and blood still seeping.

"He's awake!" Tate looked over his shoulder. I guessed the other two were dealing with Theo. He turned back to me. "Can you talk?"

Probably. But did I want to? No. Tate pulled me up enough for him to scoot around and drape me over his knees. He put his arms around me. Safe. I was safe now. And alive.

* * *

ONCE AGAIN, we were in our accustomed places in the sheriff's office. Tommy behind the desk, Eagan leaning against the wall by the door, Tate in one chair, me in the other. It had been two whole days, I'd been told, since the battle at the Pedernales; my fight with Theo. Two full days. They said I'd slept. And slept. Moaned a bit. And slept some more. Doc had visited three times. I didn't remember a thing.

I was vaguely aware there had been a million words spoken to me, around me, and over me, but none of them had made any sense until this morning. I was taking this moment to try to get it all straight, now that my brain was in some kind of working order, I hoped, resembling normalcy again. So many questions, I wasn't sure where to begin. I'd start with the most important.

"Hilda? Is she all right?"

Tate gently thumped my leg. "Been by four...five times. Says she forgives you for standing her up the other night. You were supposed to go to her house for supper. Remember?"

I didn't, but kind of did. Fuzzy conversations swirled in my mind. Maybe I remembered. I shrugged.

"Says she'll bring us a surprise, this morning." Eagan rubbed his stomach. "Can't wait."

Yesterday...was it only yesterday? Maybe. Yesterday, I'd realized my brothers and Tommy were all in one piece and hadn't been hurt by August or Lieb. I remembered relaxing at that thought. "What about Theo?" I asked.

"Locked up, back there." Tommy cocked his head toward my old cell. "With the others." He leaned forward, elbows on desk. "You broke his head. Clobbered him damn fine with a river rock, we're guessing. Nearly drowned him."

Tate thumbed at the cells. "Doc's got Theo patched up pretty good. Mayor's been in checking on his son."

"Already hired a lawyer." Eagan smiled. "An expensive one from San Antone I heard."

Tommy wagged his head at me. "Damn, Joe. You missed out on all the excitement last couple of days."

"We got to count all the money! Two, three times." Eagan stood straight, a grin pushing up his cheeks. "There was a bunch! Wish some of it was mine."

Tommy shot a look at Eagan like he'd wanted to say it. "We figured out how much each town lost. Sent a courier to Blanco Hill yesterday morning. Fredericksburg's already got theirs back. And the Johnsonville sheriff was here, yesterday. Got their money and, better yet, he's getting the circuit judge to come back, early. There'll be a trial in the next week or two."

"Fact is," Tate regarded me. "Sheriff's looking for a deputy. Noted your name. Gonna talk to you when you're making sense again."

I took all that in, yet not much of it stuck. Too many names, faces, memories to sort, for now. Maybe after a nap. Or two.

I turned to Tommy. "What about you?"

He picked up a pencil and outlined a mustache on a wanted poster. "I'll be here, until the Town Council votes in a new sheriff. They're thinking first of next week. I'll be home soon's I can."

A question had been burning in my brain, off and on. "How'd you find me?"

Tate studied his hands. "Lost your trail less than a mile from the cabin." He perked up and thumbed at Eagan. "Then your little brother figured if Driggs was there in the cave where he'd kept you two, then maybe, possibly, Theo knew about it too. We followed Eagan's hunch."

It still didn't make a ton of sense, but I got the general idea. I'd ask more specifics later. I looked each man in the face. "Thank you."

The door squeaked open and aromas of freshly baked cinnamon rolls, strudel and scones left no doubt it was Hilda. I stood, offering her a hug and then my seat.

She put the sack on the desk, hugged me back. Gently. "I was so worried about you. So very worried."

"See? We've been telling you, Hilda," Tate stood smiling. "Joe's got a thick head. It's hard to truly hurt that boy."

Her sparkling blue eyes gazed up into mine. I focused on her lips. A tingle warmed my entire body. Ignoring everyone else, I pulled her into another embrace, unable to resist her charms and allure. Plus, she smelled heavenly.

Spellbound with feelings renewed and compelling, I whispered, "I love you."

A LOOK AT LADY OF THE LAW
A MAUD OVERSTREET NOVEL

A new era of empowerment and justice...

In the 1870s, women have little control over their lives, but the women of Dry Creek, California, look to Sheriff Maud Overstreet, a thirty-something spinster, as a beacon of progress. When a disastrous fire levels the local school, Maud makes the bold decision to appoint a woman as fire chief, inspiring other women in the town to step forward and run their own businesses—a bakery, a charm school, and a newspaper—much to the consternation of the male town councilors.

While investigating the school arson, Maud witnesses a fatal shooting and begins to suspect an insurance salesman of both crimes. She also becomes campaign manager for two of her friends, both running for Mayor, adding political intrigue to her growing list of responsibilities. Amidst more fires, a budding romance, a rowdy town dance, the establishment of a school for Chinese girls, and the appearance of mysterious threatening notes, Sheriff Overstreet confronts each new challenge with unwavering determination.

She is, after all, a Lady of the Law.

AVAILABLE NOW

ABOUT THE AUTHOR

Growing up in southern New Mexico, Melody Groves' mind raced with characters from the Old West–gunfighters were her favorite. Now, her novels reflect her fascination—and ties—from that era.

As a New Mexico Gunfighter re-enactor, Melody loves to entertain visitors at Albuquerque's Old Town, allowing them a glimpse into earlier times. Her books reflect her passion for rodeo and her appreciation of historic wooden bars. Yes, bars—the front and back wooden structures, which Melody feels are just as amazing as rodeo performers.

www.ingramcontent.com/pod-product-compliance
Lightning Source LLC
Chambersburg PA
CBHW010826250626
47169CB00010B/2971